The Setting Sun

Kerry Williams

Skye High Publishing

Cover Design: Moonshot Covers

Interior Design: SSB Covers and Design

Editor: Swish Design and Editing

Publisher: Skye High Publishing

For my best friend, Ria.
My soul sister.
Thank you for seeing something in me all of those years ago that I could not see myself.
Here is to a lifetime of indulging each other.

Part One

Chapter One

Peter

Connie has had way too much tequila.

But it's fun to see her this way, free of inhibitions, embracing a side so many hide from their whole lives. Truly living.

She plants her hands on my chest, pushing me farther into our enormous five-star room until the back of my legs hit the plush, highbacked velvet chair, forcing me to sit and watch.

She teases her coat off and drops it to the floor, then moves to put a song on the speaker system before opening the champagne, which is chilling on the table. I know what she's doing—making me wait, making me watch—because she hasn't kept her hands off me the whole journey to our hotel room.

The electricity crackles in my veins—I am on fire for her.

She approaches me with a sway in her hips and a sly smile on her face, then drains her champagne in one swallow, and the sight of her makes me lick my lips.

Once she reaches me, Connie puts a foot on the arm of the chair, and in the next moment, she is above me. The suddenness of her movement takes me by surprise, leaving me marveling up at her as she dances for me, the slinky material of her black dress hugging her in *all* the right places.

I run my hands up her calves as she hitches her dress up to give me a better view. That warm, hungry feeling flares in my stomach, and I get to my feet to join her. Pressing my body against hers in time to the music, drinking her in, I run my hands gently up her back until they find skin, letting the electricity crackle under my touch, my lips on her throat.

My breath catches when she weaves her fingers into my hair, pulling on it so I'm looking up at her. "Tell me again," she says, her eyes hungry.

"I would burn the world for you, Connie," I tell her.

The small noise of satisfaction she makes drives me wild, and I dig my fingers into her hips.

"Be more specific," she says, continuing to push against me.

I glance at the large double doors leading to our balcony and dip my head to her ear. "I would turn the placid waters of the Grand Canal to flames, the ancient stones of the Rialto Bridge would crumble all the way to the Basilica. All gone. It would burn, burn, burn until there was nothing left." I pull away to look at her. "All you have to do is ask."

But she doesn't ask. Instead, she kisses me, and I pour everything I have into her until she pulls away.

"Say it," I whisper against her skin.

"You are a god, Peter. My god. The only god," she says against my lips.

Caressing her face, my thumb ghosts across her lip. "Damn right," I reply while looking into her green eyes, perfect except for the black rings that circle her irises.

Nine months.

That's how long I have had Connie like this, of our feet barely

4

touching the ground, while visiting a lot of those brightly colored pins on her world map. We even convinced Lorna to come with us to some of the many places we have been. We are away so much Connie had to give up her job in the coffee shop, for which I am glad. I have spent a scarce moment away from her since that night in the barn, too paranoid of what might happen to her when she is not with me. So, we travel—which is my plan until she tells me to stop.

It didn't take her long to fall in with the luxurious lifestyle I can talk us into, and while she draws the line with many things, five-star hotels and restaurants she cannot seem to say no to. Paris. Berlin. Ibiza. Monaco. Singapore. Tokyo. Bali. And now, Venice. Anywhere she's wanted, anywhere to keep her distracted.

The truth is, after coming down from my high of killing several of the Irish coven, the worry about what I had done set in.

The black rings on Connie's eyes? Yes, at first I enjoyed the fact that I had marked her but I soon became unnerved. I can tell when I touch her she is still human, the soul of the witch I fed her pushing perhaps fifty years onto her life span. Souls are the key, I know it. But the black rings—I can't explain them. She assures me she doesn't feel any different, other than being a little freaked out when she saw her eyes for the first time. I had to do a lot of damage control convincing everyone—except Lorna and, begrudgingly, also Jamie—that her eyes have always looked this way. Truth be told, she was more freaked out about her eyes than seeing me kill a bunch of people. Which, I suppose, can only be a good thing when she has me for a boyfriend.

Connie seems able to rationalize it away as "kill or be killed." Either way, I've become wary of my mission to make her immortal. When I feel her, she still very much feels like Connie, her human cells regenerating at a slightly slower rate due to the power of the soul. But still human, still mortal. The only slight difference I sense is, underneath the brilliance of her human soul, there is a faint signature I can't put my finger on. It's not the witch—I could recognize that—but something new. An unknown, and it makes me nervous. Without her permission to take another soul, I won't be able to figure it out, but I promised myself I would never do anything against Connie's will again. Especially kill someone.

Connie is twenty-one tomorrow, and I have to take her home for at least a week before deciding on where to go next. I know she will figure out what I am up to at some point, but I'm hoping to have more time.

When Connie is long asleep, I stand out on the balcony that overlooks the Grand Canal, quiet and serene, in the dead of night. With a glance, the clouds overhead clear and I see the twinkling stars reflected in the water. Gracefully moving my fingers in the air as if playing the piano, the ripples spread across the water as I trace the stars' reflections. Sometimes the problem with absolute control is simply that—no excuses.

These days, if I destroy something, it is because I want to. The unseemly urge to set fire to everything around me happens more often than one might think. It often comes out of nowhere. Someone pushing past me in the street or a wrong look at Connie, and the heat rises against my skin, and the faint whisper living in the back of my head that tells me to burn it, *burn it all*.

Sometimes I like to pretend the voice is Anna's. After all, the fire came after she died. But it doesn't quite fit. It's more like she was holding onto that last terrible piece of who I am. Deep inside of me, that monster has always been lurking, and it has nothing to do with my sister. She is gone. Another push of my hand and a wave undulates down the water, sending the abandoned gondolas against the banks of the canal.

As I push back through the heavy, floor-length velvet curtains and into the room, Connie stirs a little as I finish the last of the champagne, then take a seat and put my headphones on. These last few weeks, the nightmares have been back, and I'm in no hurry to wake up surrounded by sweat-soaked sheets. I avoid sleep for as long as possible until I am so exhausted I don't dream at all.

Instead, I sit and watch over Connie, her now long shiny hair splayed around the pillow. Her brow furrows, and she lets out a hard breath as her head twitches. I ease off my headphones, watching her closely as she swats at something invisible in front of her. Her breaths come heavier now, her frown deepens as she shakes.

I am at her side in an instant, grasping onto her shoulders. "Connie. Connie, wake up. It's just a dream."

Connie's eyes flutter open, the panic fading to relief in an instant when she sees me and realizes we are in the safety of our hotel room. She brings her delicate hand to her chest to steady her breathing.

"That was a nightmare." She brings her hand to my face. "You were there. Something terrible was about to happen." Connie shakes her head, trying to recall, before saying, "We were somewhere unlike anyplace I've ever seen before. There was this mist all around us..." she pauses like she's thinking then blurts out, "...and a cross. I could see a cross. Something bad was going to happen."

My eyes widen, but I try not to give anything away. A huge black cross, looming and dreadful, is what has been plaguing my nightmares of late. That and fields soaked in blood and bone. Thousands upon thousands of sacrifices.

"What else did you see?" I ask.

Connie's eyes snap up to mine, immediately suspicious of my question. "What do you mean? It was just a nightmare."

I move off the bed, rubbing my eyes. I want her to be right

about it being only a nightmare, a coincidence, something not real or tangible.

"Peter, remember what I said about honesty. Tell me..."

I glance back at her wide eyes looking up at me. She is so different from the person I met four years ago, but then, I suppose I am too.

"That is my nightmare, Connie. I have been having nightmares about a dreadful dark cross, and blood. In my nightmare, I am always at the center of it. That's why I haven't been sleeping. I can't escape it, and now, it's moved on to you."

Connie doesn't say anything for a while, so I move back to sit by her side, threading my fingers into hers.

"Tell me what you're thinking."

"In my nightmare, *I* was at the center of it," she says, staring at our hands. "Maybe I wasn't myself? I think I was dreaming as if I were you. What does it mean, Peter? That I am having your nightmares?"

"I don't know," I answer honestly, moving my free hand over her heart and feeling it beating against my palm. "If I do this... if I make you immortal, Connie, I think you will always be connected to me, bound to me in ways I have no way of anticipating."

"Is that why you've been putting it off?" she asks, her voice timid.

So she does know what I have been doing.

I give her a small smile. "It's part of the reason," I admit. "I don't want to have that type of hold over you. I always want to be your choice."

"You are my choice."

"Maybe we should wait a few more years, Connie."

"Why?"

"Because I don't know how to do this without sacrificing

people, and I don't know if you would ever forgive me, or yourself, for doing that."

"It can't be the *only* way."

"I am pretty sure it is, Connie, and even if I do it, I don't know what it will turn you into. We just don't know enough about it. There's no precedent. I can't find any real accounts in history, and what we can find, it's hard to tell what's a myth and what isn't."

Connie stares at me for a while, her eyes becoming hard. "We? You spoke to Lorna about this?"

"You know she knows what you want." I say, a bit perplexed by her question.

"I didn't know she was helping. And what? She *is* okay with you sacrificing a whole load of people?"

"Of course not, but she's practical. She knows there probably isn't another way I can manage on my own. She's just assisting with the research options, trying to help me figure it out." I smooth down her hair. "I know you don't want me to kill anyone. So we're looking for alternatives."

Something in Connie's eyes shifts. "But you would, wouldn't you? If you knew I would be okay, you would do it tomorrow. Just kill whoever it took to give me what I want."

"You know I would." I smile at her without hesitation.

She doesn't return my smile at first, and when she does, it comes strained as she shifts onto her knees to look down at me, kissing me with such tenderness. "You say I taste like honey," she whispers, and I murmur a quiet yes into her lips. "Is that what my soul would taste like, Peter?"

I am on my feet in an instant, putting some distance between us. "Please don't do that. It's not like that. I don't want to think of you that way."

"Like what? Like I'm food?" She cocks an eyebrow at me. "Is

that how you see everyone else now? Like they are food?" She gestures to the empty balcony, the city beyond.

"Of course not."

"I heard you say it to that Japanese witch, how her soul smelled."

Rue.

Even thinking about her soul makes my mouth water.

Connie crosses the room, making me look at her. "Peter, I know everything is different now for you. But you have to remember who you are. We can't lose sight of our humanity."

I don't have the heart to tell her this is very much who I am. Or that, without her, I wouldn't hesitate to kill whoever looked at me wrong to feed the addictive taste, that voice that buzzes away at the back of my mind.

Instead, I kiss her, letting the buzz of electricity rise in my veins at having her in my arms, and throw her back to bed.

Chapter Two

Connie

The agitation rolls off Peter in torrents. It's clear from the way he picks the edge of my nail as our taxi takes us back to Wixford, his eyes firm and scowling at the rolling countryside outside our window. I know he hates coming here. Every time he returns, he has to visit his aunt and uncle, which, in turn, reminds him of Anna. When we are back, he feels her absence more keenly. His grief for Anna is a different beast from the grief he felt for Brady. After Brady died, Peter drowned in sadness, but losing Anna was different. Now, a constant simmering rage lies under his skin, crawling there. Festering and infecting him every second of every day.

It would be better if we didn't come back, and at some point, that will happen. One day, I will leave this village and never come back. I will put my mortal life behind me and walk this Earth for an eternity with him. I can sense in Peter that day is close. I can feel it in myself too because every time we return, I'm slightly more at odds with the place.

It's strange. I've always wanted to escape. Wixford is the same, day in and day out, the monotony always overwhelming but...

Well, I guess I have come to see it as a port in the storm. The only piece of normal I have left. There are no doubts in my mind that Peter is what I want, but I'm not quite ready to give up my final slice of reality—Jamie, my mum, the only home I have ever known. It's the one place where we maintain a shred of restraint. In our travels, under the mask of cities, Peter grows under the anonymity they provide, more and more happy to use his influence to take what he desires.

My fingers trail along the cluster diamond necklace he gave me for my twenty-first birthday this morning. I dread to think how much it is worth and push down the knowledge that Peter probably has not paid for it—and the realization I don't care enough not to accept it.

I wonder if there is much I wouldn't let him do for me. *At the same time, is there something wrong with me for feeling this way?*

I turn to watch him staring as we drive past his now inhabited old house, the white of the outside repainted and pristine with a couple of fancy cars parked outside. The shaking of his knee rocks the whole car.

"Would it make you feel better if we went to see her first?" I offer, placing a calming hand on his knee.

Peter turns back to me and, without a word, nods. I pull out my phone and drop my mum a quick text, then tell our driver the slight change in destination.

The car hasn't even come to a stop when I see Lorna appear at her front door, her face breaking into a huge grin at the sight of us. We've only been gone for two weeks, but I can see her visible relief at our return. Peter barely lets the taxi stop before he is out of the backseat to greet her.

Lorna flies down the front path and into Peter's arms with a warm embrace, hitting with enough force that he takes her up off her feet, laughing.

A tiny pang of jealousy barbs me when the hug she gives me is a tad less enthusiastic. In my heart, I know I will always be somewhat jealous that my once best friend is now Peter's best friend. Don't get me wrong. Lorna loves me as much as she always did. But she loves Peter more. That's the thing with Peter —when he has you, he has all of you. There's nothing to be done. I can't hold it against either of them. They both lost a person they loved, and they have to hold onto each other for her memory.

"How was Venice?" She beams at both of us, her smile infectious.

"It was beautiful. You would have loved it," Peter tells her.

"Yeah, but being the third wheel isn't always easy."

He slings his arm around my shoulders. "You are more than welcome to join us." He winks, and Lorna rolls her perfectly lined eyes.

"You do know that if by some miracle in your wildest dreams that did happen, I would be far more interested in your girlfriend's body than yours."

My cheeks flush at Lorna's words but, on the other hand, Peter's eyes sparkle. "That is in no way a problem." He laughs, and we both slap his stomach.

I know it's a joke, sort of.

In our nine months since what happened in the barn, Peter and I have talked a lot about Sorcha and what happened in India. Peter confessed he'd seen her again in Wixford before he came for me. And that he didn't kill her. Again. At first, he explained he wasn't even sure if he could kill her or if he could be killed himself. It became apparent there is something more than that on a whiskey-fueled night when he confessed he was not sure he even wanted to kill her, only that he had the desire to put her in her place.

"What? Do you mean like some alpha bullshit?" I had questioned him.

He'd shrugged, suggesting he didn't know for sure.

Peter had a tendency to kill those who had the answers, although they were never forthcoming with those answers. All he knew was he was way more powerful than her, and he knew it bothered her a lot, not to mention the fact that he would choose me again and again over her.

We've seen neither hide nor hair of Sorcha in all these nine months.

It was my mistake to mention it was more Sorcha as a person to which I'd had the objection anyway. A notion that piqued his interest, obviously. He'd spent the next night pointing out Parisian girls we might be able to seduce. It was quite fun plotting out what we would say, making each other laugh with our seduction techniques, but ultimately, I said no, and Peter hasn't mentioned it again. Yet I know he is once again biding his time, merely waiting for me to say yes.

Either way, I don't think even Peter would go so far with Lorna. Although we never can quite tell with him. It had come as a surprise to me when he asked if he should point out men rather than girls, if I preferred. Again, while fun to consider, when I said no, the matter wasn't brought up again.

But, as time went on, the constant hedonism became intoxicating, each hotel he checked us into was more lavish than the last.

I allowed myself to take more.

There was always more.

I'm glad to be home for a while.

To ground myself.

"Wow! Connie, your necklace." Lorna's squeal breaks me out

of my thoughts as we walk together, her fingers lightly running over the bright diamonds. "This is your birthday present? It must be worth a fortune."

I laugh at Lorna's choice of words, which are all too knowing, as usual. She's careful not to say it *cost a fortune*.

We slip into comfortable, excited chatter as Peter stays a few steps behind us, letting us catch up as we make our way to the coffee shop. Lorna gets me up to date with what has been happening with her, which isn't much, other than her little brother getting into a fight at school. She also tells me she will come with us for our next trip. That isn't unusual for her to do, although it does make my heart catch a bit and wonder if this will be the last time I'm in Wixford. The last time I will see my mum. I have no doubt that when we do disappear, Lorna will be with us.

We soon come upon the intoxicating aroma of coffee and the familiar sight of Mike behind the counter. Giving Peter and me an enthusiastic greeting, I direct Lorna and Peter over to a table so I can catch up with him as he makes our coffees. Hardly two minutes pass when the tinkle of the bell above the door sounds, and I look up to see familiar blue eyes, his expression filling with warmth when I catch his eye.

"You're back." Jamie closes the distance between us and pulls me into a hug. "How was Venice?" He steps back to look at me again, his eyes widening at the sight of my necklace and cutting me off before I can answer. "It seems like it suited you."

"It was a birthday present." I move my hand protectively to my neck, resisting the urge to glance back at Peter, whose eyes I can feel hot on my back.

"Right." Jamie snickers, looking up at the menu board. "I wouldn't let your mum see that, though. You will never hear the end of it."

He's probably right.

The amused look remains plastered across his face, so I cock my hip at him. "What?" I ask, rolling my eyes.

"Just, you know... blood and diamonds, is it now?"

"Very funny, Jamie."

"Not really." His smile falters a little, his voice lowering to a whisper. "I keep wondering when it will happen. When will be the last time I see you."

His eyes lock onto mine, on the blackness there, but all I see is the same sadness behind his guarded cockiness. Jamie was the one other person I convinced Peter not to hide the truth from. After all, we owed him. Leaving his memory intact was the least we could do.

"Jay. I wish I knew myself. I will keep coming back for as long as I can." I give him a weak smile. "And there is no reason why you can't get out of Wixford, come see the big wide world with us. You could bring Lauren. I'm sure she would love to see some exotic places."

Something wicked flashes across his face. "I'm sure your boyfriend would love that."

I give him a nefarious grin of my own. "My boyfriend knows what's good for him."

Jamie full-on laughs while shaking his head. "I am a small-town boy, Con. I don't know if it's for me."

"How do you know unless you try?" I push. "Think about it, okay? Even when I go, it's not the end. You have my number."

Jamie lets the warmth return to his expression, knowing I mean it. Somehow, even after what happened, we've been able to become friends again.

A hot arm slides around my shoulder, distracting me. "Were you planning on bringing these coffees over anytime today?" Peter purrs in my ear.

I roll my eyes in response as he turns to acknowledge my friend.

"Jamie."

"Peter."

This is about as civil with each other as they can manage, and even for this, I am grateful. Jamie came around to putting up with Peter's presence when he realized he didn't want me to vanish from his life altogether. And Peter—well, Peter couldn't begrudge me a lifelong friendship, especially with someone who came to his aid—despite not liking him—not once, but twice.

The barn night seems like a blurred memory now, more shades of crimson and fire than anything else. It was the most blood I have seen in my life. I hadn't witnessed the massacre at the coven in India, which plagues Lorna's nightmares with bodies. As for myself, I almost can't recall the bodies in the barn, it's mostly the blood. Everywhere. Including on me and on Peter in particular. I also remember the coppery taste of blood on my lips. Peter and I had silently watched the barn burn into the early hours of the morning. When it started to turn light, Peter retrieved his phone from his back pocket and handed it to me. As I recall those events, they seem to have a sheen of the unreal about them. Like a mirage in my mind.

"You need to call him."

"Who?" I ask with no genuine clue to what he is thinking.

"Connie, everyone is looking for you. We're covered in blood. Lorna will be with him. He's the only one with a car. We need to get back and get ourselves sorted. I will handle this."

"What are you talking about?" Peter's eyes are as wide as saucers, making him appear doe-like and blood-splattered.

He looks so appealing I can't take my eyes off him. I am having trouble following a coherent train of thought and fighting not to put my hands all over him. It's the first time I have thought of him as a god in the ancient sense of the word.

"You will see soon enough, and I need to act while I have the power to pull this off on such a scale. I can only keep the sound of sirens away from here for so long. I need to get back and fix all the damage. Don't worry. Just call Jamie."

"He won't come." Jamie told me there was no "after" this time. We were through.

"He's in love with you. He will come." Peter holds my gaze and, taking my face, his thumb ghosts along my bottom lip. "You need to understand, Connie. What we are now, we can have whatever we want. We just need to take it."

The thrill of his words vibrates through me. "We can't do that to Jamie."

"Just call him."

So, I had. And Peter had been right. Jamie was so relieved I was okay, he came. He saw. There was only fire to see—no bodies, luckily—plus Peter and me all bloody. But his look of horror turned to absolute shock when he noticed my black-rimmed eyes.

I have to give him credit for his nerve and for going for Peter.

His fist collided hard with Peter's face, and Peter didn't fight back, but he did cackle. A cracked, haunting sound. Then he laughed loudly at Jamie and his anger as Jamie hit him a few more times. It was only after that I realized Peter was still high. Lorna and I tried to pull him off as he continued to pummel Peter, blood staining his knuckles, but in the end, he was forced off when Peter engulfed himself in flames, sending Jamie back several paces. The fire burned away Peter's clothes.

Jamie hadn't had the words. Peter shook off the flames like they were nothing and advanced on Jamie, his voice deadly, grabbing the front of his shirt and pulling him close to his face. Even naked, so full of menace.

"You need to listen to me very carefully, Jamie. I can't count the ways how easy it would be for me to crush you. But I will if you lay a hand on me again. Nod if you understand."

Jamie nods his head a fraction.

"Now, we need a ride back and I will explain what has happened on the way."

Something in Jamie changed that night. He didn't only hate Peter —he became convinced he was a monster, one intent on turning me into one too. Jamie decided remaining my friend might keep me from becoming one for as long as possible. Things got better when Peter and I returned from Paris and I learned Jamie had started seeing Lauren.

Peter and I have met up with Jamie and Lauren a few times when we've been back. I like Lauren a lot. She's not afraid to keep Jamie in line, and it's nice she knows nothing about what Peter is, so our topic of conversation can never steer that way in front of her. Peter rarely says a word, so she isn't subject to his charms. Although I do catch her glancing in his direction sometimes. I ponder if she wonders what he sees in me.

"Is Lauren at uni at the moment?" I ask Jamie, breaking through the awkward silence.

"She's coming back this weekend." Jamie's eyes light up.

"Do you have plans? We should do drinks." Peter's body tenses beside me.

Jamie glimpses at Peter, the corners of his mouth twitching. "Sure, sounds like fun. I'll text you."

19

He collects his coffee and heads over to where Lorna is sitting, leaving me with Peter, who is glaring at me. "Great. Another evening with Jamie. Just what I need."

"He's my friend, Peter. Besides, he's with Lauren now."

Peter gives me an incredulous look. "Please, like he wouldn't have you back in a heartbeat."

I shake my head in disbelief.

Peter dips his head to whisper into my ear, "You just don't see it, do you? How incredible you are." He snakes his arms around my lower back.

I feel the heat rise in my face.

"You are so beautiful, Connie. I'm so lucky you are mine." His tongue traces around the back of my ear.

"Peter," I whisper. "People are looking."

"Who's going to stop me?"

I giggle, placing my hand on his chest and pushing him away. "I am. Honestly, people know us around here."

Peter leans against the counter, laughing at me. "Fine, as you wish. I'm just saying, you owe me for forcing me into spending time with someone who openly hates me."

"I'm sure your ego will manage it for one evening," I tease, and he makes a mock wounded expression as he picks up the tray with our coffees on it. "You know, if you would rather not see Jamie, you don't have to come."

Peter peers at me from the corner of his eye, something deadly there. "Don't even think about it." He growls out the words.

Heat rises up through me, something between anger and embarrassment. "Excuse me?" I whisper to him.

"Connie, I am not letting you out of my sight." He must see in my face that I'm about to say he is not the boss of me because his expression softens, and the intensity in his eyes relaxes. "Please. I can come, I don't mind. The last time I left you, you were taken."

"Peter..." I murmur. "No one is coming for me. You'll have to leave me on my own at some point."

He smiles, gorgeous and final, leaning down to lightly kiss my forehead. "Why?"

Rather than giving me a chance to answer, he walks past me to join Lorna and Jamie.

Chapter Three

Sorcha

The earth smells damp and rancid. My eyes are taking a while to adjust to the dim light in the winding underground tunnels of the coven's ancestral home. It's been a long time since I visited here—since *they* were here. I don't remember the air being quite so stale then, so different from the airy hall of the Varanasi coven. It's strange to think there was a time I called this place home.

I finally reach the round central meeting room, the ceiling so low the top of my head scrapes against it. Torches illuminate the faces of those present, making them appear sinister, like a secret society. They fall silent as I enter, all eyes turning to me and then to Glory, who keeps her fingertips leaning against the large oak table they are standing around. Not everyone is present, only the seniors. They must have been talking about some sort of strategy before I interrupted.

"I didn't think we would see you back here," Glory says, her thick Irish accent laced with humor and the corner of her mouth twitching.

"I felt that enough time has passed for you to have cooled down. You should not have sent so few. I did try to warn you." My eyes sparkle at her. I shouldn't taunt her loss, even after almost a year, so I change the subject. "How does it feel to be back in Meath?"

"Long overdue," she replies, her answer simple.

"Why are you here, Sorcha?" Gareth asks from beside her as he stands like a guard dog over her.

As if Glory needs protecting.

Some of the witches give me a wide birth, allowing me to reach the table, my fingers finding the familiar grooves of the grains.

"Rue was a sad loss," I say, keeping my eyes on my fingernails.

"We don't need reminding," Gareth barks from across the table.

Glory straightens, taking Gareth gently by the arm. "It's okay, Gareth." She turns back to me. "Rue was indeed a loss, keenly felt by everyone here. A mistake that will weigh heavy on me for the rest of my days, Sorcha. I was foolish in my belief that a witch as powerful as Rue was more than a match for a fledgling god. Is that why you are here? To remind me of my mistake?"

"No." I shake my head a fraction. "Of course not. I only want to know what your plans are now."

Glory's cool blue eyes narrow. "What is it to you? It has been many years since you traveled with us. I believed in your horror at what befell our Varanasi brothers and sisters, but I have heard since that you barely knew them. With Rue and the others perished, I have no one to verify what happened in that village in Worcestershire. So, why are you so keen to see this boy destroyed, Sorcha?"

I bring my gaze to match hers. "He is not a boy, as you well know." I lower my eyes to watch my fingers trail over a rough swirl in the wood. "The power he absorbed from Rue, what do you think that will do to something like him? He is dangerous, Glory, too dangerous."

"I lost loved ones, Sorcha. The decision does not rest easy. But we have not seen signs of any further attacks. Perhaps he is not as dangerous as you think. Perhaps you remember Varanasi wrong. Maybe he was provoked."

I feel the weight of Glory's accusatory stare. "He was half driven mad by poison," I reaffirm quietly.

"He isn't now. I will not risk more members of the coven for no good reason."

It is my turn to stare in disbelief at the high priestess. I am surprised she has given up so quickly. The loss of Rue must have hit them even harder than I imagined. "The slaughter of a coven isn't good enough for you?"

"It seems to be an isolated incident." Glory fixes her gaze. Gareth remains unflinching beside her, his curly black hair contrasting the coolness of his skin as the light of the torches chisels his cheekbones. If only he wasn't so damn spiteful, he would be beautiful.

I stare at them both for a moment. My mind racing, calculating, I look back down at the table. "That can only mean you don't know what he is planning," I say, my tone quiet, taking care with my words.

"Oh, and I suppose you do, Sorcha?" I can hear the venom in Gareth's voice.

It's hard to believe he was once more like a brother to me, and that I watched him grow up.

"He is careless," I spit back at him. "I have been watching."

"Like the snake that you are," Gareth says, not quite under his breath. It is clear he lays Rue and the others' deaths at my door.

"Gareth, please," Glory chides once more before giving the spotlight back to me, nodding for me to continue.

I know I have to play this just right. A wrong word and the coven will never agree to take action. "The girl, his human girl... it's not his intention to keep her human for much longer."

The coven members exchange confused glances.

"Why does this concern us?" Gareth questions.

"He plans on turning her into something of *his* creating. Not another creature, something new."

More confused glances, this time with hints of trepidation.

"You are right, I was not totally honest about my acquaintance with the Varanasi coven. I had only met them once before as they took great pains to call me when he arrived at their shores. They wanted protection, so to speak. I couldn't believe he was as ignorant to his situation as they claimed him to be. It was only when I saw his living twin that I truly believed what they said."

Glory pinches the bridge of her nose. "Sorcha, why did you not tell us this? Why did the coven require your protection?"

"His living twin made him extremely unstable. The coven was scared, and they didn't know what to do for the best. When it became apparent of his relationship with those whom he traveled with, the coven tried to use it to their advantage."

"Advantage?" Gareth questions.

"The advantage doesn't matter. It didn't work, and he killed them for it. What matters is, before I learned of what they were planning and Kali sent me away, she told me something that scared them all into taking such action that got them slaughtered."

"You have us on the edge of our seats here, Sorcha." Gareth smirks at me.

I smirk back. "It is not just the elements he can control. He forced the lifecycle into reverse. Kali saw it with her own eyes. Turned a plant back to seed."

Glory's eyes widen, but Gareth audibly scoffs as if my revelation is meaningless. The rage fires up my body, and I slam my hand onto the oak table, splitting it down the middle.

"He broke a fundamental law of the universe!"

The coven seems to snap to attention at the raising of my voice. I may be a lesser god, but I can command when the moment needs it.

"He was but a part of his true form then, and he could do that. What can he do now? With the power of Rue's soul in him. Do you want to wait and find out? Do you think he will stay quiet for long? Do you think something with that much energy doesn't affect *everything*?"

The timbre of my voice reverberates and echoes around the room, the following silence hanging heavy on the coven members staring at me until Glory brings her own fist down onto the edge of the split table, knocking half completely over.

"Fucking Arjun," she screams, picking up a knocked-over glass and throwing it to shatter against a nearby wall. "He should be here to clean up his own messes."

"What does that mean, Glory?" a nearby witch asks meekly.

Glory pushes her murky blonde hair out of her face. "It means the end of days," she spits out before releasing a long sigh. "It means Sorcha is right, something has to be done. His existence is too close to chaos, too far from the natural order."

"How do we stop something which cannot be killed, now that we don't have Rue?" Gareth murmurs.

Glory takes a solid breath in, steeling herself and meeting my eyes once more. "We have time. We will take time to prepare, not go in half-cocked this time. I assume you will stay here and help, Sorcha?"

"Of course." I grin.

Glory motions for Gareth to follow her, and I leave them to it, following a different path, a familiar path, trodden many times before now.

I run my fingers along the rough earthen walls, tracing the steps of my eleven-year-old self. My hair was already a pure white when my father—or the closest thing to a father I had ever known —left me here under Glory's care with little more than a promise to return and make me even stronger. A promise unfulfilled.

When the Irish coven had to flee their home to protect one of its own, I fled with them and have not returned since. *Until now.*

When I was younger, I wanted to blame Glory and her decision to move the coven for my father never returning to me. Because Glory had not continued his traditional sacrifices, he did not come back. It wasn't until I left Glory that I understood the truth, one she was too kind to tell me—I had been abandoned. I searched for many years for him, but he did not want to be found, not by me. It has been over fifty years since I last returned to Meath, and I cannot help but wonder why they are back now and what it feels like to Glory.

My room looks the same as it did when I left, books and clothes scattered everywhere, clothes from a different time, swirling pink-and-orange fabrics and monochrome minidresses. While I never killed, using my abilities had been fun. It was a liberating time to be alive. There had been hope in the air. I remember watching a man walking on the moon on my best friend's old television set. There seemed to be so much promise in the world. I rest my hand against the low curve of my room and feel the energy vibrating from Newgrange from here. There is the old energy that lies there, and then the new remnants from the events that eventually lead to Glory and her coven fleeing their home for over fifty years.

Back then, the coven had been massive, well over two hundred strong, an ancient and established coven dating back to the first witches. I didn't know the witch involved. I can't remember her face or where she ended up. The coven's numbers have dwindled over the years. Glory's nomadic lifestyle wasn't for everyone and many of them branched off, traveling apart from Glory and joining their Romany cousins, or some settling with new covens in need of a place to call home. But Glory could never forget Meath and the winding pathways of the old witch tunnels that reside beside the ancient monument of Newgrange.

"Well, look who the cat dragged in," a silvery voice comes from behind me.

I turn toward the willowy figure in my doorway. "Lily," I shriek, and in two strides, I'm across the room and pulling her into an embrace, holding my old friend impossibly close.

Lily may be as tall as me, but she's also slight and ethereal, with milky white skin and ice blue eyes, her bedraggled blonde hair hanging down to her shoulders.

"It has been far too long, my love," she tells me.

I nod, so happy to see her I can barely talk.

"Glory said you found her. I'm sorry to have missed you. I was in London at the time. I was hoping you would find us again."

"You look so well, Lily. As beautiful as the last day I saw you." I beam at her.

"Which was thirty years ago. I should be furious with you." She laughs before turning serious. "There has been lots of activity this past year, many rumors. Why am I not surprised to find you in the middle of it?"

"Rumors?" I ask, and the humor leaves her face.

"Isn't that why you are here?"

"Do you mean Peter?"

Now Lily looks confused, a smile ghosting her lips. "Who is Peter? Have you fallen in love again, Cia?"

"Didn't Glory tell you what happened in Varanasi?"

Lily nods, oblivious until I eye her enough for her to get the picture.

"Goodness, Cia, you certainly know how to pick them." She laughs.

"Don't, Lil." I shoot her a warning look. "And I am not in love with anyone. He's a monster who killed all of those people for crying out loud."

"Mmm... I saw the look in your eye when you said his name." Lily wiggles her finger at me. "I know you better than you know yourself, even after all these years."

I roll my eyes. "And it has nothing to do with the fact that you can read minds."

She examines the stuff strewn around my room, smiling to herself. "I don't even have to try around you," she muses.

"Well, do me a favor and don't mention it to Glory."

"Why?" Lily's nonexistent eyebrows rise in surprise.

"Because she wouldn't understand how I can be in love with him and want to destroy him at the same time. She will question my intentions with being involved with the mission."

Lily's playful stance turns serious. "Heavens, Cia, *that* is why you are here?" Her eyes narrow, scrutinizing me, and she moves back over to run a soft palm over my cheek, easing my face to inspect the jagged scorch scars on my neck. "Did he do this to you?"

"It was my fault," I say, wiggling out of her grip.

"It takes a lot to scorch your skin, Cia."

"I know," I confirm, giving her a look of understanding.

She moves to sit on the edge of my bed, patting the seat next to her. "So, tell me about him. What makes this guy who hurt you worthy of your love?"

I take the seat next to her. "For one thing, Lil, he is not human.

He is like me. Created by my father—" I catch myself. *I should stop calling him that.* "By Arjun. And it was never like that, not in any real sense of the word love."

Lily's brows furrow.

"I know you can read my mind, but I am being honest when I say that I don't know if I do love him, not the way I've loved before. It's something different, something hard to explain. I could curse that Varanasi coven for introducing me to him if they were not already dead."

Lily stifles a chuckle.

"Lil, you shouldn't laugh."

She composes herself. "So, what is it then?"

"Ugh, he drives me crazy. He is so oblivious it infuriates me to my bones, and he isn't remotely nice to anyone he chooses not to be. He is murderous and unhinged, and dangerously powerful for someone so bloody stupid."

Lily chuckles now. "But?"

"But..." I start. It is all too easy to be this way with Lily, even after all this time. She was my best friend for so long, before I decided to separate myself from those it would be too painful to watch die. "But despite it all, he is like me. And he is like bloody gravity. I can't escape him, Lil. I feel him everywhere. There's no detaching from him, whatever distance I put between us. He doesn't want me, though. And I want that feeling to stop."

Lily smooths her thumb against my temple. "You are in pain," she says, more to herself than me. "Physical pain. This is more than heartbreak, isn't it? It goes deeper."

I nod. "Yes. It hurts. But what I told Glory is true. He is dangerous, and what he is planning on doing to his human pet isn't natural. It is better for everyone if he is eliminated."

Lily looks at me with soft eyes. "I won't tell Glory, Cia. But tread carefully with your heart. You may find that it prefers a world with him in it to one without, despite what your brain is telling you."

Chapter Four

Connie

The warm glow and soft chatter of The Fish enfold me like a comforting blanket. A rosy heat in my cheeks from the red wine doesn't hurt either. Peter leans back in his chair to motion for another bottle, his movements languid and dripping with charm.

"Another?" Lauren giggles, her fingers dabbing her rosy cheeks. "This expensive wine is lost on me, I have to admit. As a student, I'm pretty happy with the cheap stuff."

"This is on us." Peter smiles at her, one of the few sentences he has uttered other than ordering his food this evening. The direct hit makes her blush even harder.

"How is uni going, Lauren?" I ask, trying to save her from her embarrassment and distracting Jamie from the fact that she is reacting to him.

"Really good, actually. This semester we are studying the Pre-Raphaelite Brotherhood. It's quite interesting."

"I have been hearing a lot about it." Jamie laughs, giving Peter a nod as he tops up his glass. "Including having to see a lot of sad-looking people in water."

Lauren gives his arm a playful slap. "They are beautiful. I swear you have no appreciation for culture. Anyway, Connie, I am sure you would appreciate it. You're the romantic sort, right? Didn't Peter whisk you away to Paris not so long ago?"

"Yes, he did." I smile, the heat rising in my face.

Lauren giggles, then sips her wine. "Well, I love it. There is something so stirring about it. I love the medieval influences. You know, everyone always goes to "The Lady of Shalott," but I am quite partial to a "Sir Galahad.""

I titter as Jamie rolls his eyes at her, and she shakes her head at him and says, "We don't all get a white knight, do we?"

She winks at me and eyes Peter, who is watching me, his expression betraying that his thoughts are anything but knightly.

I snort. "I know you don't fancy yourself as a white knight."

"Am I missing something?" His expression turns bewildered, and he looks from me to Lauren.

"Apparently not." Lauren laughs. "Just the wine getting to my head. I could jabber on for ages about my love of Arthur Hughes and Sir Galahad."

"I'm completely lost. Who are those people?" Peter looks to me for some kind of answer.

"You know, Sir Galahad, the quest for the holy grail and all of that..." Lauren trails off as if it should be obvious.

My smile fades as I realize where this is going, and I notice Jamie eyeing me from across the table.

"What's a holy grail?" Peter asks.

Lauren's gaze moves from me to Jamie incredulously before returning to Peter. "Are you serious? I thought everyone knew that story—"

"Peter's mother was pretty conservative, Lauren," I say. "I doubt she would've given much stock to Arthurian legends."

"What is it?" Peter asks again.

Lauren looks beyond baffled. "You know, the cup of life. It gives immortality to whoever drinks from it. Jesus was supposed to have drunk from it."

Peter's eyes snap back to me. "You knew about this?"

"It's just a story, Peter," I say. "It's not real."

"I'm real," he says simply, his dark eyes sparkling with hope.

Just what we need, a crusade.

"What on earth are you talking about?" Lauren giggles, her nerves showing a little.

Peter turns back to her with his most charming smile, and I feel it rolling out of him, the power, as the influence washes over her skin. "My mother was very conservative, and I love all things to do with history. You really don't need to worry. Don't think about that again."

Lauren nods, moving to take another sip of her wine.

The evening continues in a somewhat different vein. Jamie looks nervous. Lauren's tidbit of information has piqued Peter's interest, and both Jamie and I can see the longing in his eyes when he looks at her. She has something he wants. *Information.* So he spends the rest of the evening encouraging her to talk about Hughes and Waterhouse, and she tells him all the Arthurian legends she knows, paying particular attention to those of Sir Galahad and Merlin.

She glows under the weight of his attention and becomes more animated and loose-lipped as he continues to feed her more wine. I can't say I am looking forward to a night of Peter yakking on about a search for the bloody holy grail, so I try to think of excuses as to why it's a bad idea. I decide to drop a text to Lorna to give her a heads-up.

"I'm going to get some fresh air," I say as I rise, but Peter is on his feet in an instant, startling Lauren so much she swishes some of her red wine onto the tablecloth.

"Are you okay? I'll come with you."

"Peter, please sit down." I peek up at him through my eyelashes. "I'll be right here. I will stay in front of the doorway, okay?"

Peter glances to the front entrance, which he has a clear view of, giving me a slight nod and lowering himself back into his seat.

The clear night sky is good for my head, although I have to pay extra attention to hitting the right keys as I text Lorna.

Me: *Just to give you a heads up, Peter is going to think it's a good idea to search for the holy grail.*

Lorna: *What the hell? How did that happen?*

Me: *Lauren. She didn't know what she was saying. But I can see it in his face, he thinks this is it.*

Lorna: *But it's not real.*

Me: *You will need better reasons.*

Lorna: *Ok. I'll work on a logical argument... a logical argument against looking for the holy grail! As if I should need one!*

I snort at her last text. It's ludicrous.

The door swings open behind me, letting a burst of warm air envelop me.

"So, he has you on a short leash these days," Jamie says.

"It's since the barn," I remind him. "He's protective."

"He's psychotic," Jamie retorts, but there is no real malice in it.

I smile at him, linking my arm in his and turning to look up at the stars, slipping into a comfortable silence.

"Is what Lauren said going to get you in trouble?"

I chuckle. "Tons. He'll be going on about it for weeks. Don't be surprised if we're arrested trying to break into the Vatican or something."

Jamie laughs for a moment before becoming still again. "I guess I have to believe anything is possible these days."

"Hmm..." I agree, resting my heavy head on his shoulder.

Jamie leans his head on top of mine for a few moments before saying with some reluctance, "We should get back in before they miss us." He releases my arm and heads back inside.

Later, just as suspected, Peter is animated and excited as we walk back to my mom's house. Distracted, he lets me sway due to his leaning across my shoulders. Lauren had been so smashed she couldn't walk, so Jamie had to bundle her into the back of a taxi. *Lord,* I think to myself, ignoring Peter's ramblings, *she is going to feel awful in the morning.*

"You know, you shouldn't do that to people," I say out loud, cutting him off mid-sentence.

"Do what?" he asks, his large brown eyes the picture of innocence.

"She's not used to you. You can't just overwhelm her like that. The poor girl was a wreck."

Peter chuckles, leaning a little heavier on me with a wave of the hand. "She'll be fine. She will sleep it off. No harm done. Besides, the grail... I needed to know more. I can't believe no one thought of it before."

"It's not real, Peter. Besides, even if it was, do you know how difficult it would be to find, to try to verify any true accounts?"

"No harder than anything else we've been investigating. It's all myth and folklore, Con. This is a lead. Something to focus on."

"It's a wild goose chase," I say, my tone dry.

"I don't know what else to do." He pulls me closer, dropping his voice to a whisper as the look on his face turns mischievous. "I could take out Wixford, claim all those souls, and push them into yours. Maybe a fire, or a hurricane?"

"You would never," I refute, pushing him away from me without any real force, the smile that plays on my lips betraying me.

He catches my hand, spinning me around once, twice, light like I'm a prima ballerina. "Whatever you say, my love." He smirks before guiding me in close to kiss me. A warm, reverberating kiss I feel deep down in my stomach.

My mum is already asleep when we arrive home. She seems to sleep deep and hard these days. Although her new boyfriend tends to stay away when Peter and I are back.

My bedroom looks like a different place now. Although Peter doesn't own much stuff, it has far less space with the addition of a double bed. Plus, Peter is chronically messy. His clothes lie scattered everywhere as well as half-finished books and overgrown plant pots dotted across the floor and along the windowsill. In addition to random souvenirs we've brought back from our travels, there is also bric-a-brac Peter has picked up when he found it interesting. The window is forever open when we are here, letting the cool night air play with the thin curtain.

I lie outstretched on my front, lazily tracing the way the candlelight reflects across a crystal ball, the fractures of the spectrum of colors ghostlike with their fragile movements. I can hear

Peter pottering around behind me. He's wearing only his jeans and is smoking a joint Lorna gave him.

He is all mine, I think. *Sometimes I want to eat him up.*

"You probably shouldn't smoke that after drinking so much red wine. It will make you sick."

"It calms my nerves," he says as he comes to lie next to me, the earthy smell filling the room with him, his eyes wide as he looks up at me.

I move my fingers to trace the freckles I love so much and chide, "You have nerves now?"

He doesn't answer straight away, taking me in for a moment. "I can't sleep. It helps."

I can't argue there. The fact that his nightmares are catching is another unknown factor we cannot account for. I've dreamed it a few times more since the first. Even more like Peter, I had seen the blood-soaked ground between my toes, but the skin wasn't my own —it was his. A dark and terrible place surrounded by death, and Peter is always at the center. If I don't dream it, Peter does.

I pick up a small antique globe, an oddity Peter procured from somewhere or other. Spinning it slightly, looking at the gold scroll lettering and wanting to change the subject, I ask, "So, where to next?"

"I suppose Spain would be the obvious choice."

I roll my eyes at him. "You can't be serious. Do you honestly think the real holy grail is in Valencia?"

"It's worth ruling it out."

"And what..." I wave my hands around, "... you are just going to walk into the Cathedral and take it?"

He bites his thumb. "Why not?"

I eye him for a moment, the thrill of the idea washing over me. "You could pull that off?"

"I think so."

"It must be heavily protected."

"You're probably right." He grins. "I think I can handle it, but we can make more of a plan when we're there and see the setup."

The wine must have gone to my head more than I thought. "You know if the supposed holy grail is stolen, there will be uproar on a global scale."

"If it doesn't work, we'll put it back."

Sure, as simple as that. We will go and borrow the holy grail, no big thing. I rest my chin on his shoulder.

"Peter, you have gotten used to getting away with things, just taking what you want. But this isn't like walking into a hotel room or ordering champagne. This is something people will notice."

"So?"

So? I wait a beat before I carry on, our shadows dancing against the sloping wall of our room.

"Is that what you want? That kind of attention on a global scale. What if a new coven notices?"

"Connie." He drops the joint he's smoking onto the floor to go out, then rolls over to thread his fingers through my hair. "As much as you say the words, I don't think you truly understand what I would do to make you mine forever. There is nothing I wouldn't give, no line I wouldn't cross. And this way, I get my wish. *You.* And you get your wish, that no one has to die. Everybody wins."

I let his words float across my mind. They are reassuring, but I can't help noticing the gleam in his dark eyes. I know that devouring look all too well.

"Tell me that it's all for me. Be honest, that this isn't because there is a part of you wanting to cause trouble."

Peter's nose ghosts along my jawline, his breath making my skin prickle before his lips find the sweet spot. "Is that what you think of me?" he asks.

"Oh, I know you are trouble," I say before giving in.

Chapter Five

Peter

"Wrong way."

The night is cool, the candles long gone out, and Connie is sound asleep beside me. I slide my hand up my face to find it soaking, my hair clinging to the moist skin. Sitting up and looking around the quiet, still darkness of Connie's bedroom, I try to take in a deep steady breath. Just a dream, another nightmare, although not quite the normal terror. The same blood and destruction but something different this time, right at the end. *"Wrong way,"* the words echo in my head. I try to claw back to the memory. *What does "wrong way" mean?*

Connie stirs, wrapping her arm around my waist. "You okay?" she asks sleepily, her hands moving to the sheets and her eyes opening more when she finds them soaked through with sweat.

"Sorry..." I groan. "Nightmares again." I rake my hands through my hair, getting out of bed to let the air cool me.

"It's so hot in here." Connie moves to follow me, pulling the sheet off the bed.

40

"I know. It's the bloody nightmares... they make me cook. I feel like I'm boiling from the inside."

"Well, just make sure you don't start any fires in our bed." She yawns, bringing the balled-up sheet to her nose before throwing it into a pile in the corner. "Is it weird that the sheets smell nice to me? Kind of sweet."

"That is extremely weird." I pick up the joint from the floor I'd dropped earlier and move to the window. Leaning right out into the night in an attempt to bring my body back to a normal temperature, I look out across the fields and sleepy houses. A view I've appreciated so many times before.

Only tonight is different.

A light flickers off in the distance, a cool silver spark. Blinking, like morse code. I watch, letting the joint slowly slip from my fingers and fall to the garden below. The light flickers closer, brighter. A feeling, a strange sensation of familiarity. The light gets closer, until it starts to take a form, beginning to weave through the trees of the woods close to Connie's house.

"Con," I beckon her from her task of changing the sheets.

She pads over to the window and looks out in the direction of the bobbing orb. "What is that?" she whispers, the goose bumps rising on her skin, nothing to do with the chill in the air.

"I think it's here for us." Something deep in my core stirs, a connection, something that reminds me of someone, a feeling of belonging. "I think it's Anna," I say, hot tears filling my eyes.

"Is it a spirit?" Connie asks, but I don't answer as I break my fixed stare from the orb.

I rush into action, needing to get to her. Grabbing my jeans, I shove them on, throwing a hoodie at Connie.

"Get dressed. We're going." I go back to stare at the light snaking closer to the garden. *I'm coming, sister,* I think, then glance back to Connie, who has made no move to put any clothes on. "Con, I can keep you warm, but you need some clothes on. Let's go."

"Peter."

The way she says my name is so fragile it might shatter. The sound stops me in my tracks.

"Didn't Anna... She didn't go on. She's part of you now. That's not her."

The tears rise against my will and, for some reason, my throat burns. She hasn't meant for the words to hurt, but I feel them cut into my chest in a deep gouge. I gaze back to the window, giving an involuntary shudder. "It feels like her."

"What if it's a trap? What if it's witches, or Sorcha?"

The light is in the garden now, and I look between it and Connie. "I need to go to it. I can't explain it. Please come with me. Please, please." I hear my voice shake as I beg. Connie is right. *How can it be her? It feels so like her, but I took her life—it's mine. Her soul is part of mine.* But I can feel the pull and the connection like I always did with her. *My other half, my twin.* A tear escapes my eye and rolls down my face.

Connie crosses the room to catch it, saying nothing, only lowering her face and pulling on the nearest clothes to follow me.

We slip out of the house in stealth, although I tend to keep Connie's mum in a harmless state of sedation when we are here. Another person in Connie's life who hates me. Although I cannot bring myself to care.

Outside, the orb—a familiar silver light—bobs around Connie's apple tree. Sharing the same space with the orb, the feeling of familiarity is even stronger, and the tears surge to the surface again, so strong I whisper, "Anna?"

The orb glows bright and bobs out of the tree, gliding toward us and then dancing around us. Connie's grip on my hand is tight, the shine of the orb reflecting in her eyes. It doesn't feel like danger. It doesn't feel like a trap. My chest aches with the emotion of being around it. I could live a thousand lifetimes and still mourn my sister.

"We need to follow it," I mumble to Connie.

She doesn't say anything but walks beside me, the silence between us filled with anticipation as the orb leads us out of the garden and back in the direction of the woods. It casts a different type of quiet into the night. The calmness after a night of snow, crisp and delicate. Neither of us talks for fear words might break the magic.

The orb bobs into the woods, weaving in and out of the trees and sometimes circling back around us. We can't have walked for long, but the ache inside grows so strong I begin to wonder if I've died and am going to heaven, going to see my sister again, and not in the throes of poison, unable to comprehend what is really happening. *Maybe I can hug her one last time. Tell her I love her. Tell her goodbye.*

It takes me a while to realize I am crying, actually crying. The pain in my chest threatening to burn me whole, leaving only ashes. My sister's soul may have completed me, but my heart will never be whole. I struggle to take a breath, and Connie stops following the orb to throw her arms around me, letting my shaking body lean against her. Not saying anything except my name, and it's a balm. If I could hear only one sound for the rest of my life, this would be it.

I push the ache of my broken heart away.

I can't let it in.

I can't break like that again.

The orb simmers beside us. At first, I think it must be getting impatient, but soon it stops dancing to instead glow brighter, stretching in length like a doorway to another galaxy, the light so blinding Connie and I have to break apart to shield our eyes. I take an instinctive step in front of Connie. The light so luminous I almost fail to notice when it changes. It's no longer an orb—it's starting to take form.

The shape flickers into focus, hazy and blurred at the edges, shifting into something much taller than me. Something that looks human, sort of, but the skin retains a glow with a remnant of the orb that lingers behind their shoulders. They are a pearlescent kind of creature. Two large eyes with gold banding around the skin of one of their forearms. As the light of the orb wanes, the features appear human. More masculine features begin to sharpen on the tall, beautiful creature in worn earthen clothes.

"You are Peter," they say, their voice calm and commanding at the same time. The final glow of the orb fades to reveal someone who looks like a man, dark-haired and wide-eyed, the gold banding even more prominent now that I can see properly.

Connie takes a step from behind me.

"Son of Cassandra," they state.

"How do you know that name? Who are you?"

"Someone with a vested interest in the outcome. I am Boots."

"Boots?" Connie questions.

"I have had many names. Boots is my favorite." He smiles, and it makes the orb light glow around his shoulders again.

"Are you a god?" I ask.

"No."

"Are you an angel?" Connie asks with quiet trepidation.

"Like I said... I have gone by many names over the years. I will explain as much as I can, but I do not have much time. I am not supposed to be here. I should not be interfering."

"Interfering? Why are you here?" I ask, taking a step closer to him. Up close, his wide eyes are not dark, but the irises are ultra-light, almost like crystal. "You are not human, are you?"

"I would have thought that was obvious." Boots laughs.

"How did you do that? Why do you feel like my sister?" Boots flinches at the question but does not answer.

"I apologize. That was not my intention. I only meant to make myself friendly. I can take many forms, more often than not, I appear comforting. I did not mean for it to be painful. I came here to tell you that you are looking in the wrong direction. The answers you seek will *not* be found in Valencia."

Connie looks from Boots back to me. "How did you know that?"

"It is my job to watch, but I should not be interfering."

"Then why are you?" I eye Boots with suspicion. In turn, his wide eyes stretch wider.

"Because there are some who would want the Son of Cassandra to succeed. You know there is a lot in a name, Peter."

"How did you know her?" I ask, ignoring his riddle.

Boots cringes. "I didn't," he replies, rubbing his left arm the way someone does without thinking when reminded of an old wound. As I glance at the skin beneath the cuff of his sleeve, I notice there is no gold banding on this arm, although there might have been once. It is now burned away, and his skin is covered with the deep canyons of burn scars.

"What are those?" I nod to his forearm.

"That's not what is important. The point is, you are going the wrong way."

"Was that you in my head?"

"Of course," he snaps. "You need to listen to me."

"Well, what is the right way?" Connie asks, with a shred of impatience in her tone.

"Across the Atlantic, in a city called New Orleans, there is a witch there who will help you. Her name is Marie."

"No, no witches. The witches want to kill me." I hold my hands up, there is no way any witch will help Connie and me.

"Listen to me. It's different there, a different thread of magic not recognized by the traditional witches. It is darker magic, new magic. One less concerned with the natural order. Marie *will* help."

I shift uncertainly to look back at Connie, who gives me a little shrug. "Obviously you know what I am trying to do, for Connie. You are okay with that?"

Boots averts his gaze. "My approval is irrelevant. There are wider things afoot, and the future is not set in stone." He seems to debate his next words. "Mankind is on a precipice. What happens to you could sway the outcome. I have watched for a long time, and when you watch for that long, you cannot help but care. The natural order... sometimes you don't want it to win."

Connie gets a possessive grip on my arm. "We just want to be left alone."

Boots blinks at her, then looks back to me before he continues, although he doesn't need to say the words. "You know that will *never* happen for you, don't you?"

I don't answer, but my stomach plummets as Connie looks up at me.

"I am sorry, boy. It is a lot to put on your shoulders, but the one you call father didn't know what he got his hands on when he met your mother." Boots takes a long breath, the first I have noticed him take. Whatever he is, he looks tired and battle-weary. "It shouldn't have happened, but it did. And maybe it happened for the best. Maybe some good can come out of it." He seems to be talking to himself now.

"Boots," Connie snaps him out of his reverie.

"Yes. The point is, Peter, your being here set off a chain of events. Or, perhaps, continued a chain of events started way before you were born. But when you were brought forth to this planet, it changed everything. Old secrets started to wake up." He shakes his head. "Either way, we stopped interfering a long time ago, and I shouldn't be here now."

"You keep saying that," I say dryly.

"That's because it's true." He pushes his hands through his long, dark hair.

I hadn't noticed before how it looks almost liquid. Something stirs deep inside of me, a deeper kind of recognition.

"I should go," he says after a moment.

The words tear at my insides. For some reason, it feels like a loss. "Boots."

He stops and his orb eyes meet mine, his eyes like crystal, and that deep feeling brings the tears back into my eyes.

"I have to go, Peter," he says as he takes my hand. "I am sorry I could not have known you more. What a creature you are."

"This can't be the last time I see you," I say before I know I am saying it.

Boots moves his free, gold-banded hand to the back of my neck, bringing my forehead to his, the cool skin there and his eyes somewhere between a burning passion and stark desperation. "Maybe. In another life. Go to New Orleans, that is the way."

In the blink of an eye, he is gone.

I stare into the space between the trees where he stood only moments before with nothing to do but sink to my knees, my fingers finding cool comfort in the earth. I feel like I am slipping, drifting into the abyss. It was a moment with Boots, but his absence is devastating. The loss of my mother, my father, my sister... I killed them all.

"Peter, Peter." Connie's cool skin grasps at the hot surface of my chest.

My head drops back into her hand. *"Burn it all, Peter,"* the voice in the back of my mind tells me. I am fire, but Connie's hands feel cool. They soothe, bringing my temperature back down.

"Peter, come back to me."

My focus shifts and I find the jeweled green of her eyes in the sea of stars. "Connie." I snake my arms around her waist, pulling her down to the ground with me. Noticing the cinders around my knees kindling the dry leaves on the ground, I wipe a hand quickly across them. Breathe Connie in.

"Peter, what was that?"

I shake my head, resting it in the crook of her neck. "Kali was right. She was right all along. He was an angel, Con, or an alien. Whatever you want to call it, it's all the same. An ancient being, one of the first. The very things that started human life here."

Connie shudders.

Once more, I wish I could read her mind as she looks down at me to pull me back to my feet.

"Let's get back to the house" is all she says though.

I let her pull me up, and we walk back to the house in silence, the bare floor of the woods dry against my feet. The fire is well and truly subdued with Connie's cool hand in mine. The interaction with Boots seems more unreal with every second that passes until, if Connie hadn't been there with me, I might think I dreamed it. Boots' features are already becoming blurry, leaving the lasting memory of the brilliant light and feeling of being so close to my flesh and blood lingering.

We quietly pad up to Connie's room. I'm exhausted when I sit at her desk chair and rub my eyes. Boots may have brought us a trail to follow, but my mind swims at all the new questions now left unanswered. Why would an angel care for the lineage of my mother? Care so much that they are prepared to upset the natural order. He said that, with my birth, old secrets had started to wake up, but he gave no indication of what.

I look around me for something to drink. Reading my mind, Connie hands me an old bottle of whiskey that has been fermenting on the windowsill.

"You okay?" she asks in a hushed voice, wrapping her dressing gown around my shoulders, more for comfort than anything else.

I take a deep drink and meet her eyes. Those beautiful jewels I have tainted. "Are you sure about this, Connie? About me? This shit is going to follow me everywhere, forever."

"This again?" She kneels at my feet and takes my hand. "I told you I am with you. That will never change. I will always choose you."

"You are too good for me," I whisper.

"How can you say that? Peter, a literal angel cares about you. Surely that counts for something?"

"Hmm..." I take another swig before passing the bottle to Connie. "He must be some kind of renegade angel. Did you notice the burns on his arm? He even said he was breaking the rules by interfering. I just don't understand... it felt so much like Anna. My head is all messed up."

Connie pushes the hair out of my eyes. "What next, Peter? What do you want to do?"

I stare for a moment, thinking. "Let's do it. Forget the grail, let's go to New Orleans. As soon as we can."

"This is it, isn't it?" Connie's lip trembles for a fraction, just long enough for me to catch it.

I almost don't want to ask her to do this. To make her leave the people she loves breaks my heart. To hurt her in any way is at odds with all my instincts. I want her to be happy. But more than anything, I want her with me. So I smooth my thumb over her cheek, look into her eyes, and tell her, "It is."

She takes a visible swallow, and her eyes become wet. "Do I have time to say goodbye?"

"Of course," I tell her.

Whatever you ask, I will give you are the words I don't say.

Chapter Six

Connie

"What an earth do you call this?"

My mum holds up what I can only presume is the end of the joint Peter dropped out of the window last night. I pretend to get a closer look to better scrutinize it, even though I know it is a rhetorical question.

"It looks like weed to me," I say.

Her face turns different shades of purple, gearing up to give me a piece of her mind.

"It's Peter's," I tell her coolly before she has a chance to shout at me. Might as well throw him under the bus. She doesn't like him anyway.

I can almost feel him roll his eyes as he continues to potter around the kitchen, making breakfast. She turns on him, ready to let loose, but he doesn't even look up.

"Don't bother," he commands, starting to plate my breakfast.

Without a second glance, my mum drops the subject. Kind of handy, that, sometimes. Instead, she sulks off into the living room. I sidle up to him, taking the coffee he's made me out of his hands.

51

"You know, you could try to be a little more discrete," I say, knowing he won't take any notice.

"Here." He slides me a plate of what he has been making. Scrambled eggs with rocket and oven-roasted cherry tomatoes he's grown in the back garden. On the side is sourdough bread, which he also made. "Breakfast of champions." He smiles.

"Wow. This looks delicious." I grab the fork, ready to dig in.

"Hmm..." He catches my face to give me a long, slow kiss. "You're delicious."

His kiss makes me breathless. I would think after so long together he would stop being able to do this to me, that his effects would diminish over time. Except, just when I think I can't love him any more, I do. Part of me still finds it hard to believe he won't get bored of me one day. Perhaps that's why he has been so hesitant with my immortality of late. It would suck to have an ex as an immortal, following you around for all of eternity.

"You know..." I glance sideways at him as we eat, "... I need to spend some time with my mum before we go. She has always been there for me, through everything. I need to say goodbye."

Peter only glances at me for a second before going back to his food. "Are you going to tell her? That we aren't coming back."

My throat feels thick. "I don't have the heart. I don't know how I would even begin to explain it. I think I am just going to say this trip will be longer. At least prepare her for that."

He nods.

"Peter..." I draw out his name with care.

He stops eating and looks up.

"I need to do this without you, have this time with her." I can see it flash behind his eyes, the hardness of what he really wants to say, but it only lasts for a second before he dips his head again.

"Okay," he agrees, sliding off the stool at the breakfast bar. "I'll be upstairs." He walks past me, taking a bottle of wine out of the refrigerator.

It makes me squirm. I wish he wouldn't drink during the day, but I let it go. He won't leave the house without me, and upstairs, on his own, he will be incredibly bored.

I make my way into the living room, where my mum is watching television. She looks up at me in surprise as I approach, lingering by the door.

"Hey." I have no idea why I feel so shy of my own mum all of a sudden.

She eyes me suspiciously as I take a seat beside her. "What's going on?"

"We're leaving soon."

"Already? You've only been home for a week. Surely, he has to run out of money at some point and you two will have to get jobs. Or, you could think about going to university again."

The thickness in my throat is back again. Taking her hand, I say, "I've told you, it's hard for him here, Mum. Everything reminds him of Anna." I fight with myself to say the words. "I doubt we will ever settle here."

My mum doesn't say anything, and I can't bring myself to look at her. I know in her heart of hearts she already knows this, or at least suspects it, but neither of us has said it out loud before. I wish it didn't hurt so much, and I fight to keep the tears down. She doesn't need to know that when I say goodbye to her this time, it will be the last.

"So where are you off to this time?" she asks after a while, regaining her composure.

"New Orleans."

"I've never heard that one on your wish list before."

"This is one of Peter's, and it's probably going to be a longer trip. You know, to make the journey worthwhile. So I was thinking it would be nice if we could spend some time together, just me and you."

I chance a look at her, and her beaming smile makes my heart break.

"That would be lovely, Connie. What do you have in mind?"

"For starters..." I smile, leaning into her arms, "... let's make use of this lazy Saturday morning and hang here, watch rubbish TV, and catch up."

So that's what we do. Drink loads of tea and laugh at the television, Barney coming to lie between us. She tells me all about her new boyfriend, who happens to be called Pete, and how happy he makes her. I'm so pleased she has someone for when I am gone.

In the afternoon, we open our own bottle of wine, which we sip in the kitchen as she makes us some lunch. We giggle over gossip like we used to, my mum being more than happy to listen to me moan about some of Peter's more annoying habits, like leaving wet towels everywhere and having to have all the windows open all the time.

"Or leaving muddy footprints all over the kitchen floor," Mum chimes in, laughing after her second glass of wine. "What does your boyfriend have against shoes, Connie?"

I shrug my shoulders. "He just forgets to put them on, Mum."

"Just like he forgets to close doors. I swear that boy was born in a barn. It's a good job we live in a small village, anyone could walk into this house."

"Don't get me started. I think he has gone through about ten phones this year. He leaves them everywhere."

My mum laughs again, running her finger along the rim of her glass. "He's an excellent cook, though," she concedes. "I will give him that one. You have to appreciate a man who knows his way around the kitchen." She raises her glass to me, which I clink, and her expression turns more serious with the blush of her cheeks. "I know me and him don't always see eye to eye. But I do love seeing you so happy, Connie. You are so different this time around."

"What do you mean?"

"I don't know what really happened in India between you two. Before you left, I could see how much you adored him, and it's no secret what a charming boy he is, when he wants to be," she adds. "When he came back, I know I wasn't happy about what happened with Jamie. But, I don't know, your confidence, Connie... you just glow. You have always been beautiful, but I've never seen you look so sure of yourself. Now, when I see you two together, it's how he looks at you." She thinks to herself for a moment, her hand to her chest, and I have forgotten to breathe. "You're not this puppy-eyed girl anymore. You are this incredible woman, and I am just glad he sees that too."

I cross the kitchen and throw my arms around her, holding her so tight she could break. "Thanks so much, Mum. I am... I am so happy."

"Then I am happy for you." She hugs me back.

When I trundle upstairs in the late afternoon, I half expect him to be asleep or to have climbed out the window to go to Lorna's, but to my absolute surprise, he is up, sitting at my desk on my laptop. His eyes rake over me as I enter.

"I spoke to Lorna," he tells me.

"I was half expecting you to have gone over."

He shakes his head. "We can go tomorrow." He swigs the near-empty bottle of chardonnay, looking completely ridiculous.

"So, what did Lorna say?"

"She thinks about two weeks. To get everything in order, buy the tickets, visas, and all that stuff." He lets out a long sigh, turning in the chair to face me. "She made a good point... the name Marie isn't much to go on."

"Oh, yeah, I never thought of that," I admit.

"Yeah, well, me either." He takes another long swig before handing me the bottle.

Why not?

I take it from him. *I guess we are both ridiculous.* "Maybe Boots told her, and she'll be expecting us."

"Maybe. But we also got thinking to what Boots meant by this new magic, one not so concerned with breaking the natural order, and that maybe if this Marie isn't expecting us, then it will at least help us narrow things down."

"And?"

Peter smiles his devilish smile, which is all too inviting. "Voodoo."

"Voodoo." I grin back at him as he pulls my hand to straddle him on the chair.

"Have you heard of that before?"

"Only in books and TV. Nothing real."

He rests his hands on the top of my thighs, leaning his head back onto the top of the chair. "I guess we'll find out how much is real when we get there. It's always hard to tell from the internet. But if there's any truth in what I have seen, this magic is a lot darker, more open to possession, less guarded."

"Sounds interesting." I raise my eyebrow. *It sounds scary.*

"Mmm..." is all he has to say to that. He looks lost in thought.

"What else did Lorna say?"

"Not much."

"Oh? She had nothing to say about Boots?"

"Of course, she had lots to say about Boots."

"Like?"

He moves his hands to rub his eyes before taking the wine bottle from me. "Just the same questions that I have no answers to. How did he know my mum's name? Why does he care about what happens to me? Why is a frigging angel telling me to go to New Orleans? I have even fewer answers than Lorna." He pinches the bridge of his nose. "He said a lot was in a name. Lorna thought that was interesting. She said Cassandra is associated with Cassandra of Troy."

"The Greek myth?"

"That's the one. Anyway, Lorna told me what it was, and I can't say I'm a huge fan of the theory. My mother said some pretty wild things in her time. A lot of things that no one believed. She even told Anna about my influence long before either of us knew about it. Anna, of course, didn't believe her until... well, until she did."

"You never talk about her," I say quietly, taking the bottle from him and setting it down on the desk behind him.

Peter's body lurches, and he brings his forehead to rest on my shoulder. "I don't blame her for what she did to me. But that doesn't mean she was nice."

I lean my head to rest against his, threading my fingers through his golden hair.

"She was cold." He thumbs the top of my leggings, still not looking at me. "I was a mistake, Connie, a terrible mistake that she made. What she did was do everything she could to neutralize the threat. Keep me hidden, teach me the way things should be. It wasn't love... it was fear. That was my childhood. And when she died, I turned into the thing she tried so hard to prevent anyway. I don't want to talk about that."

"You are not a mistake, Peter, and you can talk to me. I'm not scared of you. I love you, all of you."

He pulls away to look at me, and the softness in his eyes is enough to kill me. "Say it again."

"I love you," I tell him, peppering his neck with kisses. "I love you, I love you, I love you. Forever. I love you, forever."

He wraps his strong arms around my waist. "That's all that matters now."

———

Sometimes I wonder if Peter and I are merging into one person. Now that Peter is whole, I am not the thing that keeps him level. I'm not his balance. I am something else. Now that he is whole, he is something else. We are both different people to the teens who met under the stars years ago, creating our own cycle, constantly feeding into each other, never tiring, never wanting to be apart. Peter can't let me go, and I don't want to be away from him. I can lose days with him. I have to remind myself I need to spend time with my mum, to say goodbye. Not spend days tangled up in bed with him. Even on those days, I feel better knowing he is still in the house, waiting for me to come back to him, talking into the night, trying to fight off our collective nightmares.

As the first week passes, I become increasingly aware of the one goodbye I truly don't want to make. For some reason, my mum's ignorance makes it easier. Jamie will know this is *the* goodbye. I only hope I can convince him he should come when all is said and done.

I watch Peter stir in the late morning sun beaming in through the window. He had wanted to make my last days in Wixford sunny ones. It's good to see him sleep—last night had been bad. I'm hoping whatever we find in New Orleans will drive off the night terrors. I hate to wake him, but his leg is heavy on my abdomen.

Once he's off me, I shuffle out of bed and slink to the bathroom to make myself look half-presentable. I push my now long, unruly hair out of my face. My dark hair has turned a shade or two lighter from traveling to sunnier places, and my skin is more sun-kissed.

The black rims of my emerald-tinted green eyes have taken a little getting used to, but my features are a tad more defined from losing weight again—not that I'm as skinny as when I came back from India. I have never felt happier about the way I look. It's strange to feel this way, completely comfortable in my own skin.

When I get back to my room, Peter is wide awake, propped up on his elbow, reading a book he seems to have been reading forever.

I gently kneel next to him and kiss the top of his head. "I need to go and see him today. Before I lose my nerve." I move and start getting dressed before he can distract me. "Can you just not be a giant pain in the ass for once?" Peter doesn't say anything. I had a feeling this would happen, but when I chance a look at him, he only looks surprised. "What?"

"Nothing. I mean, I knew you would. But I felt sure you would ask me to stay behind. That you would want to see him on your own."

I pick a pale blue sundress, shrugging my towel to the floor. "I thought it would be pointless to suggest. Anyway, maybe you could just, you know, loiter. Like maybe, just wait outside or something."

Peter laughs. "You make me sound like a stalker."

"More like a shadow," I muse, pulling my hair high into a bun.

Peter chuckles again, getting out of bed and pulling on whatever clothes he finds on the floor first.

"What's so funny?"

"You know, Jamie called me a creature of the night once. I guess he wasn't too far off."

"He's strangely astute," I say, my tone lighter than I feel while trying not to think about the knot in my stomach and trailing my fingers across my necklace. "When are we going to see your aunt?"

Peter comes up behind me and wraps his arms around my

waist to watch me apply my makeup in my wardrobe door mirror. "We can go before the flight."

I stop applying my lip gloss. "That's it?"

"What do you mean?" he asks between placing kisses on my neck, which send shivers down my spine and goose bumps across my body. "What else is there?"

"We've only seen her once since we've been back. She was so glad to see you. She'll be devastated when you tell her you're not coming back. That she didn't get to see you more."

"She won't be because I'm not telling her." He meets my eyes in the mirror. "Don't look so horrified, Con. You're not telling your mum either."

"It's different. Your aunt knows."

"Con..." he drops his hands in exasperation, "... don't do this. I don't know why you want me to say it. I know it makes you disappointed in me."

"Peter."

"I don't care. I don't care about saying goodbye to her. I don't owe her anything, and I don't want to have to deal with the emotional situation it will create. She only pretends she cares because she feels guilty. It's easier this way. But..." he continues before I have a chance to argue, "... there is somewhere I need to go before we leave. After you see Jamie, if that's okay with you?"

It feels like years since I knocked on the solid black wooden door of Jamie's house. In reality, it was only a little over a year ago I was coming here often. Eating dinner with his mum at their dining table, like she insisted they always do. Jamie's mother dotes on him, has ever since his dad left when we were thirteen. Jamie always claimed it was a good thing his father left and talked about how he hated him, but I know it hurt him in ways he could never speak about. I haven't seen his mum since we broke up. My heart races as I knock on the door, and I hope she isn't home. Part of me hopes Jamie isn't home either. I glance behind me. Peter, true to his word, is waiting on the wall behind the conifers.

I am just about to give up when the front door swings open to reveal Jamie in his shorts.

"Hiya, Con. I thought you were the postman. What are you doing here?" He ruffles the hair on the back of his head.

I take a big gulp. I should have practiced what I want to say. Or maybe Peter was right. Maybe it's better to not say anything at all. The only problem is now I am saying nothing, fumbling over my words. *Just say something,* my brain tells me.

"Fuck," Jamie curses under his breath. "You're here to say goodbye, aren't you?"

I still haven't said anything, but hot tears dampen my eyes. I can only nod as they begin to spill. *I didn't know it would be so hard.*

"Shit," he exclaims.

Jamie closes the distance and wraps his arms around my neck, pulling me close. I can smell the nostalgic scent of his aftershave, feel the stickiness of his skin from the heat.

"I'm not ready for this," he tells me, his voice quavering. "Was it what Lauren said? What's changed?"

"No." I break away from him, finally finding my voice. "We have a lead. It feels different, more final." I don't have it in me to ramble. I simply look up into his pale blue eyes.

His hand moves up to take my face, thumbing under my eyes. "I can't say goodbye to you, Connie."

"Then tell me this isn't goodbye." I take his hand. "Promise me that you will come and see me one day, when this is all over."

Instead of fighting me, he nods. "Okay, yes. When you call, I will come." He gives a gentle laugh, shaking his head a little while looking up at the sky. "I will always come."

I chew my lip and smile despite myself. "You're too good for me," I tell him.

He doesn't say anything, only looks at me, a thousand things he wants to say flitting through his eyes. I move and hug him again, possibly for the last time.

"Maybe you will come back," he says without any conviction.

I hold him a little closer. "This was never permanent. He only kept coming back here for me."

I feel Jamie's body tense underneath me. I know in my heart what he wants to say. To choose different, to stay, to pick him. To let Peter go. That, in time, I will burn for staying too close to the sun. For a second, a fraction of a second, I wish I could.

We don't say much more—there's not much left to say.

When I emerge from Jamie's driveway, Peter is still leaning against the wall, watching me with concern. I try to rub away the evidence of my sadness from my tear-stained face, feeling guilty about what he must think about me crying so much over leaving Jamie. Rather than make me feel guilty, he smooths his thumb down my cheek and asks, "Do you want me to make it rain?"

The lump in my throat comes back, and I have lost my words again. All I can do is nod and bury my face in his chest. His arms wrap around me as the first drops hit. Heavy, soaking rain drenches us in minutes. So heavy my tears mix easily with the downpour. After letting me get my grief out of my system, I look up into his bottomless brown eyes. They're still full of concern and warmth.

"Better?"

I nod. "Thanks for that." I smile, gesturing to the sky, the rain clearing up as suddenly as it came. "You always know what I need. So, where do you need to go?"

"You'll see," he tells me, looking a touch dubious, then leads me back in the direction of my house but forking off early and entering the woods.

At first, I think he must be trying to find the spot where we met Boots. After a while, however, I realize where we are headed, and I start to pull back on Peter's arm.

"I know," he says, not looking at me. "I just need to see it one last time. You know, I was so certain Boots was Anna, and I kept thinking that I never really had a chance to say goodbye. I don't know if I'll ever be able to, not truly, but I figured this is the only place to try. I've never really said goodbye to either of them... my mother, Anna... and I can't let them go."

I give his hand a squeeze. "I don't think you can ever truly let the people you've lost go. It's important that we keep the memory of those we love alive. Especially Brady and Anna."

"Even if it hurts?"

"Even if it hurts. Peter, I get it about your mother and all. We should talk about Anna more. I know it hurts, but you loved her more than anything, and the more you talk about her, the easier it will get. I think it will start to hurt less." I'm rambling again as Peter pulls me along. "The more you deal with it, the less... you will be less..."

"Less what?" Peter looks down at me out of the corner of his eyes, looking somewhat amused.

"Less angry." I breathe out.

"I seem angry to you?" The corners of his lips turn up, and I know he is not taking me seriously anymore.

"Not to me. But I can see it in your face when you don't think anyone is watching. The drinking, Peter, and this mask you wear like you don't care about anything. I know you are angry. God help the person who makes you snap."

He rests his arm around my shoulders. "I'm not angry, and I'm not going to snap. You don't need to worry."

"Why not? You worry about me."

He doesn't answer as we make our way to the edge of the tree line and the back of the grand house comes into view. I see that it's been repainted a brilliant white, and the top windows—once wooden, flaking, and overgrown with nature trying to reclaim the house—are now framed with clinical white facias and refitted with large glass panes to let as much light in as possible.

The overgrown wild garden is now blocked from view by wooden fencing, only the top of a climbing frame visible over it.

Peter stands and stares at it. I can imagine what he is thinking. This isn't his home—it's lost the identity it carried to him.

He will find no closure here.

He separated from this place a long time ago.

"It's a good thing you sold it. That there is a new family here to love it," I offer, feeling like I should say something. "Make happy memories."

He exhales a long, deep breath, placing his free hand onto a nearby tree. "You're right, but I need to say goodbye too." Under his hand, the bark springs into life, pushing vines traveling up its trunk and sending the Viburnum into overload, the petals shedding all around us, landing like confetti in our hair. "Goodbye, sister. I am so sorry for everything. I-I hope you have peace. I hope you feel that in here." He moves his hand to his heart. "I will carry you everywhere, always. I wish every day that you were still here. I would give it all up to have you back, to have you back for a minute. I only hope I don't disappoint you."

Trapped between sadness and beauty, I move my hands up to catch the petals on my open palms, enjoying the velvet touch of them on my skin. He's so sad it hurts to look at him, so instead, I turn my face up to the branches, letting some of the petals land on my eyelids, my arms stretched out as I twirl around. The petals break free of my hair and chase me in the wind. When I open my eyes, he doesn't look so sad anymore and, smiling, he catches my hand to spin me some more. He keeps spinning me as the petals dance around me until I am thoroughly dizzy and he is laughing.

I become so dizzy I stumble and he has to catch me so I don't fall over.

"Seventeen years, Connie. This was my world for seventeen years, and none of it was real. *I* wasn't real, and then I met you." He looks at me, my gentle, soft, loving Peter. "You are the home I never knew I missed. I wasn't real until I met you. I wasn't living until I met you."

Chapter Seven

Sorcha

The cool waters shine like crystal in the afternoon sun as I dip my feet in and out of them while lazing on the riverbank of the Boyne, my hair splayed out behind me as Lily weaves daisies into it. The warm sun on my face is a perfect contrast to the cool on my feet, and for a moment, I allow myself to feel content. To feel happy and relaxed in Lily's company and not think of battle strategies for a moment.

Glory has been sending out members of the coven on reconnaissance—emissaries to the great covens of the world—to ask for assistance, to share knowledge and power of their most powerful witches. Not an easy mission, given the falling out Glory's coven experienced over fifty years ago when some great rule had been broken.

So, while we await news, we have had little to do but bide our time and speculate.

"Do you remember what happened here?" I ask Lily, breaking our comfortable silence.

"Not really. It was all kept very hush-hush from everyone.

Strictly need to know." Lily clucks. "To be honest, I haven't thought about it in a long time. I find it best not to dwell on the past. No good can come of it."

"I can't even remember who it was."

"Doireann," Lily states. "It was Doireann. I don't know what she did, but whatever it was, it made our home unsafe. She was never the same after we left."

"What happened to her?"

"She died." Lily's eyes become distant. "Of a broken heart." She stops her braiding and looks across the lush countryside. "It is so strange being back. I was born here, you know? It almost feels like I am haunting the place. Like reopening an old wound." She views me with caution as I sit up. "Did you ever go back? To where you were born, I mean?"

"Only once." I push my fingers through the grass. "Right after I left Glory."

"How was it?"

"It didn't feel much like home. It had been too long. But the grove was still something to behold, beautiful and strange. I always felt so connected to it. However, I felt more of a burden to the coven there, a reminder to them of what they had lost."

Lily strokes the side of my face. "It was not your fault, Cia. You cannot keep carrying this guilt. Human bodies are not built for that type of ceremony. Your mother's death is not on you. Arjun... he did not know the consequences, or he did not care. Either way, you have to stop blaming yourself."

I look down at my hands, tracing the pattern of my tattoos there. "His mother survived, you know, for seventeen years. His mother and his twin."

Lily's eyes widen, but she doesn't say anything.

"I just keep thinking, Lil, maybe after all this time, maybe it is me. There has to be a reason. Maybe Arjun was right to leave me because it was my fault that my mother and father died, and my brother. What if there is something wrong with me?" I take a deep breath before I go on. "And I can feel this thing, deep down inside, telling me Peter should be mine and me his, and yet he doesn't want me. I must... I must be broken."

"Oh, my love." Lily shuffles closer, wrapping her long arms and legs around me.

"I hate this." I laugh, half shrugging her off and looking up to the clear blue sky. *I have to pull myself out of this wallowing.* "I hate feeling so weak. I shall talk about him no more. He is banished from my mind."

"Cia." Lily grabs my cheeks so rough that the blood rushes to my face. "You are a lioness. But someone has to *see* who you really are. Those walls you have built so high... it's not a bad thing to let someone in every now and then."

Mmm... it's never worked out so well before.

I have only been in true love twice in my one hundred and nine years. The problem with being immortal is that partners never last. Even the witches die in the end. A pain I have locked away and promised myself never to visit again.

"You are the only one I love, Lil," I tease, getting to my feet and splashing into the shallows of the river.

"And I, you. One day, you will open your heart again. I know you will. That's the thing with being what you are... those feelings you have are as strong as the powers you possess."

I kick the cold water at her. "In case you haven't noticed, I am not all that powerful. My influence is small... it wouldn't even cover Meath."

"It doesn't need to. I was quite happy with the pub providing us free drinks all night." She shrugs.

"Hardly much of a threat to this world."

"Since when have you wanted to be a threat, Cia? You've

never liked violence." Lily regards me, curiosity in the tilt of her head.

It's true. During our life together in the sixties, Lily and I got swept up in the youthful energy of the time. I used my powers to party and create stunning illusions people would become lost in. I could get us into any clubs we wanted, where we were never short of admirers. Lily is still a hippie in her heart, despite the wisdom of her years and her nomadic lifestyle. I can only imagine the weariness of knowing others' thoughts.

I stroke the burn marks adorning my neck. I've never liked violence, true, but some violence is intoxicating when it has a form, when it fills your chest with desire, a desire to push, to take, an incredible orbit that pulls you in and destroys everything you are. There is something about that kind of violence that cannot be looked away from.

I hadn't seen the bodies of the coven in Varanasi. Fire was already devouring the temple when I arrived, huge plumes of flames engulfing everything they licked at like awful golden wings. The fire smelled of *him*, heated my skin from where *he* had burned me. The fire brought to life all the vibrations in all the places in my body that had known him. It was then I knew.

I will never be free of *him*.

And I so desperately do not want to feel like that.

"Lily," Glory calls from the top of the hill to us. "Gareth sends word."

Lily and I look at one another, then scramble up the hillside and into the tunnels. Lily's forehead is furrowed when I glance at her, and I gather there must be lots of busy minds up ahead. The main hall is full of people, not just the seniors, and the great oak table has been restored. The room settles into an easy hush while Glory waits, her features dark in the candlelight.

"I know we were not expecting our emissaries back so soon,

and many are still on their way or enjoying the hospitality of other covens, telling them of our request for help." Glory's eyes find mine in the dim light. "Osogbo, Cuzco, Jordan, Oregon, Whanganui, all the major covens, as well as a few minor ones too. These missions will take time. As you know, we have not had contact with our brothers and sisters in many years, but I am sure you are all aware of the events in Varanasi, and even if you are not, then you all know what happened to Rue." Glory takes a long breath, the candlelight catching her long caramel-toned hair. *She still knows how to hold her crowd.* "We still wait on these outcomes before we move. But Gareth has returned."

The coven shifts about in excitement, and Glory raises her voice above them, clearly excited as well.

"Gareth returns to us with a great ally, a witch so powerful I am sure her allyship will tip the balance in our favor."

The rest of the coven murmurs, struggling to crane their necks to get a better view of the figure walking down a corridor with Gareth by their side. Something looks off. They appear tiny and deformed. The energy from them, strange, unlike any witch I have encountered before, a murky low vibration cast all around them.

I whisper into Lily's ear, "Whoever they are, they are very old. What are they thinking?"

Lily shifts uncomfortably. "I cannot tell. They are not thinking in words."

"What? How does that make sense?" I whisper back as the witch comes into better view.

Closer, it becomes obvious she is not deformed. From the distance, I hadn't noticed the small merlin perched on her shoulder. She bears pockmarked cheeks, her dark hair is tied back, and her eyes are as amber as the falcon's. I shudder at the sight of her.

"She has a strange energy," Lily whispers to me.

"This..." Gareth states with delight, his arm gesturing to the tiny witch, "... is Morgan."

There is a hushed murmur across the coven, and I am about to ask Lily what that means when I hear her speak next to me.

"*The* Morgan?"

Gareth's eyes sparkle. "Yes, Lily, *the* Morgan. She will align herself with us in our cause before returning to the forests of England."

"England?" I hear myself say. "England has no coven anymore."

"Morgan is the last of an ancient line, Sorcha," Glory explains.

Morgan's falcon-like eyes rest on me.

Glory continues to address the coven, updating them on the progress of the others, but everyone watches Morgan with rapt curiosity, though she pays no notice and says nothing. The falcon on her shoulder is so still I'd think it stuffed if not for its fluttering heartbeat.

"Are you sure she is entirely human?" I whisper back to Lily now that everyone else has started to talk.

"I was sure she was a myth," Lily whispers into my ear. "If the legend is true, then she must be around two thousand years old."

My gulp is loud enough to make those in front of me turn around as I clasp my hand across my mouth. "That cannot be possible," I mutter with speed and louder than I mean to, getting a few more evil looks. "Even Kali was nearing the end of her years."

Lily shrugs. "It is just a legend, most likely exaggerated."

"Humans don't last that long," I whisper.

"I know, Cia," Lily sputters, rolling her eyes.

Morgan's energy feels human. Yet strange, old. Too old. A thought occurs to me as I grab Lily's elbow, and ask, "Morgan, as in Morgan le Fay?"

Lily doesn't answer, only smiles.

Wow. She truly is a legend. No wonder Gareth is beside himself. I can't imagine how he pulled this one off. I know he is talented for a witch so young, not quite yet out of his human years —although he could pass for twenty-five—but this seems too much. A good part of me thinks it must be some kind of trick and this can't be the real Morgan le Fay. *Why would a legendary witch unearth herself after two thousand years of hiding from the world?* Yet I can't deny what my own instincts are telling me—*yes, this witch is human, and old.* Her vibrations so unbelievably low, twisted, and bent out of shape from time under the prolonged exposure to magic.

Glory brings her speech to an end, dismissing the rest of the coven and nodding her head in my direction for me to join her.

Lily gives my arm a squeeze and heads in the direction of her room while I push my way through the crowd to where Glory and Gareth are waiting with Morgan.

Up close, she is even more sinister-looking with her nails turned black and claw-like, her skin sallow and loose. Only her beady falcon eyes reveal how sharp and all too knowing she is.

"This is Sorcha." Glory motions toward me as I make my way over. "Sorcha, it would be useful if you could brief Morgan on everything you know about this new god and his dealings in Varanasi."

Morgan is tiny, not even five feet. Her amber eyes huge.

"Are you the real Morgan le Fay?" I ask.

The witch in front of me cocks her head at me, even more bird-like, while her small falcon remains eerily still, peering at me with the same expression of confusion.

"Morgan has not spoken in many centuries," Gareth informs me, keeping his eyes on Morgan, while she, in turn, watches me.

I cannot help but wonder how a mute witch will aid our plans, or if she is an aide to encourage other covens to join us.

Gareth continues, "Sorcha is a new god too, but she is no threat, Morgan. She is aiding us. Shall we?" He gestures to a nearby lounge area full of comfy sofas and armchairs.

I want to sit as far away from Morgan as possible, but she chooses a red plush armchair right next to me. The worn green cloak she dons seems to shift as if it has a life of its own. Morgan brings her lips into a smile, revealing yellowing teeth. I can see where the stories of old come from when it comes to witches.

"There is no time like the present," Gareth presses.

The fire in his eyes triggers the warning from Lily to echo in the back of my mind. Peeking back to the time-ravaged face of Morgan, a portent to be careful with my heart, that maybe I have underestimated what I'm getting involved with. With the eyes of Morgan, Glory, and Gareth heavy on me, I open my mouth and share everything I know about Peter.

I talk on through most of the evening, only stopping when Glory or Gareth interrupt to ask a question or clarify a point. Morgan's eyes never leave me. Only after a while do I notice something catching my eye, a movement, and as I look down, I notice Morgan's sleeve has moved up. I catch sight of an adder wound tight around her wrist moving up her arm, out of view.

Chapter Eight

Lorna

The plane's wheels touch down onto tarmac, jolting me awake. Peter's heavy head bobs onto mine, and I wiggle out from under it. Without my head to prop him up, he turns his head and rests it on Connie's instead, where it lies snoozing on his chest, her arm wrapped around his stomach with his protective arm around her shoulders. They look like perfect pieces of a jigsaw puzzle, slotting together as they sleep while the plane coasts down the runway.

I rub the sleep from my eyes, feeling groggy and shabby, the way one can't help feeling after a monster journey. After almost fifteen hours, a transfer, and one more transfer to go, I'm ready to never step onto a plane again. It is long and beyond boring. Peter moans incessantly about the food, my bones ache, and I feel envious of Connie's tiny body and her ability to curl up in her seat. The only saving grace with long haul is free booze, which allows us to slip into an alcohol-induced slumber for a good few hours. Of course, waking up with a banging headache is not ideal.

I give Peter a big shove and try to act casual.

"Are we there yet?" He sits up, groggy, stirring Connie as he looks around and takes in the fact that we are still on the plane.

"Almost," I tell him as he gives me a closer look. I can only assume he's thinking I look terrible.

"Are you okay?"

"My head is pounding."

"Here, let me fix that," he says without hesitation, sliding his fingers into my hair at the bottom of my neck so no one can see the golden light as he heals my headache in an instant. "You should drink water too. You are super dehydrated." He hands me a bottle of water from by his feet.

"Are we in New Orleans?" Connie asks, peering out of the window.

"Atlanta. One more transfer and we are there," I remind her before downing the water.

"Another plane." Connie moans as she reaches up to crack her back. "I can't wait to take a shower and rest in a real bed."

Peter reaches and wraps his hand around her ponytail, pulling her closer to kiss her, whispering things I do not want to hear, so I put my earphones in while we wait for the airplane to reach the terminal.

It took me a while to get used to being a three.

Connie has been my best friend for as long as I can remember, and then came Anna, who I loved so much it burned as bright as fire in the depths of a darkness that can never last. And then came Peter. All things end with Peter. He might be the last thing I ever love. A different love from what I felt for his sister. As with most things involving him, my feelings about him are complicated. Seeing Anna's face in his every day is bittersweet. He will do or say something so like her that my heart almost splits in two from the pleasure and pain of feeling like she is still with me. Their mannerisms and turns of phrase are almost identical.

Peter, in himself however, is so different from everything she was that it can be scary. Maybe it is the influence, but all the same, I do not want to stop loving him. Unconditional love or not, witnessing his relationship with Connie serves as a constant reminder to how he is Anna's opposite. Reckless, selfish, in absolute control of everything around him, while at the same time, his self-control hangs by a fine, constant thread. A dangerous mix which, I hate to admit, is intoxicating to be around.

As he grows in power, he becomes a more and more exaggerated version of himself. Ever since the events in the barn, Peter has wrapped Connie up and worshipped her in a way so different from before. Connie has become more confident and surer of herself as a result of his constant indulgence, yet I can't help but worry about the pressure that brings on her. Although, the lifestyle they have found themselves in seems to suit Connie well and keep her distracted from the burden. *I wonder how long that will last.* I only hope it will ease when we find an answer to the impossible question we have been trying to figure out.

And yet I know they make a conscious effort around me not to be wrapped up in each other to such a sickening extent. I dread to think what they're like when they travel on their own.

Of course, the duration of waiting for our connecting flight is spent in a bar drinking rye whiskey. So by the time we stumble off the plane in New Orleans, we are all half-cut and nonsensical.

The New Orleans air is sticky and sweet, hanging close and intoxicating in itself. The force of it on my face in the dying day hits hard after the stagnant air of the planes. It has been an eighteen-hour journey, and I am tired, dirty, and super drunk.

Standing on the curb of the Louis Armstrong Airport, I realize I have no idea what to do. Connie and Peter sway on the spot with lazy smiles of people who do this all too often, her hand lingering on his chest, laughing as we wait for a taxi. A taxi that will take us to a hotel, where we will continue to get drunk for a few days before we all realize we have only a name and a few suspicions.

"Guys..." I blurt out, laughing a little at the situation, "... you do realize we have traveled for eighteen hours on four planes across three countries, all for a name. Marie. How many Maries do you think live in New Orleans?"

"Thousands," Peter states, throwing his arms out with drunken drama and not looking the least bit concerned.

"But we only need one," Connie confirms like it is so easy, pushing her fingers into his light hair as he relaxes into her.

"And do you have any ideas on how to find the one?" I grin.

"Oh, I have a few." A wicked expression passes his face as he looks around at our surroundings, pushing Connie into a pirouette before pulling her after him. "Follow me, both of you. I have an idea."

With that, he takes my hand too and marches us out of the taxi queue and across the tarmac. Connie seems to catch on quicker than me, clocking where we are headed and clapping her hands together.

"Peter, tell me we are not doing what I think we are doing," she says, but the skip in her step betrays her words.

Peter wraps his arm around her shoulder, and then mine, pulling us both so close I can smell the rye whiskey on him. "We don't know Marie, and she may or may not be expecting us. So we have to make sure she knows we are here. And the only way of doing that is by being loud... very loud."

He releases us to step into the car rental area, approaching the front desk and saying whatever it is he is saying to the guy that works there.

I eye Connie, incredulous, and ask, "Is he seriously going to take a car?"

Connie shrugs. "I guess so. Beats waiting in the queue, I guess."

Peter comes strolling back out, swinging keys around his finger and wearing the smuggest look.

"Yeah, great plan, Peter. You do remember none of us can drive?"

"All the more fun." He laughs, walking us over to a black Chevrolet.

"A little conservative for your tastes, isn't it?" I comment dryly as I climb into the back, and Peter positions himself in the driver's seat.

"I did think that," he says, pretending not to notice my sarcasm. "But, watch this..." He clicks a button on the dash, and the roof slides down around us.

Before we have a chance to react, Peter slams the car into reverse, spinning the car so fast it takes out the car rental sign behind us with a monstrous crash. Connie and I squeal as we come to a stop and rush to put on our seat belts. Peter laughs with wild abandon, then glances back at me for a moment to flash his maniacal grin as the rental shop clerk runs outside to inspect the damage.

"You are fucking crazy, Peter," I scream at the top of my lungs.

"Let's let New Orleans know we are here," he shouts back, then cackles in Connie's direction before he hits drive and sends us away from the parking lot and onto the freeway, careering between lanes.

Connie reaches her hands up to catch the air as if on a roller coaster.

It's hard not to be swept away, not to feel invincible too as he cranks up the music and we all dance along to the heavy beat. Peter brings the car under relative control, and we speed into downtown New Orleans.

Our new home for the foreseeable future.

We party for three days and three nights, non-stop, hours filled with rye whiskey, mezcal, and drugs Peter is able to acquire. If we get sick, Peter can heal us straight away, always monitoring our heart rates. I wonder if he is so used to their rhythms that he would be able to pick them out in a crowded room. He's like our personal life support so we can push our bodies to do more.

Far from letting New Orleans know we have arrived, we haven't much left the sanctuary of our luxury hotel, or the bar that looks like a gilded carousel, almost moving with the rushing of the drugs coursing through our bodies. Laughing and talking louder and louder until we are asked to leave, where we retreat to the lemon-striped walls of Connie's and Peter's room.

I have only been into my room to drop my bags.

As the dawn breaks on day four in New Orleans, I need a break. Draining the last of my whiskey, I rub my tired eyes and watch Connie and Peter for a moment. Connie is in the middle of the room, in her own world, dancing to a song, twisting and turning her tiny body in time to the music, while Peter lies on the floor stretched out on his back, resting his head on his arm to watch her.

It isn't a dance of seduction. Connie's eyes are closed, her arms raised above her head, her hips rocking in slow languid movements. She isn't specifically dancing for him, but this is how things are with them now. When she moves, he moves. I notice he taps his lips in time with the beat of her movements.

"You forgot to bring your guitar," he mutters after a while.

Connie's eyes open. Crouching next to him, she states, "I have never brought it with me. I can live without it."

He props himself up on his elbow. "But music makes you happy. Playing music makes you happy."

Connie lowers herself to kneel, giving him her best smile, one that reaches her eyes while lighting her face.

"It's different this time. You need one. I will buy you one. Really buy you one, not steal it. A good one."

Connie bites her lip. "You don't have to do that, Peter." Her hand moves to her necklace, running her fingertips along its sharp edges.

Peter chuckles. "That's what you think I did, isn't it? You think I stole that. I didn't, you know. I bought it. You should know that. It was for you for your birthday, so I wanted to pay for it."

"You don't need to spend your money on me." Connie wraps her hands around the back of his neck, fingers splaying against his skin.

"There are some things worth paying for. I want to give you everything you deserve, Connie. You are already giving up so much for me."

"I don't see it that way," she tells him, inching closer.

I should go.

It's been four days since they have been alone. When I feel the shift in the air indicating things are about to escalate, I slip out of their room undetected and head for my own. Looking in the mirror, I feel like I've been awake for three years, not three days. I try to tame the lion's mane that is my hair before giving up. I look around the luxury room, now feeling alone. The hotel is beautiful, full of chandeliers and old-fashioned New Orleans' opulence. Somewhere I would never have been able to stay in a million years without Peter, but I know the hotel is part of his plan. It is somewhere we will get noticed.

Now that I am on my own, I feel sobriety heading my way and it doesn't feel good, so I douse myself under the shower for at least twenty minutes, letting the water wash away the last three days. *I am tired.*

So much so that I am asleep before my head hits the pillow.

When I wake, it is dark, and New Orleans is alive underneath my window. I haven't had the chance to take it in yet. I'm not sure what day of the week it is, but the street below is bustling. My stomach grumbles so loud it echoes in the silence of my room, and I realize I am ravenous. I throw on whatever is closest and am out the door, out of the hotel, and into the sticky night air.

The air feels different here. It hangs close all around. The streets are alive with all sorts of people laughing together and hanging out at the front of bars. They glow under the neon lights. The city feels alive, more so than any place I have ever visited. It seems to have a pulse. I decide in an instant that I like it and let my nose take me to the nearest restaurant.

I squeeze myself in at the bar, catching the eye of a barmaid. "Can I eat food here?" I ask her, praying she will say yes.

"Sure thing, *cher*. You want a menu?"

"Yes, please, and rye whiskey to start."

She cocks a perfect eyebrow at me. "I'm gonna need to see your ID there."

Panic floods me as I pat myself, but luckily, I am wearing my jacket with my passport in it, which I dutifully pass to her.

She examines it and snickers, handing it back to me along with a menu. "You is just a babe. What are you doing out here on your own ordering a rye whiskey?"

I let out an embarrassing snort and scan the delicious-looking food choices on the menu. "I have only been here for three days. My friends are back at the hotel. I got hungry."

"Mmm..." she answers, still looking amused. "Where are you from?"

"England," I tell her, distracted as my stomach grumbles.

"And what brings you and your friends to New Orleans, Miss England?"

My stomach drops, and I feel exposed, like I should not have come out on my own. Maybe we were being louder than I thought.

My face must give me away because her expression changes and she turns away from me. "I am sorry. I didn't mean to intrude. I will leave you to decide on what you want to order."

"No," I breathe out. "Don't go." I hold my hand out across the bar. "It's okay. You just took me by surprise, that's all. Actually, we came here to look for someone."

"Oh yeah?" She comes back to face me appearing curious. "Who ya looking for?"

I chuckle and try to relax. "Someone called Marie. Do you know her?"

She lets out an easy laugh, leaning her palms against the bar. "I know a few. You are in the French Quarter. You will have to give me a bit more if you want to find your Marie."

I nod, looking back at the menu and feeling more at ease. "It sounds crazy, right? I'll have the barbecue shrimp," I tell her and, with a nod, she takes my order and walks off to serve someone else.

I feel a touch disappointed when she doesn't come back, someone else bringing me my drink and food instead.

I linger in the restaurant, ordering another drink before I take a slow walk back to the hotel, marveling at the metropolitan hustle-bustle of the streets. New Orleans seems like a good place to be different. The sounds of jazz, the smell of gumbo, the vibrant characters walking the street—they all tantalize the senses. Perhaps this is a good place for Peter to be as it seems to be a city bent on indulgence.

When I reach the hotel, I feel next to human again. Although not quite ready to go back into the fray that is my friends, I best check on them, make sure they haven't eaten each other or something. When I knock on their door, there is no answer. *They must be asleep.*

I have a vague memory of the concierge saying something about a heated rooftop pool when we checked in, so I dip back into my room to change into my bathing suit and check it out. It's not until I am on my way that it occurs to me that it will probably be shut.

I am pleasantly surprised when I push the large double doors to the pool and find them open. Looks like I am in luck, although the pool sounds deadly quiet. Almost too quiet. Dark and deserted except for the white underlighting that glows around the pool. When I hear a splash, I almost jump out of my skin.

"Great minds think alike," Connie calls out to me. She is sitting at the edge of the pool, wearing a tiny gold bikini, holding up a glass in cheers. "The water feels great. Come and join us."

As I step closer, I see Peter in the water, pushing himself back to come and bob along next to me. "How did you manage this?" I ask, thankful he is wearing swimwear.

The ghost of a smile passes his lips as he floats on his back, moving his gaze away from me and to observe the heavens. "Do you really need to ask?"

I don't answer him and instead go sit by Connie, dipping my feet into the warm water as she asks, "Would you like some champagne?"

"Please," I reply, and Connie hands me a glass, sloshing champagne into the pool.

"Have you two slept?"

Connie shrugs. "I think so. Where did you go?"

"It seemed like you two needed some alone time." I gesture to

Peter, who is still floating around on his back. "I went to get something to eat. I was starving. I don't think we've eaten since we got here. Have you eaten?"

"We had some strawberries," Connie tells me, sipping her drink and reaching behind her. "I have some here." She passes me the half-eaten basket of strawberries.

I eye her. She looks great—our tiny, glowy Connie—but I can't help but worry. "You need to eat, Con," I tell her, keeping my voice hushed. "You can't survive on Peter alone."

"I know that." She laughs, shaking her head.

Peter is at our feet, pulling on Connie's foot. "You said my name?"

"Yes. Can you please remember to feed your girlfriend? What, you don't need to eat anymore?" I chastise him.

"I eat," he muses, his dark eyes meeting mine, something wicked there. "I can eat for hours." His eyes flick to Connie, who rolls her eyes, and I kick some water at him for his foul brain.

"Fine." He laughs, holding up his hands. "You..." he points to Connie, "... let's get you some food."

But instead of getting out, he kisses her ankle bone and yanks her into the water, submerging her completely. She emerges, spluttering and letting him know he is in for it, throwing herself on top of him so she can dunk him underwater too. This lasts for a few minutes before they both turn on me, pulling a foot each so I plummet in, still holding onto my glass.

The water feels great, and I have my bathing suit on so I can't be too angry, but what a waste of champagne. When I surface, Connie and Peter aren't looking at me, and they aren't laughing anymore. They are both looking at two figures watching us from the edge of the pool. I clock Connie's hand on Peter's arm.

"I hear you are looking for me." It is a statement, not a question. She is tall with dark, immaculate skin, hair in short braids, and an angular beauty in modern dark clothes. *She doesn't look like a witch.*

"You are Marie?" Connie asks.

"I am. It is known new travelers have come to this city in strange circumstances, staying at a fancy hotel and racking up debts worth thousands of dollars, which don't seem to be paid. No records, no credit cards, no name. Very nice." She smiles.

Peter's face gives nothing away. We've been told Marie will be a friend and not a threat, but he seems to be weighing his options.

Marie clasps her hands in front of her, and it's only with her movement that I realize I recognize the figure beside her as the waitress from the restaurant. I open my mouth to talk, but Marie continues.

"Trust me... I would usually think it is none of my business. Many strange sorts pass through this city. Some unpaid bar tabs are no concern of mine. But then I heard you were looking for Marie. I can only assume it is me that you are all looking for?" She smiles again, this time looking more unsure at our collective silence and the mistrust rolling off Peter. She turns to the girl next to her. "Then again, if I am mistaken, I apologize and will not intrude any further."

"We were sent by Boots," Peter says as she turns to leave.

Marie and the barmaid's heads snap back in our direction, Marie's brow furrowed. "What do you know of Boots, boy?"

Peter casts a weary look from Connie to me, then back to Marie. "He didn't tell you we were coming?"

The barmaid glances at Marie, who makes some sort of a hiss in the back of her throat before saying, "Boots is my spirit guide. If you are already in touch with the beyond, then what do you need me for? I help those in need of guidance, so if you are already in touch with the spirits, you do not need me, strangers."

"Marie, wait." Peter changes tactic, holding his hands up and moving through the water with caution toward her. "Boots did send us. This isn't a trick. And something tells me you are more than just a guide, something you don't advertise often, not truly, not everything. I am something too, something I imagine you won't believe. Not at first."

Peter reaches the edge of the pool and, hauling himself up, stands over Marie. She is unable to look away, too curious or too captivated to say anything. Peter's movements seem off, though, too slow, too predatory. His hand moving to the back of Marie's neck, slow and commanding, he says, "You need to listen to me—"

"Peter, stop," Connie shouts, breaking Marie's concentration, and Peter's, as she too wades to the edge, hauls herself up without quite the same grace, and moves his arm from Marie. "Allies, remember?" she murmurs.

"What is this?" Marie looks thoroughly confused now.

"Boots really did come to us," Connie continues, leaving Peter hovering behind her.

I see his back muscles tense.

"But we are not in touch with the beyond. We met Boots as a person, not as a spirit. Well, kind of a person. Not a human person, but he looked like a person. Like an alien or angel, wearing a human skin."

Marie now looks beyond horrified. "Boots is a spirit. What are you talking about?" she stammers.

"I'm not doing a good job of explaining myself." Connie looks to Peter for help.

He runs his hands through his hair. "We really do need your help. Boots sent us. He said you could help us, that you would know how to turn a human into an immortal." He looks to Connie.

Marie's eyes boggle. "You are all crazy. I should not have come here. I cannot help you." She looks like she can't get out of our sights fast enough, and I am a bit peeved that they are too drunk to make a coherent tale of why we have searched her out.

I make for the edge of the pool. We've come all this distance, and she is going to walk away from us. Peter looks back to Connie and me.

"Just tell her, Peter," I whisper.

He looks torn, but Marie is almost at the door.

"He is a god, Marie," Connie shouts, sounding confident while walking toward Marie, only the slightest stagger in her step. Marie rakes her eyes up her almost naked body.

"I do not believe in gods, girl." Marie laughs at her, and the barmaid snickers behind her. "I have met a lot of strange creatures, but there is no such thing as a god, even in my religion."

"You can help us, or... he can make you," Connie says through her teeth, taking us all aback.

Marie studies Connie for a moment before looking back at Peter. "Pretty scrawny god, ain't ya?"

The barmaid laughs again.

Now that I'm out of the pool, I see Peter roll his eyes before holding his hand up and letting fire burn like it is nothing, spreading against his skin, across his shoulders, and into his other hand.

The barmaid stops laughing.

Marie scrunches her nose at him. "I've seen fire magic before. It is a pretty trick."

"Pretty... until I burn you alive." Peter scoffs before realizing this is not the right tact to be taking. "Okay, fine." He breathes out, letting the fire go out on his unmarked skin. Instead, he turns his hand up to the sky, and with a sweep, the clear night fills with thunderous-looking clouds, rolling in terrible and looming in the sky above us.

Marie and the barmaid appear unnerved now, shuffling

together for protection against the menacing sky while Peter looks a lot more pleased with himself.

"Stand back," he tells us, giving us a mere minute before the lightning hits the top of his outstretched hand and ricochets down his body, the purple bruising firing down his arm and then healing before our eyes.

Marie takes a step back from him as he brings his hand up for her to view better. The electricity washes over his palm, back and forth, golden and crackling.

"What are you?" Marie whispers, the glow of the sparking current illuminating her face.

"I told you. I am a god. It's okay, there hasn't been one like me in a really long time."

Marie looks hard at his hand. "And *I* am supposed to help *you?*"

"Yes."

"How?"

"We have a lot to talk about," he says as the rain starts to fall from the swirling clouds.

Chapter Nine

Peter

"You don't feel like a witch," I tell Marie as we make haste to enter a closed shop front.

The windows are shuttered down, and she wastes no time locking the door behind us to the still-bustling New Orleans night.

Marie makes a noise of detest. "That is because I am no witch. I am a practitioner."

"Of Voodoo, right?" I ask, taking in the sight of the shop. The contents I can only describe as magical wares—black candles, Ouija boards, chicken bones, as well as talismans and rabbit's feet —while the smell of incense fills my nose. It's the kind of stuff that caters to tourists.

Marie gives me a long look, and it's clear she is a little more relaxed in her own domain. "Do not speak about that which you do not understand."

Rather than switch the main lights on, Marie lights a few candles and an antique oil burner behind the counter. I like the look of it, and the smell is pleasing, and under its soft glow, I can see Marie better. The confidence she wears so well is betrayed by the hammering of her heart. Whatever she can feel in me, it must be something she does not recognize. In this moment, she sees me as a threat and can't quite decide what to do about it.

Rather than examine the trinkets as Connie and Lorna currently are, I cross the shop to the counter Marie now stands behind. Her friend stands by the door, watching the girls. Her heart is hammering too. Connie doesn't want me to do this by force. These should be people who want to help.

"If you knew anything about Voodoo, you would know that I do not recognize any so-called god who walks this Earth. I believe in one creator. You are not Bondye, so... what are you?"

I shrug. "I suppose god is just a word. I did not create this Earth, but I can create. I can create life in plants, I can create the wind that blows, fire that burns, and I could burst the banks of the Mississippi with just a thought." I slide my hand over hers, and she doesn't move, only lets me drink in all that she is. I feel her cells, alive and singing, strong and sweet. "I can tell that you have lived on this Earth for thirty-three years, that you are connected to magic but in a different way to witches, something a little more turbulent." I close my eyes to concentrate, to figure out the high vibration of her soul. "Something closer, less practiced, something wilder." I open my eyes again to find hers wide and inquisitive, watching me. I try to push down my hunger and decide not to tell her how her soul would taste like buttered popcorn. "My name is Peter. I can tell you everything you want to know about how I came into being, but please, we do need your help."

Marie stands there for what feels like eons, regarding me before letting out a long breath and turning my hand over in hers, bringing my palm up and studying it for a while. "You certainly look very human, Peter," she says after a long time.

"What would you expect? Wings or horns?"

Marie snorts. "I suppose I asked for that," she relents, running her finger across a large break in one of the lines of my hand.

"I was dragged into this world by my human twin when she was born. Part of an old ritual that has long been outlawed. Something about needing a human half. I am, I guess you could say, contained in a human form."

Marie cocks her eyebrow at me, then glances at Connie and Lorna before asking, "And where is your twin?"

"She is dead."

Marie doesn't say anything, instead runs her free hand across the beads of sweat forming on her forehead. Looking back at my palm, she states, "*Cher*, there is a lot of violence here." Her eyes return to me, almost sympathetic. "And I know nothing of gods. I'm sorry, I really am. But I am curious, so much so, by your being here. But what you need is an old witch, someone much more knowledgeable about the old ways. This is way above my pay grade."

I turn my palm back into hers to pull her closer, pleading now. Against what I know is the right thing to do, I allow the smallest vines of my influence to wrap around her wrists. "Marie," I say so soft I can hear the seduction in my own voice. "The witches do not want me here. I was..." I swallow hard, "... a mistake. The witches want me gone from this Earth. They think I upset the balance. The violence you see... that is them. It is not what I want, nor is it what my friends want. We are looking for a way to live our lives in peace. The witches don't think a creature like me should exist."

Marie's laugh takes me by surprise, and she withdraws her hands and comes out from behind the counter. "That certainly is rich. The witches curse you for being an unnatural creature, despite the fact that their ancestors created pretty much every unnatural creature that walks this planet." She shakes her head in disbelief. "So high and mighty they are. They think magic is theirs alone for the controlling, yet they take no accountability for their history."

"Unnatural creatures?" Lorna chimes in, coming to stand next to me now that Marie seems to be relaxing. "There are more?"

Marie glances to Lorna, then to Connie, who joins me on my other side. Marie motions to the girl by the door. "Lisette said you were only just twenty-one. Is your friend here the first of his kind that you have met?"

They nod.

"As far as we know, Peter is only the second god to walk the Earth for over two thousand years," Connie tells her.

Marie releases a jostling laugh. "I can believe it. For I have never met a god before, but I have met many other of the night's children. Vampires, spirits, wolfmen. I also met a fae once... incredibly rare, almost extinct. So you two are extremely lucky to be in the company of a god, the rarest of all creatures. And all these creatures, every single one, were put on this Earth by witches. They were once revered and now shunned." She flaps her hands to her side before rubbing her forehead. "There is a reason the Voodooists separate themselves from witchcraft. We are far more accepting than those stuck-up witches. They consider them-selves the gatekeepers to all things, and if a creature is no longer relevant to them, then their place on this planet is no longer needed."

"Vampires exist?" Connie asks, her eyebrows raised.

"Indeed, they do. Some of the oldest date back almost two thousand years, which is an interesting coincidence since you are telling me gods have not been here in over two thousand years. Which raises the question, why are you here now, god known as Peter?"

"Just Peter will do fine," I tell her. "Please don't go around calling me that... it's weird. The practice may have been outlawed, but my father, he found the ritual. He succeeded one before me, but she wasn't strong enough, so he did the ritual again, and there was me. I was told by the coven in India that the old gods were tethered to their people, their ruling coven, and my father wanted to do the same with me if he thought I was strong enough. To use that power."

"If this Indian coven helped you before, why can't they help you now?" Marie questions.

I look at Connie, and her emerald eyes encourage me that this is a moment for honesty. I take a deep breath and confess. "Because I killed them all. It's a long story, and I am certainly not going to say there is a reasonable excuse for what I did, but there were circumstances around what happened. I didn't set out with the intention of killing anybody. But..." I pause, considering. *I suppose it is important for her to know.* "But you should probably know, the old gods... they became more powerful through human sacrifice. A lot of people died back then at their hands. Souls make us more powerful. The old gods had so much power they could change their human forms. I don't want that power for myself, Marie. I-I don't want followers, and I am certain I don't want a religion. All I want is a life." I pull Connie to my side.

"I want a life with Connie as close to human as I can make it. Since I cannot die, I just want to make it so she can't either. If I attempt it, it will require bloodshed. We are here for another way. And then, I will never darken your doorstep again. We will live quietly and peacefully."

"I see," Marie says after a long minute, rubbing her temples. "This is a lot to take in. I need some time to consult with the spirits. What is your relation to Boots? Why would he come to you?"

I shrug. All this talking is making me exhausted and in desperate need of a drink. "Something to do with my mother. And a vested interest in my outcome."

Marie mulls on the words, her next question an unexpected one. "And how old are you, new god?"

"Peter... really is fine. I'm twenty. I will be twenty-one in June."

She nods and runs her fingers along a nearby Ouija board on the counter that looks old and battered. She retrieves a metal object from the top of her jacket pocket, and a red stone glints off the top of it as the candle flames close by flicker when it makes contact with the board.

The metal object vibrates on the board while Marie's fingers pet it. "Peter, did something happen last year? At the start of spring, maybe in May, something significant."

My body tenses and heat rises in my face, running up my arms, as my anger flares.

Just set fire to the shop. Burn her and this city down. Kill them all, and you can start again with the ashes. This is not her business.

The voice calls for blood—her blood. The buttery taste of her soul would wash down so easily and make me feel so much better, quench my thirst in a heartbeat.

"It's okay, Peter." Connie's cool hand slides into mine. "Marie, Peter's sister died at the end of April. As you can imagine, they were very close."

"Not just close," I manage to get out, although my throat feels like gravel. My eyes stay on the floor, and I am so thankful to be holding Connie close now. "She was already dying and there was nothing I could do about it. But I held her under the water until she drowned." I hear Lorna sniff behind me. "I did it so that I could take her soul. Hers and mine, we were always supposed to be one. What I can do now, I couldn't do it all before then. When she died, I became whole. And that is the sad truth of my existence, Marie."

The air feels thick. *All it would take is a spark for the entire room to go up in flames.*

"What are you doing?" Marie asks with a guarded tone.

"I am concentrating."

"On what?"

I trace Connie's delicate knuckles with my thumb, thinking, *Not killing you and your friend.*

No, I shouldn't say that.

"The grief is still strong. It takes some managing to keep it in. It might be wise to change the subject from my sister."

I hadn't noticed the metal object vibrating so fast until Marie slams her palm on top of it. "Right." The sudden sound makes us all jump, including Lisette. "You three should stay here for a time. You have made quite enough of a scene at the hotel. It would be best not to draw too much more attention to yourselves. Lisette, could you show them upstairs while I consult the board?"

Lisette nods and leads us behind the counter and through a beaded curtain. As I pass Marie, the thought occurs to me to ask, "How did you know? About what happened?"

Marie lets out a big sigh, holding what I can now see is a ruby-laden planchette between her fingers, then speaking with speed as if the story is a long and arduous one, "I didn't. But something started to happen last year, in May. Several of my circle heard of signs, unusual happenings, even in the world of the unusual. The spirit world was turbulent, and a very forceful spirit punched through the veil. Lucky for me, they were benevolent, useful and protected me. That spirit, Peter, was named Boots. Boots became my spirit guide when you and your sister became one."

I glance back to the doorway Connie and Lorna have already gone through, growing more nervous since I can't see her. "What do you mean by signs?" I match Marie's quiet tone, my own heartbeat picking up. *I need to get to Connie.*

"Boots was an unusual spirit, specific... very specific. I assumed he had been powerful in life and perhaps something of the supernatural himself. His guidance was always quick and driven, with never any agenda for reward. He was the first sign while I was doing a reading in May one afternoon. I had never felt anything like it, the spirits in an uproar. I was facing an onslaught, and they overpowered my last guide looking for a vessel." She grasps the planchette with visible force, the metal digging into her skin. "They very nearly broke through, if they had succeeded, I would have been possessed." She shudders before continuing. "I am lucky to use such a strong instrument. Then Boots punched through and his voice was deafening. I thought I might have died. But I'd only passed out, and when I woke, my customers were kneeling around me. They thought I'd had some kind of fit and called for an ambulance. They weren't banking on the real deal. There are not many real practitioners of the board, not even in New Orleans. Anyway, I was fine but needed some time. About a week later, a fae walked into my shop. A real-life fae... here, in *my* shop. I never thought I would see one in my lifetime as the last of their kind live in the forests of Eastern Europe. But that's just the thing, Peter. She wasn't one of the last... she was one of the first. Old and out of her time. She was terrified and speaking a dead language that I couldn't understand. I had to consult the board and spoke with Boots once more. He helped me communicate with her. She had woken up on the bayou. Do you know what else she said?"

"What?" I lean closer to Marie, something about her becoming intoxicating the more she speaks. I feel her magic—her energy flaring up around her.

"She said she was a swamp fae, that her home had been on the bayou hundreds of years before the first settlers came to America. Aligned with the native tribes who lived off the river, when the settlers came, the fae became weary and went back to the land. As far as I can tell from what she said, they kind of turn into trees. Which means she had been asleep for hundreds of years. She had no idea what woke her. Boots didn't know either. He just said there had been a shift, something which has been moving for a while. I reached out to some people I know in Germany and put her on a plane to where she can be with her kin."

Marie rubs her head wearily before continuing, "After that, I became obsessed. Boots is a fantastic guide, and I would take to the board and search for whispers, the right spirits. These signs have been happening all over the world. Old things waking up, reports of mermaids off the Syrian coast, more possessions all over the globe, unusual drownings and passings with survivors telling tales of seeing the other side and returning with unusual gifts. The supernatural scales are starting to tilt, and the further I dig, the more hushed the whispers of even stranger things, lost artifacts being looked for. Unbelievable things."

"Like what?" I ask. I don't remember moving so close for both of my hands to grip her arms, holding her inches from me.

She shakes her head. "Ancient things, from before time was time. Boots said that this world was changing once more, one way or the other. He wouldn't say anymore, but when I delved deeper, these signs were there before. Not as many, and they were more subtle, subtle enough that there were no whispers... the tremors more ripples than waves. I traced it back to a date, a quake off the coast of Osaka. So small by Japan's standards, it was barely reported. What was more interesting is what happened next. An opening in the ocean floor. This is the sight of the first artifact. The first event. Only, it wasn't the first event, was it? It was the second."

I almost don't want to ask. "What was the date?"

"June tenth, year two thousand."

"Fuck." I shake my head. "I need a drink."

I let Marie go, and she takes a step away from me on instinct. "You said you were born in June?"

"I was born on the sixth of June, year two thousand," I confirm grimly.

"You are the source," she whispers to herself, flat and strained.

I rub my eyes. I don't know why I'm still surprised I am in the middle of every shit storm. "It is obvious Boots sent me to you because he knew you would understand. That you can help."

Marie nods absentmindedly. "Yes, it does seem that way. Okay, you go upstairs. Lisette can get you a drink. I will consult with the board and follow you up."

I give her a small nod, my brain ready to explode. It's been a while since I have felt overwhelmed by yet another awful revelation about myself. Maybe it's not so awful... maybe a world more full of wonder. *That can only be good, right?*

I reach the top of the stairs to the apartment above as it becomes light, the first trappings of dawn coming in through the high windows. Connie is fast asleep on the sofa. I haven't let her sleep in four days, and the lack of sleep weighs heavy on my body as well. I can't help grinning at the sight of Lorna chatting up Lisette in the kitchen.

I try to sneak up behind her, but Lisette gives me up.

"Everything okay? You and Marie have been a long time."

"She is just playing with her Ouija set. She said you have liquor."

Lisette gives me the once over but doesn't argue and collects a bottle of Jack Daniels from the cupboard and slides it, along with a glass, across the table.

"You want ice?" she asks with her hand on her hip.

I don't bother to respond, only pop the cap off the bottle and chug down as much as I can without throwing up. Lisette looks less than impressed, but I feel Lorna put a gentle hand on my arm.

"Peter, maybe you should get some sleep."

Sleep. What I wouldn't give for a real sleep.

I look back at Connie, then to Lorna's round, honest eyes. I should tell her, so I do. "I have nightmares. And they are not pretty. The only problem is..." I confess as I down more of the bottle, "... if I don't have them, then Connie has them for me. I should be there for when she wakes."

Before I can address the confused look on Lorna's face or let her ask me any questions, I move over to Connie, pulling the blanket from the back of the chair over her. She looks even smaller when she sleeps, every bit as fragile and delicate as she truly is. The only thing that matters. Her lips flutter into a smile as I run my thumb across her cheek.

I sit back in the armchair to keep my watch over her.

Chapter Ten

Connie

The ground feels moist as I reach my fingers down to the sticky wetness underneath my bare feet. The digits do not look like my own. They are much longer and several shades more tanned. Something deep inside me tells me this is all wrong. I turn my palms over and there is so much thick blood oozing down my arm and dripping off at my elbows. I look at the large hands that are not mine in horror, realizing the ground is saturated red. Something terrible has happened here. The smell of death clings to the air, suffocating me. I want to open my mouth to scream, but no sound comes out, and it feels like I am on fire. Like I'm burning alive.

"Connie, Connie." Peter's hands are clutching my arms, shaking me awake as I look around wildly into his concerned eyes. "Shh... it's okay. You were dreaming. It was just a dream."

I turn my hands over, half expecting to see the blood there, breathing a sigh of relief when there isn't any, and collapse into Peter. "Yikes, I swear they are getting even more intense."

Peter holds me up to look into my eyes. "Were you me again?"

"Yes." I nod, leaning my forehead on his shoulder, still composing myself. "It's always you. It's clearer now. It feels more real."

I gaze at him, but he doesn't say anything, only examines my eyes. I wonder what he sees there—if it's worry I see in his eyes or something else. Since we started sharing the nightmare, I haven't dreamed anything else. I am always Peter in the nightmare, always in the center of varying degrees of horror. As he looks closely at me, I take in the signs of many sleepless nights on his face, the least of which are the dark circles under his eyes.

"You look like shit," I tell him, taking his face in my palm.

"Well, I love you too, gorgeous." He laughs, running his hand over mine. "I'm fine."

I narrow my eyes at him. "Stop lying to me, Peter."

Now it's his turn to nudge his head onto my shoulder, pushing me backward to lie his body weight on top of me. "Okay, fine. I'm terrible and I want to sleep. I am so tired."

I try to wiggle free without success. "Well, don't fall asleep on top of me. I can't breathe when you do."

His arms constrict around my waist, and I feel the vibration of his laughter against my stomach. "Please," he says, his head heavy on my shoulder.

I manage to wrangle my arms free from under him and wrap them around his neck. In truth, I could sleep more too. Maybe one nightmare is enough punishment for us both tonight. I move my head a smidgen, so my nose is in his hair and breathe him in—he smells so good, like the earth, the sun, and the air on a hot summer's day. It's not true that he crushes me. His weight is comforting. His breathing becomes deep, and I feel my eyes flutter closed, my breathing falling into rhythm with his.

The smell of coffee wafts into my nose, stirring my subconscious into waking. My eyes open to see Lisette standing over me, coffee pot in hand, while Peter remains fast asleep, drooling on my chest.

"You two are just the sweetest," she says with humor, taking a sip out of her coffee mug. Indicating to Peter with the pot, she adds, "So, he is the big bad who has the spirit world all riled up?"

"Excuse me?" I try to pull my thoughts together, straining to look around to see where Marie and Lorna are, finding no one. "Where is Lorna?"

"She's in bed." Lisette starts walking toward the kitchen. "Do you want a cup?"

"Oh my God, yes." I try to wiggle free again, only for him to constrict his arms around my waist tighter, the effort making me a little breathless. "Peter, get off. I need coffee."

He doesn't wake up but instead makes an annoyed guttural noise from his throat and rolls off me so I can escape while he sleeps stretched out on his back, his arm flopping over his face and his feet hanging over the edge of the sofa.

I take in Lisette for the first time properly. She is only a little taller than me but with a much better figure and curves in all the right places, tanned and freckled with lots of dark brown hair that sits in a messy ponytail on top of her head. She pulls a mug from a high shelf, revealing a tattoo of a pentagram on her lower back.

"So..." I say, half-biting my cheek and noting my best friend is conspicuous in her absence, "... Lorna is in bed. There are beds, then? Free beds?"

Lisette pushes the cup toward me after filling it up, her chestnut eyes sparkling. "She is in my bed if that's what you are angling at." At the smile pulling the corners of her mouth, I let myself smile too.

Good for Lorna.

She pulls another cup from the shelf before looking at me again. "Does she like coffee?"

I laugh. "She practically runs on the stuff."

"Good. I can't trust anyone who doesn't need caffeine to function."

"Agreed."

"How does she take it?"

"Like me, lots of milk, lots of sugar."

"Cool." Lisette grabs the stuff out of the cupboard, handing me the sugar, and pours Lorna a drink. I instantly decide I like Lisette as she takes care making a morning cup of coffee for my best friend. "What about him?" Lisette nods toward Peter. "Shall I make him one for when he wakes up?"

"Heavens no. Avoid giving him coffee at all costs."

"Oh. Why? What happens?" Lisette asks with genuine concern.

"Nothing, he just doesn't shut up." I relax against the counter to take a long sip.

Lisette gives an easy laugh, shaking her head as she stirs Lorna's coffee. "You know, I didn't even know something like him existed until a few hours ago. A god, one who walks and talks like anything else. He's not what you would expect."

I smile.

Sure, what would you expect?

Not something who sleeps with his arms wrapped around his girlfriend, someone who drinks too much and can't handle his caffeine. I suppose it's true that Peter is not what one expects when thinking of a big bad upsetting the spirit world. He is no big bad at all.

She doesn't say anything else before she takes Lorna's coffee and heads off through a nearby door.

Almost as soon as her door is closed, the door we entered the apartment through swings open with a large bang, jerking Peter awake to a somewhat disheveled Marie standing in the doorway.

Marie's eyes land on Peter, staring, looking lost.

"What's happened?" Peter whispers.

"Boots is gone." Marie looks like she wants to cry. Her steps are slow as she walks over to Peter and sits on the coffee table in front of him. She drops her head for a moment, seeming to be lost in contemplation before straightening up again. She looks so tired. Peter shifts himself up to face her too. Her voice sounds quiet and fragile, nothing like the Marie from last night. "He hasn't been my guide for long, but his absence feels... devastating." Marie cocks her head at Peter. "An angel, you say?"

"An angel, perhaps. He didn't confirm it," Peter says softly. "But it is likely he is a first creature, something that came before witches, before humans."

Marie gives the slightest of nods before looking at me. "Girl, this is what you want? An immortal life can be as much a burden as a gift."

My heart rate launches into overdrive and my throat goes dry, and I move to sit at Peter's side. "Yes, it is what I want."

Marie stares at me hard. "There are always consequences for going against nature, girl. Always. The spirits... they are so unsettled. Something is happening in their world as well as ours. These are strange times." She takes a deep breath. "I have decided to help you, both of you. It seems the course that I have been set on, and I will see it through."

Something feels unsettling about her choice of words, as if she is doing it out of some sense of obligation rather than wanting to. I look to Peter for any indication he is forcing her into it, although his influence makes people willingly compliant. He already looks too excited.

"You know a way? To create an immortal?" Peter is pretty much bouncing up and down in his seat.

"I know only one way, and it is not something I am capable of. But I will arrange the introduction as it is not a gift given lightly. It could take some time. You are all welcome to stay here, unless you enjoy the extravagance of that ghastly hotel where you have taken up residence." Marie arches an eyebrow, scanning the empty kitchenette. "I see Lisette has wasted no time in making your friend feel welcome."

Peter looks around, only now noticing Lorna isn't here, and then raises his eyebrows at me. His face is enough to make me crack up.

"I'm as surprised as you are." I laugh, and when I do, my stomach gives an audible grumble.

Peter looks at me in surprise. "Looks like we need to get breakfast."

I nod. I can't deny I'm ravenous. I have well and truly come back down to Earth from our first few days in New Orleans. Actually, I can't believe we've been here almost a week and not seen a bit of the city yet.

Marie yawns. "I am going to get some sleep. If you go to the café on the corner, Frankie's, tell them Marie sent you."

Marie's people are different from those of the coven, young-looking and high-spirited. Peter tells me the Voodooists have no method of extending their lives, unlike the traditional witches.

They live once, and they live good. Marie and the others don't know much about old gods, the Voodoo religion much too young to remember them. Peter calls its magic young and wild. Unconcerned with order.

Marie uses her Ouija board and ruby-encrusted planchette only a few more times in the week that follows, asking the spirits to track down who she is searching for. This introduction holds the answer to our question. After a week, she finds them and is then able to procure more traditional means of communicating.

She makes a call.

A phone call she insists Peter isn't around for.

She says the negotiations will be tricky, and she will have to play it by ear because the introduction is by no means a friend.

Good or bad, we fall back into our old pattern while we wait. The city is alive with decadence and jazz, and it calls to Peter the way the waters of the Ganges once did. We spend hours and hours in the heady jazz bars of New Orleans, Frenchmen being one of our favorite streets, saturating ourselves in rye whiskey. All we need to do is mention Marie's name, and we have friends everywhere. And stares.

I have never seen Peter dance so much. He is all black jeans, open shirts, and huge smiles. The locals seem to adore him. Rather than going under the radar, he is becoming more of a spectacle. Relishing the hands that pass over his skin, people not only look at him, but they start looking for him as the week turns into two. More and more people make a beeline for him in the bars, wanting to talk to him about anything. Everything.

The boy who once had trouble forming sentences is now a man who has so many hanging on his every word. It's a funny world.

Lisette has become our fourth, although I sometimes wonder if Peter and I are as unbearable to be around as her and Lorna, with them barely able to keep their hands off each other. New Orleans is not a city that discriminates. If the city had a soul, it would be the same as Peter's, as wild as the Voodooists who live here.

I sit at the back of Frankie's, the little café on the corner where Marie and her friends spend a lot of their mornings. There are seven of them with Peter, who is at the front of the shop, telling them some random story about what happened last night.

All their faces are focused on him, howling with laughter at his tale.

I stop my people-watching out the window and turn to study him. His facial features are a little sharper now that he barely eats, and his blond hair falls into his eyes as he talks while spinning on the spot and causing fresh laughter. I laugh with everyone else, happy because I haven't seen him like this with other people in a long time. Carefree. Peter is never carefree anymore. Wild, certainly. But I can almost feel the influence ripple out of him, crash and recede against the walls of the building, urging all of those around him to let go. I watch him as the grin eases across his face, and his smile is *so* wicked. I wonder if they all adore him like I do. Every eye in the place zeroes in on him.

My own smile falters and fades.

Because they do, every one of them.

Adore him.

They are not like the other witches, the ones who are granted protection from what he is. They are all enraptured. He catches the sight of me at the back of the café as I stand, my face falling. Peter's face turns serious, so they all turn to me too.

"Everybody out," Peter commands and, dutifully, they all make their way out of the shop, filing past me, leaving me standing here studying him.

"What are you doing with these people?"

"Just passing the time while we wait for this mysterious introduction. Waiting is very tedious." He smiles.

"Peter, it's not fair to make all these people fall in love with you."

Now he looks confused. "That's not what I'm doing."

I drag my fingers across the table as I take a slow seductive stride toward him. "Yes, you are," I tease and draw close, running my hands up his chest. "I can see it... I can feel it. This whole city is falling in love with you, and you are making it happen."

He doesn't say anything, only looks at me with dark, intense eyes.

"They are all drunk on you," I whisper.

His eyes flick down to my lips as he breathes in heavy, saying only my name. "Connie." His voice low and husky. The sound is a drug.

"Shh..." I push my fingers through his hair and allow myself to feel it too, all that power he emits like a beacon. "Just own it, Peter. Own it like you own *everything* in your path."

I nibble the bottom of his lip, and his reaction is shoving me back into the nearest table, his hands grabbing my thighs so my legs wrap around him in one quick movement. I have to grab the back of his neck to steady myself.

His smile dances across his lips. "I what?" he asks with amusement.

I lean back, arching my body into his. "You own everything," I whisper into his ear. "And everyone."

He pulls back to look at me, something close to wonder on his face at his own power being fed back to him. "*Fuck*" is all he says before devouring me.

Right here.

In the café.

At midday.

It dawns on me that I need to get a grip of myself as I pick up my underwear from the floor of the café. I know I shouldn't find it quite so sexy that my boyfriend can pretty much control everything in the world. Definitely not so sexy that he will command everyone out of an eating establishment so I can have my way with him on a table in broad daylight.

Shit, it is so sexy, though.

"So, the whole other-people-being-in-love-with-me thing," Peter starts with caution. "That doesn't bother you?"

"It appears the answer to that question is a resounding no." I giggle, moving to help him do the buttons up on his shirt. "They all want you, and you want me." I peer at him through my eyelashes. "There is something quite powerful about that feeling."

"You are incredibly powerful." He chuckles, pushing the hair back from my shoulders.

"I'm not really, though, am I? It's all you." I half smile.

"Connie." He takes my hair in a fist, pulling it to one side before placing goose-bump-inducing kisses down my neck. "You are so powerful. *You.* You bring me to my knees. What is more powerful than that?"

I laugh, putting my hand against his chest to push him away. "Come on. Let's not get me excited again. We should go and apologize to Marie."

I take his hand and lead him back to Marie's magic shop. The chattering of voices sounds from upstairs, where they must have all retreated. Although it is unusual for no one to be behind the counter.

As I mount the final step and start to push the door open, Peter's solid arm slams into me. I hit the door, trying to grasp my elbow where white-hot pain travels up my arm. As his arm pushes past me, I can only hear his ragged breath and my own shout.

It happens in the blink of an eye.

What I see first are the vines. Literal vines grow out of Peter's skin, and I'm unable to decipher where the skin ends and the vines start. The vegetation is around the neck of a small figure who stands in the middle of the room, no one saying a word.

"What the fuck are you?" Peter growls.

Marie, coming to her senses, steps forward, holding her hands up. "Peter, this is Deva. This is who I asked here. The invitation... the introduction. Deva is a vampire."

The muscles in his back ease and he relaxes his arm, the vines retracting to nothing.

Well, that's new.

I have never seen him do that before.

Chapter Eleven

Peter

The silence in the room feels deadly. Eyes flit between me and what I have just been told is a vampire. Breaking through the silence is the frantic pumping of everyone's heartbeats, all except one, of course.

"I'm sorry, I-I..." I stammer out while the vampire wears an expression of mild amusement. Which is a good thing, I suppose, given that only moments ago, I tried to strangle her. "It was just... I was confused. You don't have a heartbeat."

Her eyes sparkle. I have caught her off guard.

"No, my heart has not beat since the day I died over two thousand years ago."

Her voice is thick with an accent I don't recognize. It's musical, its vibrations with a low undercurrent like a cat's purr ripples across my skin, making all my hairs stand on end. She is an ancient and lethal creature.

"I had to come. When Marie said that a god was alive and walking the streets of New Orleans, I had to see for myself." As she talks, she takes some measured steps closer, sizing me up, appraising me with her keen eyes. "See if the stories I was told as a girl were true, that the gods walk among us. Violent, bloody creatures. Slaves who, left unchecked, would eat every soul in sight, caring only for the people they are bound to. So, are they?" Her smile brings large dimples to her cheeks. "Are the stories true?"

Something about her is captivating. She has no heartbeat, no smell, and I want to touch her, to see what she would feel like. "I heard vampires only feed on the blood of virgins." I grin. "Is that true?"

Deva cackles and it is high and rings around the room, breaking all the tension that had formed. Everyone takes a collective breath and laughs along with us. Under the noise of their laughter, she whispers so only I can hear, "You smell like sex, god."

Now it is my turn to guffaw. "And you smell like nothing, vampire."

She chuckles again and tosses back her face, coming to life when she does. It's infectious, and I wonder if it is part of a vampire's charm. To make people want to agree with them—influence but less.

"There is no soul inside of you, is there?" I ask even quieter.

"I suppose that can be expected when one has been dead for as long as I have, Peter, can't it?" she muses, still seeming entertained by my being. Her outfit, made of earthy batik fabric, seems to cover every inch of her flawless skin, only showing the slightest tan of her heritage. Her face is the one thing on show with her black hair tied up in a crown of braids. For lack of a better place to touch, I run gentle fingers over her cheek.

So weird, so very far from human.

I must shake my head subconsciously.

"What is it that you feel?" She gazes up at me with rapt curiosity.

"You are ageless, like your body is frozen, preserved in time." I run my fingers across her jawline, down to her neck, trying to find a chink in the armor. A way to let me in. I meet her eyes again. "Do you have to drink human blood? Is that what keeps your armor in place?"

Deva giggles a bit, moving her own fingers across my hand and down my arm. "My armor? I have never heard my skin called that before. I need blood, yes, but it doesn't need to be human. When I was a new vampire, I lived solely on the blood of Sumatran tigers."

I laugh. "Is that why you purr?"

"I purr?" She takes her hand off me and moves it to her chest in consternation. "I do not purr."

"You do. I can hear it in your voice. A low frequency. It sounds just like a cat's purr."

She laughs again, unguarded and without inhibition, and I like the sound. I like her.

"I guess you are what you eat. And what is it that sustains you? Do you really eat souls?"

"Yes. But I don't need to. I can just eat and drink like a regular human. I mean, I never feel full anymore, but I can survive."

She shakes her head in disbelief. "Who would have thought?" she says to herself more than anything before taking my hand once more. "Your skin is so hot, so human, how can it contain what you are?"

"I have a twin soul. A human one. It keeps me bound, anchors my energy," I tell her, watching her feline-like movements.

"Fascinating," she states, her eyes alive as she studies me. She is tiny, like Connie, only buried in a swath of fabric.

The sound of Marie clearing her throat brings us out of ourselves. I think even Deva forgot we are standing in a room full of people.

"It is good to see you two getting along. You never know quite what will happen when two species meet for the first time. I'm glad to see you are..." she quirks her eyebrow, "... receptive to one another."

I chance a glance back at Connie, who looks pissed. *So much for not being jealous.* My eyes then find Lorna, who is shaking her head at me. She doesn't look annoyed so much as if she shouldn't expect anything less—which, I think, bothers me more.

"Deva, you are very welcome here. It's not much, but let me show you to your room. We can discuss more this evening after you are rested."

"Thank you, Marie." Deva smiles, allowing herself to be led away from me.

I spin around, catching Connie by the arm and pulling her downstairs. There is no chance I am letting history repeat itself here. I leave her on the second to last step so she stands above me.

"Connie—"

"Really, Peter?" she starts in on me. "Do you just want to fuck anything supernatural that walks?"

I can't help but bark out a laugh. It's strange to hear such words come from Connie's mouth.

"Wow. What happened to not being bothered?" I snicker. She is actually kind of cute when she is mad.

"You couldn't keep your hands off her." She puts her hands on her hips as she leers over me.

"I touched her face in a room full of witnesses. I'm not going to do anything, Connie. She's a vampire, for crying out loud. She feels different. I was curious." I let out a breath. "I won't fuck her, or try to, or be stupid enough to suggest we both do." I chance a smile at her, but it's obvious she doesn't find my joke remotely funny.

She shifts her weight, folding her arms across her chest. "You think I don't know you well enough to know what you look like when you want something. You are so obvious."

"Con..." I cock my head at her, leaning my foot on the bottom step to draw myself level with her. "She distracted my attention for a moment. Yes, I will be honest with you, meeting a vampire with no heartbeat, no smell, she threw me off guard for a minute. Do you want to know what *you* do to me?" I take her hand, letting my electricity crackle over to her.

"Why don't you tell me?" she suggests, a smile starting to tug at her lips.

"You distract me all day, every day. My every waking moment is consumed by you." I slide my hands around her back. "If you'd let me, I would fill your every minute. You would never be away from me, rid of me. Am I making myself clear, Miss Prinze?"

Connie rolls her eyes, but her stance has softened, thankfully appeased. She grabs my chin so I can't look away from her. "You are *mine*, Peter. Do you understand that?"

Her eyes are so serious and commanding that I am honestly lost for words and can only nod.

"Good."

"Good," I repeat, following her back upstairs, feeling altogether a lot more tired. *It's been a weird morning.* Only as we move back into the apartment and Connie moves away from me to go talk to Lorna and Lisette does Deva's presence in New Orleans start to register. I move toward Marie, who is sitting at the table by the open window, staring out at the street below, her expression pensive.

"Do you mind?"

I break her reverie, and she tears her eyes away to study me, inclining her head the smallest amount. Marie's eyes stay keen on me as I lower into the chair, and I take a turn to watch the busy crowd below.

"You said you only know one way of creating an immortal. Deva is that way, isn't she?" I don't look at Marie, not quite believing I am going to say it, but I do. "For her to turn Connie into a vampire."

Marie scrunches her face up as if tasting my dislike of the notion.

My stomach is doing somersaults. This is what I asked for. However, it seems so wrong. Deva is intriguing, but to imagine Connie like her, cold and stripped of all the things that make her so delicious... I shudder.

"It is what you said you wanted, for her to have an immortal life," Marie reminds me, her eyes serious and her words hushed. "I told you there is always a price to pay."

I push my hands through my hair before rubbing my eyes until I can see spots. How can I begin to explain to the person who has taken a huge chance on me that I'm not sure if this is the right way? For us to find a different way.

"Peter." Marie puts a gentle hand over mine. "You and Connie do not need to make this decision today. From what I know, a new vampire has not been made in a very long time. Magic has been leaving this world for a while. There is no certainty Deva will agree to it either. She mainly came to meet you. Both of you, take your time and get to know her. If she does sire Connie, she will be part of your lives forever." Marie pats my hand, looking quite weary herself. "This morning went extraordinarily well, better than I expected it to. Take the win."

She gives me a sympathetic look, and I nod.

"Thank you, Marie, for doing this."

She dips her head and moves away as I look over to Connie, who is busy chatting away with Lorna and Lisette. I slip in behind her, wrapping my arms around her waist.

"Let's go back to the hotel," I whisper into her ear. "Get away from the noise for a while."

Turning to me, concern is etched all over her face. "Is everything okay?" she asks, placing a reassuring hand on my chest.

True to what she's said, she knows me all too well. I wish I could shake the knot in my stomach.

"Of course. I just want you to myself." I take her hand. "Let's go."

She lets me lead her out of the crowded apartment and onto the street. Although stifling hot, it is good to be out in the open air. She keeps her hand in mine as we hurry back to our hotel. While we haven't stayed much, all our stuff is stored there. I try to imagine how it would be to not feel it in her skin when she needs to drink more, not hear the sound of her heart in my ear when I sleep. I so love to sleep wrapped up in her, the sound so loud in my ear. To live a life without that. Yet it would still be one with her.

We enter the sanctuary of the hotel room, and it is an absolute mess. I'd forgotten how we left it—empty bottles of booze everywhere, remnants of weed and cocaine all over the dresser. I'd told the front desk not to send in any maids. I realize I am still being selfish—this is all I want. I can't begrudge her eternity. If this is how she wants it, then I will learn to live without her heartbeat, that sweet taste.

"Let me have it, then," she says, moving to sit on the edge of the bed. "You've been sulking the whole way back."

"I'm sorry. I don't mean to sulk." I give her a wan smile. "Busy thoughts is all."

"Hmm..." She becomes thoughtful. "Come here and tell me." She pats the bed beside her.

I take a seat next to her as she folds her legs underneath her and ask, "You understand why Deva is here, why Marie invited her?"

Connie dips her head. "Yes, I get the idea. This is the plan, right?" She shivers a tad. "She is what I have to become to be immortal, so that we can be together."

"You don't have to do anything, Connie." I move my hand to her chest, where a soul has pushed on, what, fifty years to Connie's life? Just one soul on its own.

She looks a little confused. "You don't want me to?"

I take a long breath. It feels like whatever I say, it will come out wrong. I stand and pace in front of the edge of the bed. "It seems... extreme," I settle on, which is incredibly weak.

"Extreme? Peter, are you having second thoughts?"

"No. Of course not." I kneel in front of her. "I'm just saying let's not rush this. We have time. Let's be certain this is what *you* want. That you really want to become *other*, something so different to what you are now."

Connie laughs, moving up to her knees and taking my face in her hands. "I honestly thought you might be into it, you know, having me as a sexy vampire. I know you are curious."

I lean into her hand. "Not at all. I love you as you are."

Connie's face falls serious again, and I recognize the signs. Her confidence is cracking. She thinks I don't want forever.

"Peter—"

"Connie, I am worried for your soul. About what happens to your soul if you become that thing." I close my eyes, as she runs her fingers into my hair. "Deva said that she died. What if you have to die?"

The recognition dawns all over her face as I peer into her eyes. *I don't want her to die. Not even for a minute, not for a second, not for me.*

"Peter..." she starts again.

My throat feels thick. "You can't die, Connie. Not even if it's for a second. I won't allow it."

She takes a big gulp, pulling me close to her and wrapping her arms tight around me. "You said there wasn't a line you wouldn't cross if it meant forever. You have to let me take that risk too. I would do that, Peter. I would die for you."

The words feel like a knife, physically painful, and cold in my chest. "Don't say that," I whisper, desperate never to hear her say it again. "I am not worth it."

Connie pushes me away a tad to look at her, about to make some kind of argument about how these things go both ways, no doubt, but I cut her off.

"Please, Connie. For me, let's just think about this. Really think about it, and talk to Deva. If it's what you want, what you *really* want, then I won't stop you. I will love you beating heart or not, but this must be *your* choice. This won't be me making you immortal... this will be Deva making you immortal."

Connie's brow furrows. "That bothers you, doesn't it?"

"Of course it does," I admit.

"Is that what you're scared of?" She looks incredulous, and I am surprised she still can be. "You think that what we have might be broken if Deva turns me."

I laugh because it sounds a bit stupid when she says it out loud. "We have no idea what vampire bonds are like. That's something we should ask her about. But, yes, there is a part of me that thinks that. Connie, what we have... it's not just like being in love. I don't know if it's because of what I am or what I did." I stroke her cheekbone, her black-rimmed eyes. "There is part of you that is alive, living inside of you, that I put there. You should let me try one more soul. I think it would work."

"Peter."

"This connection that I have to you... I don't want to lose it. I can find you anywhere because of it."

She laughs. "So why do you always have to be in the same room as me?"

But I don't return it. "Because it hurts me to be apart from you. Back in India, Connie, it felt like I was dying when you left me. I know it was my fault, but it felt like dying."

"You've never told me that before."

"It was my fault, not yours. Look, just promise me, with Deva. We don't have to do this. There must be another way."

Chapter Twelve

Sorcha

The coven has become a hive of activity. Support arrives from all over the globe, so many that the coven's vast tunnels can't cope with their volume. I can only imagine the locals' confusion at so many strange foreigners in their midst. Not that this part of Ireland isn't used to tourists, but I doubt Newgrange has seen quite so many in one go.

Word of the infamous Morgan le Fay joining the side of the Irish coven and their coming attack on the new god encouraging them to join the fray, covens from all over the planet are coming together for the first time in an extremely long time. All this magic collected in one place sets my nerves on edge, and Morgan's presence seems to rile them further, her lingering silence somehow validating their campaign. Our campaign. Yet I can feel somewhere deep in my bones this is something more than that. Morgan's magic is old, so old, and it stirs something in them. A connection to something more primitive.

The niggling thought that I may have done the wrong thing weighs heavily on my chest. Glory and Gareth have become more reclusive with each day, discussing the finer details of the plan amongst themselves and Morgan only.

I have never been particularly nervous, but my nerves feel frayed.

"What is bothering you?" Lily comes to sit next to me. Her cardigan is way too big, and she wraps it around her to fight off the morning breeze.

Perched on top of the mound, looking down at the river in the brightening light, I am thankful for its coolness on my skin.

"I doubt there have ever been so many witches collected in one place. Newgrange can feel the magic... I can feel it in the earth. It almost feels like it could throw the planet off its axis," I tell her.

"I know. I can feel it too." Lily smiles, joining me to gaze upon the monolithic tombs in the distance.

"What is it about this place, Lil?"

Lily fixes me with a hard stare. "You don't know? It is a source... a point of contact... a place where magic was first known."

"I have no idea what you're talking about." I laugh, leaning back to gaze up at the sky and feeling more comforted now that Lily is with me.

"I don't either half the time." Lily leans back too, resting her head on my arm, her eyes wide and sparkling at me. "You have to be the most beautiful thing in the world, Cia. I would give up every sunrise to see your face."

My heart skips, and I turn on my side to gain a better look at her, running my finger over her cheekbone. "Lil—" I start, cautious with my precious friend.

"I know," she cuts me off, smiling still. "You are desperately in love with someone who does not deserve you. I am happy to be your friend, your sister, but just know, I love you immensely, unconditionally."

"Oh, Lily." I pull her close and bury my face into her neck, promising myself I am not going to cry.

I do not cry.

And I cannot let myself love her back, not in any way.

"Shall we get back inside? There is a lot of movement this morning. I think something has happened."

I nod and let her help me to my feet. Almost as soon as we step back into the tunnel, Glory is at my elbow, her face serious.

"Good, here you two are. We are meeting. We have news," she says before pushing ahead and walking to the central room, which is now so crowded we can barely fit. The younger members are not here, nor are all the new arrivals. I imagine the most senior witches will be who reports back on the happenings.

Glory takes her place up front. "We have had news. A message has been intercepted, and we know the new god is in New Orleans. The time to move is soon. Over the next few days, we will finalize the plans with who is to go to New Orleans and who is to stay behind."

There are murmurs across the room, and I exchange a confused look with Lily, who opens and shuts her mouth. My stomach feels like ice.

"Who comes and who stays?" I whisper to her. "We are going to need everyone if we want to win. It has been over a year, so he will be even stronger now." I shake my head. "What is she think-ing?" I say more to myself.

Lily dips her lips to my ear. "I don't know what she is thinking. She has placed a powerful block on her thoughts." Lily's eyes are wide, and fearful. "Gareth too."

I didn't think my stomach could sink any lower. "What are they planning, Lil?"

Lily shifts her shoulders, but her concern is clear. A doubt I have never seen in Lily. Glory has been her high priestess for as long as Lily has been alive. I take her hand and push my way through the crowd. When Glory catches sight of us, her eyes narrow.

"Sorcha, we need to talk. Come with me."

I keep a tight hold of Lily's hand as we walk into the side room, away from the din of the main room.

"Glory, we need to know what the plan is. Have you found a way to kill him? These people need to know what they are walking into." Glory's eyes shift to Morgan, her heartbeat controlled, so I ask, "Morgan? Does she know how to kill him?"

"Morgan will lead the attack, Sorcha."

"What? How can a witch who cannot speak lead the attack? How are you going to put that on a plane?" I gesture to the whole of Morgan's grotesque form, her statue-like merlin.

"Morgan has considerable influence, Sorcha," she says, her tone wary.

I narrow my eyes at her as she looks away from me.

"I need you to stay here. You too, Lily."

"You can't be serious," I retort and hear similar words coming from Lily.

"You are not exactly useful against him." Gareth smirks.

"Bite me, Gareth," I say, and he snarls back at me.

"This isn't helpful." Glory stands between us. "Look, if it makes you both feel better, I am not going either."

My face falls. Glory, the leader of the coven, is not going. I could understand when she sent the others before—Rue was more powerful than anyone—but without her? We need Glory.

"G-Glory," I stammer. "I don't understand."

"Of course you don't. You only think of yourself," Gareth bites out at me. "You have the ignorance of a child."

"Gareth," Glory chides, placing a stern hand on his arm. "Perhaps I can speak to Sorcha alone for a moment."

Gareth gives her a long look but complies as he, Lily, and Morgan walk out of the room. Lily shoots me a look that I better tell her what is going on later.

"Glory, I have to go. This is my fight."

"No, it is not. Not anymore, Sorcha." Glory pinches her nose as if I am being impossible.

"How can you not be going? You are the leader of this coven."

"Gareth and Morgan will do just fine." Glory lets out a breath. "Besides, we need contingencies in place."

"Contingencies? You mean if this goes wrong? All the more reason to send everyone." I start to feel a little panicked. "If they go into this fight thinking there is a chance they will lose, then they are already lost."

"We are sending the strongest from all the tribes, Sorcha. There is no need for you to worry. We *will* succeed."

There is something about Glory. She's too calm, her heartbeat too steady. "How is it that Morgan will kill him?" I ask.

"Morgan can handle it. That is all you need to know. She is a first witch. Her magic far surpasses anyone here."

"Morgan will handle it," I repeat, the awful truth starting to sink in, a sickness washing over me that I haven't felt in years, not since my first sacrifices. "You don't plan on killing him, do you?"

"We have been planning this for months... we *will* succeed. Morgan knows the ritual."

My head is spinning, and I stumble forward to catch myself on the table, my breathing too hard. "No, no, no, you can't be so stupid. You can't think you can contain him."

Glory stares down at me, the defiance sparking in her warrior-like eyes. "A god like that needs a tether. It is the *only* way."

My tears finally spill, leaving me gasping for air, and I am not above begging. "Glory, no. Please, no. Don't do this."

"Sorcha..." Glory crouches to where I am crumpled on the

floor, "... he will restore this coven to the most powerful. With him in our service, we can change the world."

I cannot believe her words. "No. No. No."

"Just leave it to us. You will be safe here, and so will Lily."

I blink back my tears, watching Glory rise. *Lily, she is my consolation prize?*

"You... you are sending the most powerful witches. Why? If your plan is to enslave him?"

Glory doesn't say anything, and her face gives nothing away.

The feeling is crushing, and the words are sticky in my throat. "No. No, no, no." *I can't believe this.* "Glory, *no*, please don't tell me you are sending them there to fatten him up. Please don't tell me you are sending those witches to their deaths."

Glory's eyes soften a touch. "It is for the greater good. The tether ritual requires sacrifice. We believe he will need more than one. I am sorry, Sorcha. I know what you are thinking, but this isn't some power play. This is the *only* way. It's not about power but about bringing a force of nature to heel."

"Glory," I cry out. I sound like an animal, but I don't know what else to say.

My chest feels like it might split in two thinking of all those deaths and Peter not destroyed but instead the coven's prisoner. It is only now I start to register that this whole time, they've been referring to him as the new god, never by his name, making him appear more of a thing, something deserving of a life of servitude.

"What will you do with him?" I manage to splutter out.

Glory gives me a wry half-smile. "You wanted him dead. Why does it matter to you?"

I clutch my chest. *Lily was right.* My heart cannot take seeing him that way. Whatever their plans for him, they are not good, including sending their own like lambs to the slaughter.

Please, Peter, do not give them what they want.

Do not give in to that darkness.

Right then, I decide I have to get away, to warn him.

In a second, I am on my feet, running to the door, slamming my body into it. The earth shakes, but the door doesn't move. As I pull and pull, a deep guttural sound comes from me with the effort.

Behind the doors, I feel the magic reverberating. *Morgan.* I turn to see Glory watching me with curiosity as she tilts her head in my direction.

"Now you want to protect him?" she muses.

"Not him," I spit out. "All of those people, Glory. They don't deserve what is coming."

I try to run past her again, but she grasps my arms, sending agony coursing through my body as I realize why Glory has been so still. Golden bands of binding rope are stretched across her hands, anchoring and forcing me back, and leaving me bound in my place against the wall.

Her expression softens with affection for the first time as I struggle and cry against the bonds. "This is for the greater good. Sometimes you need to make the hard decisions." Glory caresses my face. "You have Lily. Try to be happy. The new god is not your concern anymore."

She leaves me here, bound and shaking, affixed to my spot on the wall. Knowing this—an army of witches being sent for sacrifice —is *all* my fault.

Please, please, just don't fall for it, Peter.

Chapter Thirteen

Peter

The electricity crackles and sparks as I trace my finger down Connie's arm, watching it saturate into her skin. Her chest rises and falls while she breathes in the sensation. I wish I could know what it feels like. I have to be so careful with how much we do, and monitor the effect it has on her body.

"Do you think you will still be able to feel like this if you change?"

"I hope so," Connie murmurs, opening her eyes to look at me.

We moved back into the hotel over the last few days.

"One day, this is what it will be like every day for us." She smiles.

Our whole morning has been in bed, lying curled up facing each other, talking, and keeping each other awake.

"Sounds like heaven," I tell her. "Do you think you will want that? Just you and me? Like, what if we disappeared somewhere? Lived on our own island. No one else, no influence, no world... just us. Our own corner where time counts for nothing."

Connie bites her bottom lip. "Is that what you want to do? When this is done?"

I nod. "I think so. I want to rest, to stand still for a moment. To be still with you."

She giggles. "What about Lorna?"

"What about her?" I arch my eyebrows. "I don't think Lisette would be a fan of me whisking her away. She seems happy now."

Her smile is back as she reaches her hand up to my chest. "Just me and you."

"Just me and you," I confirm.

Saying the words, I realize how much it's true. New Orleans is fun, but the stares get tiring after a while, the excess, the people. I haven't had quiet in so long. I haven't tended a garden or been silent in forever. I realize how close I am—*we* are—one step away from what we want. Maybe if we could disappear, I would be at peace. If Connie is my only company, then that murderous voice at the back of my head would quiet. I would fill myself on her alone, and I could be content.

"Deva says that when I am a new vampire, I will have to feed a lot at first," she says quietly, and the thought makes my chest constrict.

It's true. Deva told us it doesn't need to be human blood, but it must be fresh, and it has to be strong. So, living on bunnies or something similar will be out of the question. She'll need a carnivore—the bigger the better. Deva also assured Connie it doesn't have to mean killing anyone, but accidents happen, especially at first.

I thread my fingers into hers. "Maybe it could be my blood," I say lightly, not wanting to look at her expression. "I can't die, Connie, so there are no risks involved. I kind of like the idea, you know? That despite what Lorna says, turns out you can survive on me alone."

Connie chuckles. "It is a romantic thought..."

"Really? Your version of romantic is pretty twisted, then."

She playfully slaps my shoulder. "What I mean is... would that even work? You're not human." She giggles. "Maybe I would end up a vampire-god hybrid and become most powerful of all."

I kiss the inside of her wrist, pulling her a little closer. "I wonder what it would taste like?"

"What?"

"My blood." I can't help but wonder if blood has a flavor like souls do.

"I'm sure you would taste like heaven, Peter," she says, only a hint of mockery in her voice.

"I'm serious," I say as I position myself above her. "If you do this, that's what we will do. I want to be that." I smooth her dark hair from her face, and her emerald eyes sparkle, igniting the fire growing inside of me. "I want to be that connected to you, Connie. I want it to be me. Let it be me."

Connie takes a shallow breath. "Okay," she whispers before capturing my lips with hers in a swift move, catching me off guard. She bites so hard on my lip that it draws blood, and my breath hitches as I push harder into her, her legs wrapping around me. *I could stay here forever.*

Just let her go through with it.

I try to push down the feeling that this is the wrong way.

Connie forever, any way, is the right way.

We've promised to go on a double date with Lorna and Lisette tonight, and Connie wants to catch up with Deva beforehand, so I have to haul my ass out of bed and pretend like I'm interested in any of these things. I would much rather stay in the hotel today, though. I've grown tired of being around so many people.

But Connie keeps distracting me.

In the shower.

In the elevator.

Very distracting.

By the time we're out of the hotel, we are over two hours late, and I think Connie might actually be annoyed. Which would be amusing, except it also peeves me a little about how she cares so much about Deva. Far from Connie's first impression, the situation with Deva is completely different from the one with Sorcha.

After the initial shock of learning that something that was already a myth when she was born—a god—is very much real, Deva was intrigued by Connie and me as a couple even more than me alone. She insists on calling us mates and is fascinated by our bond. Somewhat worry-inducing, she has no idea what will happen to that bond if Connie is turned.

She has spent a lot of time talking to Connie about this bond rather than the practicalities of becoming a vampire, a discussion that feeds into Connie's extreme romanticism. Connie, being human, has no idea what a mate bond is or the power of it. Although the notion fucking exasperates me no end, I did feel a little guilty when I well and truly crushed the idea, reminding Connie we are not of the same species. She is human and humans do not have mate bonds. So, despite Deva's fascination with what we have, the mate bond is bullshit. Connie had looked like I'd kicked her dog or something else she would find a travesty.

"What we have is better, Connie," I try to reassure her. *"We chose each other. That is better, isn't it? Fuck fate. I chose you, Connie, I always will."*

The two-thousand-year-old vampire is surprisingly friendly and not cryptic about anything. Marie said it was clear early on that Deva would facilitate our request. All of Connie's questions were answered, and Deva explained the process of transitioning. Again, something that sets my blood on fire—it sounds extremely intimate and something I will be completely left out of.

Connie seems more and more set that this is the right decision. I flit between feeling relieved our task is almost done and wanting to scream for her not to do it.

She is mine. She is mine. She is mine. I won't allow it. I won't allow her to go through with something that will change her into anything but wholly mine.

My selfish heart screams not to let Deva have one piece of her. The more rational side tells me to get it done, and then we can be finished with all of this.

I have conflicting emotions about the vampire. Part of me is insanely jealous and borderline psychotic, at times thinking this is some great plan to take Connie away. I have to actively remind myself this is what we asked for.

I only just catch the end of what Connie is saying as we make our way over to Marie's apartment. Something about Lorna. "Yes, I think Lorna probably will stay here when we leave." I tell her, catching her drift, and then click my tongue. "I think her and Lis spend more time in their bedroom than we do, if such a thing is possible."

Connie smiles. "Ah... young love," she jokes with a spring in her step as her glossy hair ripples about her shoulders. "I'm happy for her."

"Me too. Her heart was so broken. Her pain... it was hard."

Connie gives me a sideways glance. "You've never spoken much about it. What you did for her."

"I didn't do much. Mainly kept her distracted, numbed her with booze and influence to keep her in one piece until the pain was more manageable." I squeeze Connie's hand. "But she is doing much better now, even though Lisette is like the anti-Anna... far too wild."

"Far too much like you," Connie teases.

I roll my eyes. "Anyway... Lorna can live without me now. My job is done, and she is healed as much as I can manage. Lisette can take it from here."

"Spoken like a true benevolent god," she jibes again.

I scrunch up my face in distaste. "Don't." I push her away from me. "I am the destroyer of worlds, remember? Not the healer of broken hearts."

"I promise I won't tell anyone."

I roll my eyes again as we step into Marie's shop. Marie is behind the counter with her head in her hands.

"Everything okay?" Connie asks as we near the counter.

"Sure. Just a headache. You two go up."

As we move past, I come to a stop to look at Marie, feeling a little sheepish. "I could... um... just take care of that, if you want?"

Marie raises her eyebrows, and I take it as a small sign of consent and move my hand to the nape of her neck, where my hand glows to relieve the pain.

As I do, I turn to look out the window. Her headache is nothing to do with a lack of water but the pressure in the air. The sun is hanging like a giant orb over the still New Orleans afternoon. It feels like a hurricane is coming.

"Holy shit." She laughs, her face looking much brighter.

Connie chuckles along with her, already used to me curing every trivial ailment she has.

I am much more concerned with the serene view, as I state, "A hurricane is coming."

"What?" Marie chuckles. "There is no storm."

"I hadn't noticed the pressure before. Can't you feel it?" I ask her, but she shakes her head.

Maybe I'm losing my touch. I try to let it go. She's right, it doesn't look like a storm is coming outside. Instead, we mount the stairs to find Lorna eating a bowl of cereal at the table.

"Look at you two," she says through her mouthful.

"Look at you," I joke as I go over to kiss the top of her head. "We thought we'd lost you for a second."

"Lisette is at work." She cracks her neck, giving me a pointed look. "My bones hurt."

I can't help but scrunch my face at her in mock disgust. "I have to heal your sex injuries now?"

"Have pity on me," she says with puppy dog eyes.

I slide my hand onto her shoulder, trying not to focus too much on where she has bruises. "Jesus, what have you two been doing?" I ask, causing color to flood her cheeks, which, in turn, makes me laugh.

Okay, that was a bit mean.

"Consider it payback." Lorna smirks at me. "For having to put up with you two for so long."

"Hey, what did I do?" Connie protests as she looks around the room for any sign of Deva.

"Oh, Deva went out." Lorna reads her mind. "When you two didn't show, she said she was going to the bayou... something about alligators. I was only half listening. Sorry."

"That's your fault." Connie slaps my stomach hard.

"Ouch." I frown at her, prompting an eye roll.

"You guys want to go?" Lorna asks. "It's supposed to be really beautiful. Lisette talks about it all the time. We could go and catch her up."

"We have no way of finding her," I remind Lorna. She might have a phone, but none of us has thought to ask. I gave up on them when I lost my last one.

"She's a vampire... won't she just, like, smell us coming or something?" Lorna snorts.

Connie shrugs. "Dinner isn't for a few hours. I'm game."

I look out the window, my apprehension knitting my brow. No signs of a hurricane. "Okay, let's go."

Chapter Fourteen

Connie

It's great to see Lorna so happy. She positively glows as we follow Peter down to the bayou. As we edge out of the city, I notice his back muscles are all tensed while Lorna chats beside me as happy as a clam.

"Peter," I call out, feeling a little guilty for cutting Lorna off. "What's wrong?"

"Nothing," he says. Waving his arm without turning round, he adds, "Just some weird weather."

Lorna and I glance at each other and then at the pleasant light of the fading afternoon around us.

"What? Here?" Lorna asks.

Peter slows his walk, turning to us while he scan the trees. "Yes, here. I don't think Deva is out here. We should go back."

My heart picks up a beat. The air seems quiet. Peter's brow stays furrowed. "What is it?"

He turns to look into the deepening tree line of the swamp. "I am not sure."

His feet resume forward motion and, despite what he is saying, Lorna and I follow him until our feet hit boggy swampland.

"Eww." Lorna lifts her feet as the water squelches around her flip-flops.

I'm grateful to be wearing my boots.

"Something is here," Peter whispers as we continue through the wetlands.

"Shouldn't we go back? Get Marie or something?" I ask.

"It feels strange. So old." Peter stops for a moment, looking back at Lorna and me. "Marie said all kinds of things long forgotten have been waking up of late. A fae came from the bayou. Maybe this is another one."

"All the more reason to turn back," Lorna argues. "Marie was nervous about your introductions because your kinds are separated by thousands of years. This could be a volatile situation, Peter. Peter!" she cries out.

It doesn't matter because he marches forward.

As we follow, I see by the rippling of his back and the flex of his neck that a mere fae is not what we are walking into. Peter's movements become more measured, careful, and predatory.

Until we come to a clearing.

Peter straightens up at the sight of a small yellowish light resonating from across the swamp. It's swaying slightly. Lorna and I stand on either side of him in the tree line, and I notice the light isn't just a light. A small old-fashioned lamp hangs in the hands of a tiny hooded figure. Maybe two hundred feet away from us, across the swamp, it stands there.

"It's a witch." Peter breathes deep. "A very old witch. Her soul is all crooked."

"What does she want?" Lorna whispers.

"I have no idea," he replies, looking down at her. "Nothing good."

We stand and wait. After a while, Peter starts fidgeting beside me, and I look down to see he is loosening his Converse, wiggling his feet out of them and stepping his bare feet into the marsh.

"Are you mad? What are you doing?" I hiss.

His dark eyes are alert, something dancing there in the dying light of the day. "Something is coming," he whispers.

Almost as soon as the words have left his mouth, Lorna gasps as more lights emerge from the fog, around the trees. Moving in silent unison, the moments of a well-planned orchestration. At least a hundred of them come to form a semicircle at the edge of the tree line.

"Are they all witches?" I ask him.

"Every single one." His voice is barely audible, although I swear I hear a touch of glee in it. He lifts his feet in and out of the water, and I hear his bones crack.

The first tremors of terror pass through me. I notice the first figure move back, and as they do, a bird cries out as it flies overhead.

Oh God, oh God, oh God. It's too late to run.

Peter grabs my arm, yanking both Lorna and me behind him before plunging his hand into the marsh. He forces a tree into life around us, creating a protective cage for the two of us.

"Stay here," he commands.

"Peter, there are so many." The terror in Lorna's voice matches that in my heart.

"It's okay," he tells her, his eyes catching mine for only a second, a slight tug at the corner of his mouth.

The terror turns to something different, a cross between terror and anticipation, as Peter turns away from me. The feeling fills me up with absolute certainty, making me shake harder with every sure footstep he takes out of the tree line and into the clearing.

Into the path of a hundred strong witches.

"Shit." Lorna's tear-stricken voice shakes beside me. "We have to get help."

I steady my hands on the vines of the tree, which act like prison bars, to stop my trembling, then shake my head at my best friend. "No." My voice quavers too. "No, he... erm... he is going to kill them all."

Lorna's eyes go wide.

We watch, unable to look away as Peter walks on. Now, with each step farther into the clearing, the vines of the swamp spring to life, pushing him up off his feet, supporting his outstretched arms. I know it is a sign of power, to throw them off, to give them a chance to back away.

"Witches," his voice booms around the bayou, and I hear the smile in it. "You should not have come here. I do not demand your sacrifice..." he pauses briefly, "... but I will take it all the same."

It's then I see it. With his palms outstretched, at his height, he blocks out the last of the low sun. A giant, dreadful cross. My stomach drops, and I wish I could close my eyes and not see what comes next. This is the moment from our nightmares, except we had it wrong. It wasn't all Peter's perspective—it was his *and* mine. All that lies ahead for the witches is death and blood. We have never seen farther than this nightmare.

A new figure steps forward, as tall as Peter. Taking off his hood, his rage pulses out of him like a beacon. "You are an abomination. We will not allow it. The balance must be maintained."

Peter barks out a cold, hollow laugh. "You don't understand. I *am* the balance."

He lowers himself back to the ground, and I wish I could call out to tell him to stop. That this is the awful event that plagues our nightmares.

"I am the only god this world needs." His voice is commanding.

The male witch snarls.

I expect the fray to start, but everyone remains motionless. My heart feels about to burst as I press my face to the gaps in the tree. The hoods being removed reveal a hundred irate faces all glaring at Peter in anger, which is turning into disgust.

"What is he doing?" Lorna whispers.

Now he has his left forearm extended and is digging his nails into his wrist, so deep they draw blood, so hard that he drags the top layers of skin right off. Lorna makes a gagging sound like she is going to be sick as the flesh drops to the ground with a splash. Even the male witch who has taken the lead looks vaguely horrified and bewildered at the mutilation.

"Holy fucking Jesus," I say, catching the first glints of what he is doing.

"What is that?" Lorna manages to get out as we watch Peter withdraw a metal object from the exposed muscle of his arm.

His blade. Each body he marks with that knife, its soul will be his. I had no idea he'd hid it *in* his own body. For safekeeping, in case he needs it for a slaughter. The niggle at the back of my head taunts that, behind it all, this is what Peter wants. Even more, this is something he needs. That part of him that calls, and he always wants to answer, but he doesn't.

Because of me.

I have no time to answer Lorna.

At the sight of the blade, the witch makes a kind of battle cry and, from the tree line, a hundred threads of golden binding rope cascade like an ocean toward him at the same time he lifts his arms to cover their tree line in flames. The witches lurch forward, and the movement makes most of the ropes miss, but those that remain true lash themselves around Peter's arms, pulling him forward.

They are not strong enough. The poison that seems part of him now rises to his skin. Great black vines wrap around the golden threads and drag their holders across the marsh, straight to him.

They are the first.

In one swift motion, the blade finds their throats, the ground at his feet sloshing with blood as the first ten witches fall.

The main witch slinks back.

Coward.

The remaining witches spread farther out, and more binding ropes are cast, but now the witches open their capes to reveal what appears like weapons that hold the same glow as the ropes, or oozing with a thick, black, tar-like substance.

Peter's stance drops to something more animalistic. The moment the first spear pierces his side, his and my screams are matched by the sight of the swamp coming alive. Water, mud, and vines fill the clearing, consuming the witches.

It's hard to see through the haze. The sky is black now, not a star to be seen, while fog rolls in. We can just about make out Peter's form against the golden glow of the weapons and the binding ropes. Screams and primal grunts fill the air.

I catch sight of him, upwards of fifty ropes around him, bringing him to his knees. The ground beneath us shudders, and my heart stops as I see a spear being driven into his back. The first crack of lightning forks from the unforgiving sky, killing the witch who delivered the spear. Peter twists against the ropes, yanking the nearest witch to their feet and into the shallow water before he brings down his blade into their chest again and again, the blood splattering like rain across the clearing.

He scrambles to his feet, sloshing through the water as he advances on the next. Stumbling to reach them, his blade waves wildly until the swamp vines bring the witches to a halt so the blade can find its mark.

Several more forks of lightning hit the swamp.

The remaining witches must be trying to flee.

The life of the swamp seems to be dying down, the screams quieter now. The clearing becomes visible enough to see a single witch on their back trying to escape into the smoking tree line. Peter looks ripped to shreds, some arrows piercing straight through his legs and a large gash in his back from where the spear entered. He advances on the final witch, who is begging him to stop and claiming he surrenders, but Peter grabs the front of his cloak, hauling him up closer, to stab him. Again and again. He cannot stop. I only hear the ragged sounds of his breath from across the clearing and the squelching of metal in flesh.

"Shit," Lorna whispers.

Even I can't watch.

I look back into the smoking tree line, where the fire is dwindling as Peter's stabbings lessen. He comes to a stop, utterly spent, hunched over the body. For the briefest of seconds, I swear I see a pair of amber, eagle-like eyes watching and then they are gone.

Regaining his senses, Peter springs back, falling onto his hands away from what I can imagine is a big old mess of a body.

I try to find a way out of our tree fortress but find none. Lorna is now crouched down with her head in her hands.

Poor Lorna. Not again.

But I need to get to Peter.

When I look back, he has made it to the middle of the clearing. Sloshing through the water, I finally see his face covered in mud and blood. His hair doesn't look blond anymore. His shirt is ripped away enough that I can see the initial wound from the spear is already healed, although some tracks of poison are still wrapped around his arm and up his neck. His breath heavy, he bends down to extract one of the arrows, crying out in pain.

"Peter," I shout.

He pulls out a second, causing his knee to buckle so he drops to his knees for a moment before he gets back up. Tilting his head up to the sky and clearing the clouds, he reaches my tree, still out of breath.

"Peter. Are you okay?" I ask, trying to reach my fingers through the branches.

He gives me a half smile and, shaking his head and sending the mud splattering off his hair, says, "Wow. That was a lot harder than I thought it would be." He takes a deliberate deep breath, looking up at the stars for a moment. "I had to kill some with lightning. I think I might be too late for those souls. I have about ninety, ninety-three maybe."

He puts his hand to the side of the tree. Its branches instantly move to let me out, and I throw myself at him, hitting his chest hard, the force of it almost throwing him off balance, and he winces.

"I'm sorry." I pull away to look at him. "Why aren't you healing quicker with all of those souls?"

Peter reaches down to his leg. "Those arrows were a bitch. I have no idea what poison they were made from." Then, as if only just hearing me for the first time, he looks at me in surprise. "They aren't for me, Connie. I collected them for you."

His eyes so earnest, a bit like a cat who leaves a mouse at your back door. Proud of his kill.

He rises up to look me in the eyes. "Do you trust me?" he asks.

"With my life."

He kneels at my feet, easing them out of my boots with tenderness, and I take my first step onto the sodden floor of the swamp. His hands caressing my ankles, he explains, "You should feel this... be more connected to the earth." He looks up at me with his big doe eyes. "This way, you will be made by me, in my image."

He takes my hand and leads me into the center of the clearing. With every step, the ground is more blood-soaked. Now out of my hiding place in the tree line, I see the true devastation of the fight. Not only bodies on the ground, but in the trees too, some vines still wrapped around the corpses like they're being eaten by the trees as if the swamp is alive and hungry. Then, in a flurry of water, one of the bodies disappears, the ravenous jaws of an alligator pulling it from our view. Peter's eyes gleam at the sight, but my heart rate picks up in something close to terror. From the center of the clearing, it looks more red than murky green, and my head swims at the sight of so much blood.

Every part of me trembles as he faces me. I try not to look scared. I have never ever, not once, feared him. *I'm not scared now*, I tell myself. *I should not have seen this. They came for him, not the other way around.*

I look down to see the water swirl around my bare feet and realize I have been here before. In a dream—a terrible dream.

"Are you ready?" he asks, but even he looks uncertain. He peers around at the horror scene we are part of and then back to Lorna, who is still hiding in the tree. "You don't have to do this."

"I'm ready," I say, thankful my words sound steady and sure.

Peter gives himself a little nod. Shaking out his arms, his expression turns serious as the clearing comes alive with the white glow of the souls trapped in their bodies. They travel toward him, ghostly, otherworldly lights collecting on his arms and around his shoulders. For a second, he reminds me of Boots.

His body shakes, seemingly under their weight, but then it dawns on me how this must be so hard for him to give them to me rather than have them himself. His hands move quick, slamming the force of almost a hundred souls into my chest.

Chapter Fifteen

Peter

It is done.

The last of the souls—almost a hundred incredibly powerful souls—leave the fringes of my body and mix into Connie's. The fight is over, and I am tired. So completely exhausted. I cannot wait to curl up in her arms and sleep a night-mare-free sleep.

Connie's breath shallows, and her hands clasp onto my arms to steady herself. She must feel blissful right now. I would be jealous if I weren't so exhausted. *I'll sleep soon.* I know this was the moment we've been running toward, recognized it as soon as I saw the clearing. I smile at her, and the corner of her lips start to turn up, but instead of her smile appearing, she coughs.

Blood splatters my face.

Connie's blood.

Her chest shudders and, this time, when she coughs again, she leans forward to throw up all over my feet. It is mostly blood as she stumbles into me. Her body tenses as I catch her, and she drops to the ground, convulsing in my arms.

"Connie." Her head bobs back in my arms, and I realize she has already lost consciousness. "Connie," I repeat, starting to panic. "Shit. Shit, shit, shit. Lorna," I scream.

"No. I am not coming out there," she shouts back, but I see her head pop out from her hiding place. As soon as she sees Connie limp in my arms, she comes running out, not caring or even looking at the bodies she has to run past before splashing to a halt at Connie's side. "Connie, Connie, Connie." Lorna's cries become shriller as she shakes her by the shoulders.

I feel the change in Connie beneath me as her skin flares, burning like fire. The feeling ripples across me, the destruction that lies in wait so close to coming to the surface. I clench my fists to fight the sensation.

No, no, this isn't the time.

It is not *the time to set fire to everything.*

I close my eyes.

Connie is usually so cool, not an ember in my hands.

"Peter." Lorna's palm collides hard with my face. "What the hell?" she demands as I blink my eyes back to focus on her face. "You have to get your shit together."

I focus on Lorna. *I have to get it together.* "I think she has a fever," I manage to get out.

"We need to get her to Marie."

I nod, scooping Connie up and wading back through the swamp, ignoring the pain in my leg and my exhaustion. "Lor, I don't think I can protect us from what people see. I'm exhausted. I gave all the souls to Connie. When we get back to town, everyone will see me like this."

"Let's think about damage control later." Lorna looks at Connie's face, at the beads of sweat forming there. "Why did you give her all of the souls, Peter?"

"It's just her body reacting. She'll be fine." I try to sound confident. "This is the way she turns. I've dreamed it... we both have."

"I thought they were nightmares." Lorna sounds horrified at my elbow, trotting to keep up. "I thought things were going well with Deva. At least we knew the risks with that."

"I didn't want her to become a vampire, Lorna. She would have been different."

Lorna stops dead in her tracks. "You son of a bitch. You risked her life for your goddamn ego."

My anger flares up in an instant, and I swirl on the spot, looming over her with Connie limp in my arms. "I have risked nothing. Connie will live because she has to. I fucking will it so, Lorna. And if you ever talk to me like that again, I will kill you." I breathe out so fast, the words are flying out of my mouth before I register what I am saying.

Lorna looks like I slapped her, and I instantly regret my threat.

"Look," I say more gently. "I'm sorry. I didn't mean that. I love you. You know I do. This is just really fucking stressful. I know I'm horrible. Can we please get to Marie?"

Lorna doesn't say anything, only nods and carries on walking at my side, trying to keep up with my pace as we round into town.

Please. Please, please, please let my path be clear.

I push my thought out as far and with as much influence as I can. It doesn't feel like much, but we don't come across people. The people we do cross comment on our costumes, so it seems like I still have some power remaining. Although, every time I press my hand to Connie's skin, I can do nothing to bring her temperature down. Maybe because I also feel like a furnace. I stumble forward, Lorna occasionally catching my arm. I almost wish I could die, I am so tired.

Until I finally slam into Marie's doorway, breaking open the door with ease and rushing into the closed magic shop.

"Marie," I scream. The cry echoes all around the shop. Lorna and I are flying up the stairs as Marie flings open the door to the apartment.

"What in the world?" Marie's expression is beyond horrified as we storm in.

"Where were you? I sat for an hour—" Lisette rounds on Lorna, coming to a halt when she takes in our appearance. "What? What's happening?"

"Connie needs your help," Lorna pleads to Marie.

"I can't do anything to bring down her temperature. She lost consciousness about twenty minutes ago." My own voice becoming uneven, I lie Connie down on the sofa. Her heart flutters so fast.

"What happened?" Marie asks as she puts her hand to Connie's head, motioning at the freezer to Lisette.

"We were attacked on the bayou. Witches."

Marie glances up at me for a second before she continues to wrap ice in two towels, placing them on Connie's neck.

"Anyway, I killed them and... I-I... gave the souls to Connie. About ninety, I think. Maybe it was too much in one go," I say, almost to myself.

Lisette makes a choking sound beside me, as Marie looks up in horror. "You what? To what end would you do this?"

"To make her immortal, of course," I snarl.

Marie's eyes shift to Lisette in disbelief, which she should really not do. I have half a mind to close the distance and snap her fragile neck.

"Peter..." Connie's weak voice calls, her hand reaching for me.

Thank God. I move back to her side, my body feeling like jelly. The moment I take her hand, I feel all that is wrong with her. Her human body is rejecting the raw energy of the souls. My anger melts away to nothing as I gaze into her eyes, which never doubted me for a second. *Her body won't survive this.*

"Connie, I'm so sorry." I kiss the back of her hand. In her look of confusion, I see that the whites of her eyes are already starting to yellow. Her confusion turns to pain as she clutches her side. I move my hand there and feel all the cells in her failing liver. I focus my energy.

You have to fix this, Peter. You did it.

Connie's screams fill the apartment, so loud that I am screaming too. The white healing light is working, though, putting her back together. After too long of Connie's burning agony, I let go, falling full onto my back, hitting my head on the wooden floorboards with a loud thud.

Connie has passed out again from the pain.

I bring my palms to my face.

This could *not* be more of a disaster.

I cannot lose her.

After a moment, I move my hands to see Lorna, Marie and Lisette frozen in horror, staring at me as I lie panting on the floor. I'm covered in blood, mud, and God knows what, no shoes and torn clothes. A fucking wreck.

I gingerly get to my feet, turning on Lisette. "Go and find Deva. She is on the bayou somewhere. Do not come back here until you find her." Lisette looks murderous but does as I say.

"You..." I turn to Marie, "... find a way to bring down her temperature."

"Peter..." Marie says, her countenance full of sympathy, "... this is way beyond me. I cannot help her."

I'm on her in an instant, my hand around her throat. "I just tore through a hundred witches," I say through my clenched teeth. "You are a healer, right? Find a way. Or I will skin you."

I push her away from me before I kill her to make myself feel better.

Marie nods, moving back over to tend to Connie as I collapse into a kitchen chair, banging my head on the table in front of me.

"Any orders for me?" I look up to see Lorna popping her hip at me.

"Yeah, a bottle of Jack would be really helpful right about now."

She looks less than impressed. "Nice to know you are consistent, if nothing else," she bites out.

I rub my eyes hard. "Just go and find me a bottle of something, for heaven's sake, Lorna." I know she is beyond disgusted with me right now, and I can apologize to everyone when Connie is all right.

She stalks over to the kitchen, making it known how unhappy she is by slamming all the cupboard doors.

She stomps back over, sliding the whiskey over to me, holding a glass in her hand. "Do you even want the glass?"

I shake my head, taking the biggest swig I can, and then another, and another before holding the bottle up to Lorna, who stands there with her arms crossed. "Trust me, Lorna, you can't hate me more than I hate myself right now. Please. Just drink with me."

Lorna rolls her eyes, taking the bottle out of my hand and taking a long swig, then sitting in the seat opposite. We drink in silence as Marie returns from downstairs.

The apartment soon becomes fragrant with earthy herbs while she feeds Connie small sips of lemon water. Connie's heart sometimes beats so fast I place my hand on her shoulder to calm it. I can't fix the temperature, but I can fix other things, take away some of the dehydration, and keep her heart under control.

I end up sitting on the floor, my head on my knees, by the sofa where she lies.

Sleep is on the fringes of my consciousness.

I fall under.

The sound of the door opening snaps me awake. Dawn has broken, and Lisette is back with Deva. Lorna, drunk and sleepy, blinks in the sight of them in the doorway.

"I thought vampires couldn't go out in the day." She slurs a few of her words.

"When you have been around as long as I have, you learn a few tricks, and I have never been one to shy away from magic, unlike most of my kind." Deva does not elaborate further, nor do her eyes leave Connie.

Deva moves across the room in the blink of an eye. She is right in front of me, on her knees, by Connie's side. She takes my face in her hands, her black eyes soft. The intimacy of the action brings all the heat to my face, and tears burn hot in my eyes.

"I need you to turn her," I tell her through the lump in my throat.

Deva's eyes move to Connie once more, the concern there evident, but she gives a small nod, ushering me out of the way.

I get to my feet. Most of my wounds are all but healed now. More than anything, I'm so hungry. Instead of going after food, knowing there is only one thing I am hungry for, I step back to get the half-drunk bottle of whiskey as I watch Deva position herself near Connie's waist, rubbing her thumb across her wrist.

"Her heart is beating very fast. She could hemorrhage," she states, her gaze motioning me to come forward.

I swallow hard, moving to Connie's head and placing my hand

on her shoulder to slow her heart rate. Lorna's silent tears fall down her face as she observes Connie. Lisette is watching Deva with rapt attention while Marie focuses on me. I push my free hand through my hair.

"Don't move," Deva says. "You might need to hold her."

Before my eyes, Deva's canines extend into sharp points, gleaming in the dawn. As horrifying and terrible as me, she sinks her teeth into Connie's wrist. In that instant, Connie's back arches and her body convulses. Deva hastens away, but I already feel what's wrong. One of her lungs has just collapsed. I slide my hand down her chest, her labored breathing hard in my face and her body tensing under the strain of being healed.

When she is stable once more, I look to Deva, who is also gazing at Connie, heartbroken.

"It's almost like she is halfway there. She is in some kind of transition, but something is missing." She stares at me, her face turning more serious. "What on earth were you thinking? Her body is human... you have no venom to give. Gods cannot create other gods."

"I know." I try to defend myself. "I thought it would work. Kali said the souls could transform human forms."

"Yes, for you." Deva gestures to me like I'm an idiot, which is fair. "I cannot help. She is too far gone. The souls that lie within her, they will not accept my blood. You can't meet magic with magic."

"Peter," Marie's voice quivers and breaks. "Connie is dying. You should say goodbye."

"Fuck!" I roar, picking up the bottle of whiskey and throwing it through Marie's closed window. The glass smashes out onto the street below. "No." I turn on Marie, grabbing her and throwing her against the wall, leaning my arm on her throat.

Her eyes bulge in terror.

"You find a way. You find a way to save her. If she dies, this whole world goes with it. I will travel across this globe and burn everything in sight until there is nothing left, just a wasteland of ash and bones. You find a way, or I start with New Orleans."

Marie's jaw trembles as she tries to defiantly stick her chin out.

I heave her off the wall and slam her back into it. "Do. You. Understand?"

"Y-yes," she stammers, holding in her tears.

"Oh no you don't." I feel Deva pretty much pick me up by the scruff of my neck and pry me off Marie. "You are upset, but do not forget whose house you are in, god known as Peter. Do you want us to help? Or do you need these people's fear?"

Deva's stare is lethal, and I wager she could give me a good run for my money in my current state. A battle between god and vampire to top off a truly shit day.

"No," I breathe out. "It just makes me feel better."

The delicate sound of Connie clearing her throat brings us all out of the moment. Marie and I rush to her side. Marie gives her some more lemon water, which Connie sips before lying her weak head back to look at me.

Taking my hand, she asks in the weakest voice, "Was that you I heard threatening everybody?"

I laugh in spite of myself. "I'm so sorry, Connie. We are going to fix this."

"I'm dying, aren't I?"

I can hear the fear in her question.

"No," I say, bringing my hand to her face, feeling all the organs that are starting to fail. "It's okay. I can fix it. I can heal you until we find a better way."

She makes a noise in her throat. "It hurts, Peter."

"C-Connie..." My voice cracks. "No, I am not letting you die.

You can't leave me. I am so sorry, okay? I promise I will be good. Please don't die."

She trails a weak finger along my chin. "It's okay. I get to see the beyond, remember? You have to promise me you won't do what you said. You are here to heal this world, not destroy it. I believe that you are good, Peter."

"No, Con, don't do that to me." I let go of her to cover my face with my hands. *There is no way I can keep that promise. I already want to kill everything in sight. Everything can burn except her.*

I half scream, half sob as I put my hands on her. Her screams echo everywhere as, yet again, I force her organs to heal.

Chapter Sixteen

Sorcha

My legs are stretched across Lily as we sit in her room, watching television. The last week has been as quiet as the grave compared to the bustling hive of activity of the prior few weeks. The quietness is unsettling. I haven't seen Glory since the others left.

I should probably leave, get far away from here, but I prefer to wallow. If Gareth succeeds and he comes back with Peter in tow, I don't know how I will cope with the situation. Lily wants me to stay. So I tell myself I am staying for her, not for the chance to see him again. That if he does become tethered to the coven, then he will have to leave his pet behind.

The sound of hushed voices passes by at the end of the hall, one of them bearing Gareth's unmistakable thick Northern Irish accent. I am on my feet, making for the door.

"Gareth is back," I whisper to Lily. "Peter is not with him, though. I would have felt him a mile off."

Lily is on her feet behind me and, in silence, we pad down the hall to eavesdrop on the conversation he must be having with Glory. He sounds furious as we catch the end of what he is saying.

"... I cannot help but question her loyalty."

Glory takes a while to respond. "Did she explain what happened?"

"As much as I can make out, she said the ritual did not work. The tether did not stick."

My heart does a little flip-flop. *They couldn't tether him. It didn't work.*

"Shit," Glory exclaims. "How many did we lose?"

"Everyone."

Glory gets up and we hear her heavy boots as she paces around the room. "Double shit. Does anyone else know you are back? We cannot let the covens know we lost everyone. How did that happen, Gareth?"

"By the time Morgan knew the ritual was blocked somehow, he had already taken down half of the side." Gareth shoves a hard breath out. "It was too late. There was no stopping it. Some tried to flee, but there were no survivors."

I can't help but smirk. *The slippery bastard.* I step out from my hiding place along the corridor. "Quite a situation you seem to have found yourself in, Glory." It's not attractive to be smug, but it is hard not to have a certain satisfaction.

"Is this the part where you say I told you so?" She bites back at me.

"I would, but I really don't need to, do I? The question is, what are you going to do?"

Glory gives her back to me and her attention to Gareth. "We need to regroup. Where is Morgan?"

"At the tombs."

Glory gives him a nod, and they hasten to leave.

I turn to Lily, and her watery eyes are wide as she asks, "Do you think it is true? Do you think Morgan betrayed Glory?"

Softening, I take her hands in my own. "If she had, she wouldn't very well have returned with Gareth, now, would she?"

Lily nods, seeming satisfied with my answer, considering for a moment. "It's only... I haven't been able to figure it out. Why now? No one has heard of or seen Morgan le Fay in centuries, and now, what... Gareth just travels to England and finds her within a week? Cia, when I missed you before, last year, I was in Paris. We'd heard whispers of an egg, something extra rare, something thought lost, which emitted a huge amount of energy."

"An egg?"

"It came to nothing, but all I am saying is that a lot of weird stuff seems to be happening, and Morgan is one of them. It's obvious Gareth has lost trust in her. Cia, maybe you shouldn't be so hard on Glory. I know part of the reason Glory wanted Peter in the first place is because of this. The balance... it doesn't feel so balanced right now."

"Lil. You were right before like you always are. This was a bad idea from the start." I laugh, trying to ease her worries. "That is the problem with us gods, we need to learn to think with our brains and not our hearts. The coven doesn't have the means of another attack. All will be well, you will see. I doubt Peter will hunt us. We can just carry on, and I will find a way. The balance will restore itself. It always does."

I put my arm around Lily and lead her down the corridor. Maybe this will all pass. With Peter victorious again, I'm sure Glory won't want to risk any more of her dwindling coven. The other tribes will lose all motivation at such a defeat and return to their respective corners of the globe more fractured than ever. Morgan can crawl back into whatever hole she came from. I will stay with Lil and try to move on. Hopefully the feeling will fade over time or at least become more manageable. The only positive of Peter being some kind of juggernaut is I will always be able to feel him before he can feel me. It's a big world, so if he ever gets close, I can run. Run far away and never have to see him again.

If the balance tips, even more reason to stay away. I only have to be strong and fight the feeling.

"Lil, can you do me a favor?" I swallow. "Can you make it so he can never find me? I doubt he would ever look, or care, but just in case. So that I have a head start? Can you do that?"

Lily looks at me, the sadness glistening in her pale eyes. "You know I can. So, this is it? You are giving up? Just going to avoid him for what? Forever?"

"Why not?" I stare at my nails. "You know, there was a moment, the briefest moment, when I thought Glory might win and he would be here. A tiny part of me was excited to see him. How pathetic is that?"

"Not pathetic at all."

"But it is. I was never anything more than his punching bag. The last time I saw him, he promised to kill me." I brush the hair back from my face. "I must be sick. Why am I mourning that? No, I need to stop. Glory is right. This is not my fight anymore."

"Well, that sounds like a plan. Shall we raid the kitchen and watch old movies?"

"*Singing in the Rain?*"

"Of course." Lily beams, grabbing my hand as we set off for the kitchen.

And it looks like that is what will happen. The covens take their losses, crippled with grief but no anger, no talks of round two —they'd sent their best, and it is over. The only thing left to do is retreat to their holy places and wait for what comes next.

Morgan and Gareth are nowhere to be seen. Glory seems listless and grief-stricken. I wonder if she is coming to the end of her time—she seems to be fading. True sorrow can corrupt the spell that extends a witch's life.

On day three, Lily runs up to where I am sitting in my usual spot, on top of the mound, with the sun just starting to set.

"Sorcha, come quick. Glory is leaving." Lily doesn't wait for me to say anything, only runs back inside, assuming I will follow.

My heart thunders as we rush to Glory's room. *Glory is abandoning her coven? Without naming a successor? The coven will fall.*

Lily charges into the room to reveal not Glory but Gareth, leaning against her dresser.

"You," I snarl at him. "Where is Glory?"

On command, she comes into the room from her adjoining bathroom. She huffs at the sight of me, avoiding my gaze. "I was hoping to avoid this."

"I asked Sorcha to come. You cannot just leave." Lily wildly gesticulates. "Not now."

"I have to, Lily. This is the last opportunity. I can't take any chances. This is my only shot at making things right." Glory's conviction is back, all her spirit bright in her.

"What are you talking about?" Lily stammers.

"I am going to New Orleans. Alone."

Glory's words are met by absolute silence. I can't even think. Frantic for answers, my eyes search hers.

She tells me, "He is still there."

"Glory, that is suicide," I protest.

Gareth doesn't say anything, only shakes his head, looking at the floor. *He really pisses me off.*

"Actually, it is not." Glory continues packing. "I received a call yesterday. A very interesting one. It seems his human girlfriend is dying. It looks like something I can help with."

My eyes boggle at her. "You are helping him now?"

"There will be conditions," Glory says, ice in her words.

"He will never agree to give you his freedom. Do you honestly think he will submit to a tether willingly?"

"I am under the impression there is nothing he won't do to save her."

"Glory," I plead, getting in the way of her packing. "This is *not* a good idea. Please, don't do this."

Glory looks back at me, furious. "And what do you think will happen if she dies? Do you think any of us will be safe?" She throws some of her clothes into her suitcase. "We may have underestimated him, but you..." her forefinger pokes with violence into my chest, "... you underestimated *her*."

It stings, sticks in the back of my throat. *Connie is nothing, meaningless.*

Glory goes back to her furious packing, avoiding my eyes. "He will accept the tether to save the girl. It's as simple as that. Now, get out of my room."

Gareth tries to usher Lily and me out of the room, but I reach around him to Glory. "Why is she dying? What are you going to do, Glory?"

She doesn't answer, but instead, turns away to the window with a sigh so large it would seem she has the weight of the world on her shoulders.

"This is a bad idea. Please, Glory. You save her, you give him what he wants, and it will be bad news for everyone."

Glory turns, and I am reminded why she is the ferocious leader of the Irish coven as she pulls Gareth away so she can get in my face. "Do you know what our ancestors did with their old gods? They ruled kingdoms." Her cool blue eyes are so hot I'd think they could catch fire. "You brought him to our door. Limping like a wounded animal. Do you really think I don't see through you,

Sorcha? All your ulterior motives. Your petty reasons for putting my coven at risk. You want this god for yourself."

"No," I whisper.

"Do not lie to me. You can lie to Lily, even lie to yourself, but you cannot lie to me. You wanted him dead because he broke your heart. You are blinded by him, and you put everyone at risk. And now, you would deny my claiming him to bring control to a monster you created?"

"I created?" I gulp.

"What happened in Varanasi, Sorcha? He just murdered a coven in cold blood?"

"I told you... he... they were poisoning him." I back up into the wall.

"And?" Glory advances on me. "What was your part in that massacre, Sorcha? What did you do?"

I close my eyes. "The spell would never have worked. What they were trying... it wouldn't have worked. I didn't think he would kill them all. I-I was trying to save them," I stammer.

"What did you do, Cia?" Lily whispers to me.

"I... it was me... I killed his sister. His twin was still alive. I killed her."

Gareth's low breath blows out as Glory lets me go. "Well, that's just perfect."

I fight to keep my tears in check and try not to look at Lily, who is caught between horror and sympathy.

"I thought you were supposed to be against killing?" Gareth scorns.

"Gareth, hush." Glory pushes him away, calmer now. "At least we know everything now. Sorcha, you need to listen to me. I know what you feel for this creature is more complex than infatuation, which is why you need to stay away from this. When he is ours...

and he will be... you will *not* see him. You will *not* interact with him. He is *not* yours, Sorcha. It is better for everyone this way."

I feel like crumpling into a ball to curl up and sleep for the rest of my days. "Glory, please don't do that to me. You don't know what it is like for me to be around him."

Glory softens. "We will not bring him here. This is your home, not his. I would not have him so close to our younger members." She moves, taking the side of my face in the way she used to when I was younger. "He brings out an ugly side of you. You are better off away from this."

She and Gareth leave, leaving me alone with Lily, totally devastated.

Chapter Seventeen

Lorna

My feet carry me back and forth across Lisette's room, which might as well be my room now. Things have moved quickly, although I've had little time to enjoy Lisette this past week. I have been at Connie's side, trying to keep her mind busy for the short periods she is awake.

For over a week, I've had to watch my friend suffering, quietly wasting away, and being healed every day or so amid loud screams. Peter only comes back long enough to force her body into healing before leaving again. He's been hearing only her screams, not her weak voice as she asks where he is again and again. He hasn't once heard her say how much it hurts, how she doesn't understand why she isn't dead yet. She's in so much pain.

She has been moved into Deva's room, but it's impossible to stay in there for long with her—it stinks of rot. Her organs failing and healing, then failing all over again. Marie manages to keep the rest of the apartment fragranced with incense. Lisette and I keep her body clean, trying to bathe her while she sleeps to avoid causing her pain. Taking extra care to the patches that bubble and burn under the strain of the souls.

I don't know how long this can go on for, who will give in first. Whether Peter will see sense enough to say goodbye, or Marie will give in and let her die when he is not here. I know the only reason she hasn't is for fear of what Peter will do.

I am a wreck. It feels like the horror of Varanasi all over again, a slaughter followed by unspeakable destruction. Only this time, the destruction isn't of a city, but a single person. The person he loves. Her body being destroyed only to be put back together, to start all over again. They are both stuck in a cycle where he can't let go, and no one knows what to do. What he is doing outside of this apartment... well, I can't even think about that right now.

Now, we have an even bigger problem.

Lisette slides into the room, her face twisted with worry.

"Any sign of Marie?" I ask, holding my stomach to try and contain the sick feeling.

"No." Lisette clutches her chest. "She's just gone. Oh, Lorna, I think she's left the city."

I sit next to her, pushing my hands through my hair. "This is it, isn't it?" The words sound as pained as the feeling in my chest.

"Any sign of him?"

"No." I shake my head. "But it's been two days. He could be here any moment. This is the longest he's been gone."

"Maybe he's left too?" Lisette says, almost hopeful that he has left Connie to die in peace.

I give her an incredulous look. "Have you spoken to Deva?"

Lisette nods, sinking her head onto her hands. "She is on her way back to New Orleans, but she hasn't heard from her either. Marie is gone. She's fled. There is nothing left we can do for your friend, Lorna. I am so sorry." She takes my hand, holding it close to her chest. "I am so sorry, *cher*, but when he comes, you need to talk

164

to him. It is time to say goodbye. That poor girl deserves some peace."

I struggle to keep in my sob, bringing my forearm to my mouth to muffle the sound, my heart shattering into a thousand pieces. "I know. I will," I manage to get out.

She lets me cry, rubbing circles on my back. "*Cher, cher...*" she coos, pushing my hair over my shoulder. "I am so sorry for you, and for her."

I nod. "It's going to kill him, Lis. I don't know what will happen." I rub my eyes. "I don't know how to help him."

Lisette stops rubbing my back, her eyes searching mine. "*Cher,* don't you think..." she starts, her words and visage uncertain. "Do you ever wonder... if you chose the wrong side?"

"What do you mean?" I ask, wiping my nose on my sleeve.

"Just because he is a god does not mean he is good."

I blink back her words. I have never thought of him as anything other than Peter. I suppose, to Connie and me, his being a god is just a by-product.

"You don't know him like we do. He's so much more than this." I laugh a little. "He's always been a hot mess, though."

Lisette smiles, sympathetic and warm.

My heart drops at the sound of the door opening, and we both rush out to be faced with Deva, once again buried in fabric. Her eyes drift to the room where Connie is sleeping. I have never been so happy to see someone, so relieved that it isn't Peter. Lisette all but throws herself on the vampire, but Deva goes rigid, her dark eyes widening. Her expression flits to me as if she is the one that needs rescuing. Physical contact must not be something she is used to.

"Thank heavens you are here. Marie is gone, Deva. I think she left the city. She left *us*. With no idea what to do." Lisette cries.

Deva gives her the ghost of a smile, shaking her head. "She lives?"

We both grimace a little before dipping our heads that yes, Connie is alive, although "lives" is a bit of a stretch—more like, she's not been allowed to die.

Deva's expression hardens. "Where is he?" She directs her question at me.

"I have no idea. He comes and he goes. I haven't left," I tell her.

"Then you will come with me, and we will find him," she instructs before moving to the door once more.

I can't say I'm a huge fan of the idea. The feeling in New Orleans is different now. As we hit the streets, the former buoyant vibrancy has faded to gray. Whispers of serial killers are all over the city. We haven't watched the news, focusing too much on keeping Connie comfortable, so we only know that New Orleans is being terrorized.

"How will we find him?" I ask Deva as we march down the street.

"Easy. Follow the trail of blood."

"I don't see any blood anywhere." I skip to keep up.

"No, but I can smell it," she tells me without any humor.

Deva forks off from the main street, leading me down side streets and behind bars laced with rats and grime. The putrid smell of decay and piss is enough to make me want to throw up. Up ahead, in a pile of garbage, I see a bloody hand.

"Oh my God," I choke out. "Please tell me that isn't a severed hand."

"Nope," Deva says as we draw level with the garbage pile and it becomes clear the hand is attached to an arm.

An arm belonging to Peter. Who is fast asleep. In a pile of

rubbish, blood thick on his hands, all the way up to his elbows. His bare feet are covered in filth.

Deva prods his leg with the tip of her boot. When he doesn't stir, the look of disgust deepens on her face. It kind of amuses me to see an ancient vampire disgusted by the state of him.

Changing her tactic, she gives him a good solid kick to his ribs.

Which does the trick of waking him up, although he comes round slowly, rocking about like a Weeble as his eyes struggle to adjust to us.

Deva crouches down to draw eye level with him. "Well, well, well." She grins at him, sinister in a way I have not seen her look before. "I don't think New Orleans has seen a run like this since the late seventeen hundreds. Nice to see someone giving the vampires a run for their money." At that, she takes his hand nearest to her, lifts his forefinger to her mouth, and sucks the blood off it.

My stomach rolls again, and even Peter appears to be surprised at the action.

Deva makes a noise of satisfaction. "How many is it now?"

Peter stares at her for a moment, unsure of what to make of her. "About twenty. I'm not sure." His voice sounds gravelly and, from where I stand, I see his pupils dilating and contracting so much they seem to be vibrating. He looks at his blood-soaked hands, then tries to wipe the dried blood on his white T-shirt. He scrambles to his feet, staggering all over the place.

"Are you drunk or high?" I ask.

"A combination of all three," he says, holding onto the mesh fence behind him before giving up and lying back down in the rubbish.

Deva looks back at me and then back to him in the filth. "While you are out here feeling sorry for yourself and terrorizing the residents, your girl is at home, in agony, asking for you."

Peter brings his hands to his face and makes a low, frustrated noise. "She should hate me."

"I think we both know she doesn't." Deva grabs the front of his shirt and hauls him to his feet. "It is time for you to face her. She deserves so much more than this."

Peter's face crumples. "I can't say goodbye to her. I have lost everything."

It's weird seeing tiny Deva holding Peter on his feet, but she does, not with aggression but with compassion. "I have seen this world change so much in two thousand years, Peter, believe me. You may never love again, but you find a way to endure."

Peter swallows hard, giving her a nod, and she lets him take his own weight before she leads us out of the alley. Our progress is markedly slower due to Peter tripping and stumbling over everything, including his own feet. Every time I look at him, he can't meet my eye. I find it hard to feel anything right now. I'm too hollow to register whether I'm sorry for him or hate him. It's all mixed together.

Peter stands, hovering on the threshold and seeming to take big gulps until he looks at me and says, "I'm not ready for this."

The tremor in his words shakes the ground beneath us. Lisette appears from Connie's room, holding herself in the doorframe. Her gaze settles on us in realization as we stand in the doorway. I am undone. I can't help it. I throw my arms around him and let him sob into my hair. He wraps his arms around me, lifting me clean off my feet and crushing my ribs.

"I can't, I can't, I can't," he cries. "I'm sorry. I am so, so sorry, but I can't. Don't make me, Lorna."

I can't either. I don't have words. The shuddering of the earth comes to a stop, and Peter sets me down, trying to give me a resolute nod, then walks into the apartment.

Lisette straightens up to look at him. "She has been asking for you," she tells him in a quiet, soft tone.

He dips his head, wiping his face on the tops of his arms as he moves toward Connie's room. I follow halfway, then stop. I shouldn't go any farther. This moment should be the two of them. Lisette moves out of the doorway to give him space. All of us are silent, and I can only hear my heart beating as Lisette and Deva come to my side. We all watch him.

I barely hear the sound of footsteps on the porch, only registering them when Lisette's knees give way, sending her into me.

"Marie," she exclaims, her tears falling in an instant.

Peter turns to see her, surprise that she has returned evident on his face.

Her chin juts out in defiance as she meets his gaze, but I see her hands betraying her with their trembling. "You asked me to save her," she says as confidently as she can.

Whatever she has planned, she is nervous.

"I have found a way, but you need to keep an open mind."

Peter's brows furrow as he gives her a silent movement saying, yes, he promises not to straight up rip her head off with what she is about to suggest.

Marie steps back a little to motion toward someone I've never seen before. Tall and pale with long dirty blonde hair, braided in parts. Although in normal clothes, something about her is warrior-like, the hints of a tattoo peeking from under her shirt up her neck.

"A witch." The strain in his voice audible, and his teeth set so much I hear them grinding from across the room.

"Peter, this is Glory." Marie motions again, stepping back more. "The high priestess of the Irish coven."

Peter's eyes burn into Marie.

"You asked me to save her," she says again, her voice meek.

Glory holds her hands up, slow and cautious. "Peter, I am not here as your enemy. That may be hard to believe, but I can save your mate."

Peter hisses out, "What would you know of it? Why would you help me?"

Glory remains cautious, keeping her hands raised. "The way Marie tells it... it's save the girl, save the world. We don't have many options here, do we now?" Her voice stays even, her eyes meeting his without flinching. "We like this world, and we know what you have been doing here. Maybe there is a deal to be had here. One where we both benefit."

Peter considers it for a moment, and his skin appears to shudder. "I suppose my end of the bargain results in me being dead in some fashion."

"No." She shakes her head the slightest amount. Her actions are measured and full of caution. "No one here needs to die. All that I ask is your loyalty... to me, to my coven."

Glory and Marie seem to hold their breath. Peter looks from Glory to Marie, then to me. As if I have any answers for him. It feels like time stretches on for an eternity until the silence is broken by his dry laugh, a *ha-ha-ha* sound.

"Is that all?" He flaps his arms, running a hand through his hair. He is not buying what Glory is selling, but at the same time, the situation is impossible, so what choice does he have? All he ever does is take chances. Why stop now?

Glory continues, still wary. "I am not saying it comes for free. I know you don't trust me, and I do not trust you. The deal will be binding... a business arrangement. I save your girl, and in return, when I call, you come running."

Peter gives a huff. "Where do I sign?" he asks, not even bothering to hide the mockery there. He shakes his head and tears his gaze away from her for the first time.

Something in Glory shifts, and her feet become more planted.

Marie takes half a step back as Glory declares, "Let me speak plainly, Peter." She steels herself. "I do not think you a man of your honor. I know the cost of your loyalty. What you will agree to, willingly, is a tether. To me and to my coven's line."

Deva almost hisses, cutting her off with a sharp, "No." She rounds on Peter. "She means to make you a slave. You will not just answer her call... you will obey it."

Glory holds her eyes fast to Peter, and even I feel her heart racing. "I am not cruel. I do not want to destroy this world, only maintain it. You have my word." Her words are quick and solid.

I look to Lisette, realizing what this means—all of Peter's power, in the hands of another. Just like his father wanted.

"You save her first." He acquiesces.

Glory lets out a long breath, nodding and easing her stance. "Of course, but I am sure you can understand I need a fail-safe in place. Should you try to back out of this once it is done, if you go back on your word, Peter, son of Arjun and Cassandra, if you try to break free of the tether or entering into it, I will claim her life."

Deva opens her mouth to implore him not to, but he nods and says, "Okay."

"Okay." Glory nods too, extending her hand.

He glares at it for a second before taking it in his own.

"We don't have much time," Marie reminds them.

Peter nods toward Glory. "So how will you save her?"

Glory grins, and this time it's a little more ominous. "By giving you what you want. Making her live forever." She takes a few steps back to the doorway and calls out, "Morgan, you can come up now."

The light steps are almost inaudible. Her frame, when she appears, is small and strangely familiar. She looks bird-like with amber eyes and a weather-beaten face.

"You?" Peter tenses. "I recognize you from the clearing."

Morgan's face twists into a smile that sends shivers down my spine.

"She was there, yes." As Glory confirms the witch's presence at the massacre, a small bird flies to her shoulder.

A bird I have seen before, with the witches who came for us in the clearing.

Glory is with them?

"Take us to her."

Chapter Eighteen

Peter

As the little witch advances toward me, every fiber of my being tells me to rip her to shreds. Her soul is so old and powerful it smells rancid. The putridity of it turns my stomach, and I grimace having her so close. Through age and practice, she has bent magic to her for so many years that she is all twisted out of shape.

She is repulsive, and I only want to kill her to have her gone from this world. This is no soul I want to taste. I know she will be my jailer, the only witch powerful enough to perform the tether spell. Old enough to know it.

"How are you living?" I ask her through my clenched teeth.

Her smile reveals rotting teeth as she slams a pointy index finger into my chest. Every cell reacts to the touch, my skin shuddering against her foul being.

Glory eases to my side. "Morgan has not spoken in many centuries. But she is the key to your predicament." Her eyes gleam. "Everything is connected, Peter. Everything." She shakes her head a little as if she forgets herself. "Anyway, when Marie came to us

173

and told us what had happened, it was Morgan who had the answer. The transition... you are missing a piece, right? Take us to her and we will show you."

Beyond weary, I nod, standing back to open the pathway to Connie's room.

Morgan slides past me. Her oversized dress seems to have a life of its own, looking ridiculous and ghastly on her shrunken body.

I dip my head to Glory's ear. "How did a witch who can't talk tell you that?"

Glory's eyes sparkle in amusement. "Our voices are not the only way we communicate. Are you not standing in the home of a master of the board?"

I glance over at Marie, who looks wracked with worry. I feel a slight pang of guilt she is still fearing for her life. But not enough to apologize. I look away and follow Morgan into Connie's room with Glory at my heels.

The sight of her floods my face with the heat of self-hatred. Connie looks so broken. Having been unable to eat for a week, her cheeks are hollow, her skin gray. She is asleep right now, but I know her eyes will be yellowing and her mouth bloody with sores.

Morgan moves to the top of her bed, her eagle eyes examining Connie as Glory runs her hands over her arms.

Looking at me, Glory asks, "Do you want to wake her?"

I nod, a lump thick in my throat. I haven't spoken to Connie in over a week because I was too shit scared she would beg me to let her die. I hesitate for a second, then ask, "Tell me, what will she be? After."

"She will be herself. Just something in between." Glory's expression is alive with curiosity and possibility. "In all honesty, I do not know. It has never been done before, and if it were not for Morgan, we would never have thought to try it. The missing ingredient is something of Morgan's speciality, and although she has never mixed it with raw energy, she is certain it will work."

I nod, uncertain if she has answered me or not. "But, she won't die?"

Glory stares me down hard. "Disease and old age will not find her. But that does not mean she is impervious to harm as you are. She may need maintaining."

"Meaning?"

"Meaning she may also require soul sacrifice from time to time."

My face drops. *This is the last life sentence she would want.*

"Not much, and it's just a theory. She may not."

I nod and swallow the guilt of the life I am committing her too. "The fail-safe?" I ask. My heart feels like it might explode. She is so delicate, my brilliant, light, wild, terrible, *good* girl.

Glory places a pomegranate seed into my hand, although it's laced with a magical signature. "She will need to eat this," she instructs, retreating to the wall.

"Connie. Hey, Connie," I repeat her name as I touch her arms, my voice as fragile as she feels in my hands. With the contact, I feel the failing of her liver and one of her lungs beginning to collapse. Again. I am wretched, but I cannot live without her.

Her eyes ease open, regarding me like I am the new dawn, her lips turning up as she sees me.

"Are you okay?" She frowns, holding my hand up as much as her weak arm will allow to examine my fingers.

I'd forgotten I am covered in blood. Her voice sounds like sand, so I pass her some of her lemon water while helping her sit up a fraction.

"You are seriously asking me if I am okay?" Incredulous, I smooth her hair.

"I've missed you."

"And I, you. Connie, Marie found a way to save you." I bite down the lump in my throat. "I am so sorry, Connie. About everything."

She frowns at me, her face impossible to read.

"But you can live. And still be with me if... that is what you want."

Glory moves to the side of her bed, and Connie leans away from her a fraction, asking, "Are you a witch?"

"She is," I answer for her. "But she can help. You can live, and we can be together."

Connie looks up at the witch with wide eyes. "Do you promise?" she asks.

Glory nods, speaking soft words. "Do you have any questions, or do you want me to just do it?"

Connie squeezes her eyes, grasping onto my hand as hard as she can.

"Con, you need to eat this, okay?" I hold the seed out.

"I can't. I'll be sick."

"It's magic. You won't be sick, I promise." I place the pomegranate seed into her mouth, helping her sip water to swallow it. Even with this simple task, Connie has to lie down again at the effort.

Glory gets ready, her eyes now on Morgan. "Just try to relax," she tells Connie. "You might want to move, Peter."

I move away and watch Morgan place a hand on both of Connie's shoulders, working her way down the bed to remove the covers from Connie's body.

Connie becomes more alarmed as she sees Morgan for the first time, her head turning to look at me in horror. I try to appear reassuring to let her know it will be okay as Morgan runs her hands over Connie's limbs. Connie's breathing becomes labored, and I don't need to be touching her to know that one of her lungs is collapsing.

Finally, Morgan takes both of her hands and threads her fingers into Connie's. Connie shudders away as the fabric of Morgan's sleeves ripples. From the sleeves appear the shiny, silvery skins of two snakes slithering across Morgan's skin and wrapping around Connie's wrists. Connie pulls away, trying to recoil from the snakes, but Morgan holds tight as the snakes bite into Connie's skin before continuing to climb her arms.

Connie struggles to scream, but she has no breath.

Panic overcomes me as I watch the snakes cover her body, gliding and biting all over her as she tries to yell, thrashing against them.

When I move, Glory stops me. A binding rope stretched across her palm holds me to the wall while she whispers close to my ear, "Don't. The snake venom will balance the souls. Think about it, Peter. Even the gods of old used the blood and venom of the strongest animals to change their form. Anubis, Ganesha, Pan. When the gods changed, they sought animal form." I stop struggling against her, and she relents. "You can go to her, but do not interrupt the transformation." She lets me go.

Connie is crying as the snakes wrap around her neck and travel down her chest.

I take her face in my hands. "Focus on me, Connie, focus on me."

"Peter," she gasps the word through her tears, yet I can already feel her lung healing, the venom coursing through her body and turning her cells, replenishing her blood, and healing her wounds. "Ow, it hurts, ow..." Her back arches in the agony of being forced to heal again. "Peter, please. Make it stop," she screams.

I hold onto her face, trying to get her to concentrate. "Connie, love. It's almost over." I can't help but smile at her. "It's working, Connie. I can feel it."

She smiles for half a second before her screams echo around the room again. The snakes are still working their way down, wrapping around her legs now, biting as they go, her feet digging into the bed. When her eyes open again, her cries die down.

I see it.

Her right eye, the pupil changing, becoming elongated, filling her whole iris. Connie pants, the pain passing, but I don't let go. The emerald of her right eye bleeds, the rich green seeping out of the iris, stretching across the white.

In the first noise I have heard Morgan make, she takes a large breath as she releases Connie and the snakes retreat into her sleeves. She looks spent and steadies a hand on the end of the bed. She cocks her eagle-like head to appraise Connie like she is a masterpiece.

Connie pants, no longer the labored pants of someone dying, but healthy, full breaths. Her skin is white, almost like pearls but alive, with no tint of yellow. I sweep her hair back, taking the sweat off her forehead as she looks at me.

I stroke her cheek under her right eye. It's beautiful and striking, something marking her for what she is—something other, an immortal, the emerald eye of a snake. "Oh, Connie," I whisper.

My hands travel across her arms, down her hips, meeting the skin wherever they can to feel it, the faint signature of before shining like a beacon now. Every part of her alive, not immovable like Deva, but strong and enduring.

Still Connie.

Still my Connie, *but now so much more.*

I smile for the first time in what feels like an eternity. "You are fucking beautiful." She grins as I ask, "How do you feel?"

"Like shit." She laughs. "I'm tired, so tired. But I don't feel like I'm dying. I am thirsty, though."

"Here." I nod, handing her a drink.

She makes a face at it. "Can I have something that is not lemon water?"

"Whatever you want," I tell her.

She already looks on the verge of sleep. "Can I have some tea? Ask Lorna to make it… you make crap tea."

And I laugh. Loudly. Like I didn't think I would ever do again. *My Connie*. Screw it, I cross the room and pull creepy Morgan into a hug as she looks at Glory utterly perplexed.

Glory barks out a laugh too. "She will need some time to gather her strength," she tells me with an admonishing tone, which means I should calm down, but I am too freaking happy.

Connie is alive and wants tea.

"One tea coming up." I bounce out of the room to find Lorna, Marie, Lisette, and Deva all on tenterhooks.

"What's happening in there?" Lisette asks.

Shaking my head and grinning from ear to ear, I tell her, "She wants tea."

Lorna almost can't believe me as she climbs over the sofa to get to me.

"She's weak, but she is okay, and she wants tea, Lor."

Lorna shrieks, throwing herself into my arms and wrapping her legs around me as I spin on the spot. Everyone looks at us like we've lost it. Lorna is sobbing again, but I can breathe. Finally.

"I'm so sorry," I whisper into her hair. "For what I said to you, I am so sorry."

"I know." She smiles, letting me put her down.

Wow. My knees are wobbly as I follow Lorna to the kitchen, and I almost fall over.

"You should get cleaned up now." She motions to my hands and my appearance in general.

I keep forgetting that's there, the blood crusted into my nails. I'd all but forgotten about my recent killing spree in my anguish. I glance back to Marie, who appears on the verge of a nervous breakdown. *My welcome in New Orleans is well overdone. It will have to wait until Connie is strong enough to move.* I wash my hands in the sink.

Lorna clicks on the kettle and leans back on the counter to look at me. "So, how did she do it?"

"With snakes," I tell her.

Lorna looks suitably puzzled.

"Connie looks a little different, Lor. She hasn't seen yet. Maybe give her a bit of time. No doubt she will hate it. But..." I shrug, "... she is okay. That's all that matters."

"What is it?"

"One of her eyes is different... it's where the change has affected her. Just in her right eye, kinda looks like a snake's now. You know, with the big slit." I drag my little finger down her cheek. "Her eye is completely emerald with a big, elongated pupil. She looks like fucking magic."

"She has a snake eye?" Lorna's face drops a little. "Are you serious?"

"Yeah." I shrug, drying my hands. "What's the big deal?"

Lorna gawps at me, bewildered. I take the tea out of her hand and head back to Connie's room, where Glory is crouched next to her, talking to her in tender tones.

Morgan inspects the sights of the snake bites in silence, thumbing them in wonder.

Glory gives me a smile as I hand Connie her tea. I move to join Morgan, running my fingers over a bite mark on Connie's leg.

"This will heal?" I ask her, and she nods, caressing a site on Connie's arm.

"That's how you did it, isn't it? Magic and the blood of animals. It's why your soul is all twisted."

Morgan gives a crooked smile.

"You've been around a long time, haven't you?"

Morgan stops what she is doing to take me in. I have never seen anyone look so unnatural. She edges closer, and I do my best not to recoil from her as she traces a kind of pattern into my forearm. For some reason, it makes sense, like another language I can understand.

"You are a first." I swallow. "You have tethered a god before, haven't you?"

She grins again, chancing a small glance at Glory before drawing another symbol on my arm. *I must be reading it wrong.* I dip my head closer to her, sure I've got it wrong.

"Thank you?" I whisper, hoping she will correct me.

Instead, she winks and goes back to Connie.

Thank you for what?

For agreeing to be tethered, for allowing her to create Connie? Only thank you. It's a thank you that does not sit easy.

Glory stands and pushes me away. I join her by the window as Connie sips her tea, sitting up a bit for the first time in over a week.

"I expect her recovery will be quick. We should be grateful for that, although the eye was unexpected. As things can be with ancient magic. I am hopeful it won't cause her much distress."

I keep my eyes on Connie.

She's fine. She will be fine now.

"Peter." Glory brings me out of my thoughts. "I was saying we will wait for the tether until Connie is strong enough for you to explain."

I raise my eyebrows. *Here I was thinking she would be all business.* "Yeah, whatever you say."

The heat of the late morning sun filters through the window, warming my face. I feel something I haven't felt in what seems like years—rested. I'm almost not ready to wake. Although I have never needed to sleep much, one doesn't realize what they have until it is gone. It feels good to sleep again, a restful, dreamless sleep.

I open my eyes a smidgen to see Connie watching me, only just catching her smile as I close them again.

"Morning, sleepy head," she purrs next to me. I must have passed out next to her. She reaches across to push her hand into my hair, lifting it from my face.

"I must still be dreaming. Having you here with me, smiling again. It feels like a dream."

"Then it's a good dream," she says, shuffling closer.

"One I don't want to wake up from."

Her hands rake through my hair again. "You look different. Your hair is so much lighter."

I bring myself to look at her, to face my love. Her wide green eye is so captivating I can't look away. In the morning light, several strands of her hair have turned silver and shimmer, her skin now pale like snow and flawless.

"Con, I did some bad things while you were sleeping." I swallow, not meeting her eyes.

"I figured," her voice is quiet, and without judgment.

"I'm sorry," I whisper as she examines my face. "I am so sorry I did that to you. I am so sorry I can't be better for you. I'm sorry, a thousand times sorry, Connie."

"Oh, Peter." She reaches out and pulls me to her, and I enfold myself around her. She feels a couple of degrees cooler now, even more perfect. "I am alive, it's okay. I'm not going anywhere. You can stop now. Peter, you can stop punishing yourself, and everyone else."

"You are everything that is good in me," I say into her silky hair, pulling back to feel the smoothness of her cheek in my hand. "Never again, I promise. I am going to take care of you."

She manages a lazy eye roll but seems happy about it, enjoying me running my hands through her hair.

"How are you feeling this morning?"

"Still a little hazy. My joints feel stiff." She runs her hand lightly across her snake eye. "My vision is quite blurry in this eye. It feels a bit weird."

"I should probably show you," I tell her.

She tries to get me to tell her. Instead, I get out of bed and move to her side, taking her by the hands to help her to her unsteady feet.

"I feel like Bambi." She laughs.

"Yeah, you look like him too," I tease her.

She gives me the feeblest of slaps, and even that movement almost throws her off balance.

I raise my eyebrow at her. "Do you want me to carry you?"

"Absolutely not," she says and shuffles alongside me to the bathroom.

When we get there, I stop her for a moment. "Connie, before I show you, you need to know that it looks different, okay? Really different. It's not bad, but it is a consequence of the spell that saved you."

"Peter, you're starting to worry me."

"Okay, just come and see." I ease her into position in front of the bathroom mirror, standing back a little as she takes in her altered appearance, her hands clasping over her mouth while she leans forward to examine her eye.

"Holy shit," she whispers, moving her hand to cover her eye and burying her face in my shoulder. "Peter, I'm hideous. I have a snake eye. I'm a freak."

"Then we match." I smirk down at her, lifting her chin and forcing her to look at me.

"How can you even look at me?"

"Because you are beautiful." I turn her on the spot, back to the mirror, forcing her to look at her reflection. "Connie, look at yourself." I move my lips close to her ear, my body pressing against the curve of her back. "You look every inch the immortal creature you are. Incredible... one of a kind." I meet her gaze in the mirror. "Mine."

She leans in again to give the eye another inspection. Motioning to her eye, she asks, "You really want me still, despite this?"

"I want you more for it." I thumb the skin around it as she faces me.

"You really are a freak," she teases, leaning into me.

I push all the hair up at the nape of her neck, exposing her neck and shoulders, lifting it so she has to stand on her tiptoes and ghost my nose along her jaw. "You smell fucking delicious." I breathe hard.

I know I should give her more recovery time—she is just about standing—but she looks hungry too, as she heaves herself onto the edge of the sink so her legs can make way for me. She bites down hard on her lip.

Who am I to deny her anything?

Chapter Nineteen

Connie

The eye is something to get used to and I often forget it's there. My vision in that eye is only a bit blurred now, but if I am talking to Lorna, Marie, or Lisette, they tend to avoid looking straight at me. Only Peter can look at me without flinching, as adoring as he ever was. Perhaps more. He would stare at me for hours if I'd let him—the green of my eye, the silvering of my hair, the porcelain white of my skin that is always cool to the touch now.

It only took a couple of days for me to be up and out of bed, but I avoid leaving the apartment. Instead, I climb the fire escape and lie basking in the sun on Marie's roof for hours, my white skin refusing to tan. The sun feels so good. I can lose hours stretched out on my back, my hand under my head and thinking of nothing but warmth. Peter rarely leaves my side, either lying next to me, running his fingers across the silver strands of my hair that fractures the light of the sun or standing at the roof's edge, his toes hanging off the brink and watching the life bustle below us.

No more partying, making everyone fall in love with him, or

slaughter. He remains here and lets me lie in the sun. The others come up to check on me, then go. Deva leaves. Morgan becomes satisfied the transformation is complete and I am stable. I don't feel much different, maybe less fidgety, happier to remain still.

I don't open my eyes when I feel Peter sit next to me, handing me something cold. "I bought you strawberries and beer."

I prop myself up on my elbow, taking the beer from him and watching him take a swig of his own, his tanned skin now in stark contrast to my own, his hair so light it is verging on platinum, with a slight curl into his dark eyes, the spattering of freckles on his nose only visible up close. When I take my time to look at him in detail, the butterflies never fail to creep back in.

"What?" he asks when he catches me staring.

"You're not the only one who is allowed to watch."

He rolls his eyes, pushing a little basket of strawberries to me. "I bought you strawberries."

I move to sit up, but he stops me.

"Here, let me." He takes one of the plump strawberries and pops it into my mouth, wiping the juice that rolls down my chin away. Fixating on it intently.

"I could get used to this," I say. "You as my personal hunter, collector of souls and strawberries."

Peter chuckles, and giving me another strawberry, replies, "Yeah, these strawberries really put up a fight." He puts the basket down, taking another long swig of his beer. "Con, Glory and Morgan are here. They are leaving soon, going back to Ireland, but I need to tell you something before they do."

"Okay." I sit up to face him, crossing my legs underneath myself.

"So, I had to agree to something for them to help you... before they saved your life."

My stomach drops.

Just when I thought we had it all.

"I had to agree to a tether, to Glory and her coven, to be their ally."

I frown at him. "What does that mean?"

"It means that my power is not my own anymore... it will be used for the good of the coven." He looks down at his beer bottle as I stare at him aghast.

"No, Peter, you can't. How long for?"

"Forever. It will be tied to Glory's line. So as long as there is an Irish coven, the tether will hold."

I start to protest, climbing to my knees to reach him.

"It's okay, Connie. Let's not make a big deal out of it. I've been speaking to Glory, and she said it will only take me away from you two or three times a year, tops."

I am lost for words. *How can he be so calm about this? It's what his father always planned for him.*

He meets my gaze. "I know what you're thinking, and Glory is nothing like Arjun." He looks back down, tracing his fingers across the back of my hand. "I've been thinking it might be good for me, you know?"

"How can you say that?"

"Connie. I killed a lot of people indiscriminately... innocent people... when I thought you were going to die. Maybe Glory is right and I do need a tether, something that keeps it all in line."

"Is that what she told you?"

"Kind of."

"Kind of? Peter, what you can do in someone else's hands... it is dangerous."

He grimaces. "It's dangerous in my hands."

"All the more reason not to."

"I don't have a choice, Con." He smiles and it's too tender. "I don't believe Glory wants to destroy the world or hurt innocent people. I have to do this—"

"Peter..."

"Please." He takes my face, holding me in place. "Just let me do it. I give it willingly. Let me take care of you. I can take it, whatever she needs, if it means I can take care of you. It is my burden, Connie. I can take it."

"Why is it always your burden, though?" I look up at him.

He half smiles. "You're the one who has to put up with me, remember?" He rests his forehead on mine.

"She will have you kill people in her name," I whisper.

"Maybe," he responds, closing his eyes. "But I can also grow rain forests or cure droughts or a thousand other things I am too selfish to do myself. I am not the hunter, Connie. I am the arrow."

I draw him closer. "You will always be my hunter, my protector," I tell him.

After a moment, he rolls his forehead from mine. "Will you be there with me? For the spell."

At the apprehension in his face, I ask, "Are you scared?"

"Always."

As I ease my way back in through the window with Peter close behind me. The apartment is empty apart from Lorna, who is reading on the sofa. She looks up to watch me make my way in.

"Where are they?" I ask while Lorna puts her book down.

"They already left. Glory said she would meet you at the bayou."

"The bayou?" I look at Peter, panic setting in.

"Something about needing to be at the sight of the sacrifice," Lorna continues.

"You didn't say I had to leave the apartment," I implore Peter, tears springing to my eyes against my will.

"You have to leave at some point, Connie. You can't hide here forever," he coaxes, trying to take my hands as I pace.

"It's okay, Con." Lorna rubs my arm, her expression full of warmth. "I can help. Come here."

She leads me to the sofa and sits me in front of her, and, picking up her comb, she starts to work my hair out in front of me, fashioning a fringe to hang over my right eye and pinning back the rest. Although she avoids my snake eye, she looks at me with affection.

A sense of nostalgia rises in my chest, like something has changed again that can never be reset. I left home without the intention of going back, but it is certain now that I will never return. My heart may still be beating, but my human life is behind me, and I don't quite know how to be this new thing. There are no rules for this.

"There," she says, smoothing her hand along my hair, happy with her handy work. "No one will notice."

She looks up at Peter, who is standing behind her, for approval.

His mouth is set in a grim line. "You shouldn't feel like you need to hide," he says to me.

Lorna looks a little upset, and I feel it too. "I can't walk around the streets like this, Peter. People will stare."

"Who cares?"

"I care." I look at him hard, feeling self-conscious again as I move to the mirror to inspect Lorna's handy work. She's done a great job. It's a chic hairstyle to view.

With the absence of the eye to distract me, I notice how pale my skin has become. I run my fingertips down my cheek, and the skin has a sheen I hadn't noticed before, the silver strands of my hair standing out even more against the brown. Even without the eye, I look so different.

Peter moves behind me, breaking me out of my staring match with my reflection. "We have to go," he says, moving toward the door without waiting for me.

I can tell he is pissed off because he is walking too fast for my short legs to keep up, pulling me along by my hand so I am trotting behind him. The more out of breath I get, the more annoyed I become in return.

"You cannot seriously be mad at me for feeling self-conscious."

"I thought you were past all that. It's okay to be different, Connie. I am different. I don't try to hide."

"There is no comparison. You don't have a snake eye."

He doesn't say anything, only continues to march forward, looking more and more murderous with every step.

"What is wrong with you?" I ask.

"Nothing."

"Why are you mad?"

"I'm not."

"You are. Tell me." I pull on his arm, forcing him to stop. "Stop being a fucking baby and tell me."

He heaves out a long breath and puts his hands on his hips. "I'm mad at myself, not at you. For being so happy. Connie, I love what you are now, what you look like. Inside, you are still the same woman I have always loved. I was so scared if Deva turned you, that wouldn't be the case. But outside..." He moves closer, smoothing his hand across my cheek. "Outside, you are more now than I could've possibly imagined. Your heart beats so steady. Do you know that it beats in time to mine? Your skin is so cool it puts out all this fire I have to carry everywhere. You are so perfect, it's like you were made for me. But, again, in my selfishness, I didn't realize it doesn't feel like that for you. You hate what I have turned you into."

I look up into the bottomless pools of his eyes. "Who said I hate it? It's new. I'm adjusting." I put my hand over his heart, feeling its strong beat. "You never told me that before."

He moves his hand to my chest to find my own thumping heart, closing his eyes for a second to feel it beating under his palm. When his eyes open again, something close to desperation is in them. "I am so in love with you, it hurts."

His words drive through me, beautiful and painful at the same time. "You know I feel the same way about you."

I think about what my mum said before I left, how things had changed between Peter and me after we got back together. I've always assumed the events of the barn are what made Peter so paranoid, so keen to keep me close, but I start to wonder what it means to be so loved by a creature like him.

Deva spoke a lot about mates and, at first, her tales filled me with dread. She said from what she knew of the old gods, they were often created in pairs, eternal companions to exist through the eons with. I didn't mention Sorcha to her, or even want to think about if I was depriving Peter of his mate. But Deva had not been convinced Peter was right in his assumption we couldn't be mates. In fact, she was fascinated by his assertion we chose each other. She'd seemed excited by it all—gods and fate, the world changing. Deva said she'd never felt an attachment as strong as Peter's to me. Every time I think about her words, it makes my heart sing and tremble at the same time.

When we arrive at the bayou it feels strange to be back in the swamp. The brightness of the day is jarring given the events that happened here. In the back of my mind, I wonder what happened to the bodies, if they were all eaten by the alligators or if they'd given sustenance to the life of the Mississippi.

Glory and Morgan wait casually in the clearing. Glory smiles as we approach while Morgan remains cloaked and unmoving.

"Connie, so good to see you back on your feet. You look well." Glory beams.

Morgan scans over me, apparently approving of what she sees too.

I give her a half smile. Peter is crushing my hand in his. Every muscle in his body is tense.

Glory turns her bright eyes up to his. "There is no need to feel nervous. You are entering into this contract a willing participant, it will not be painful."

He gives the shortest of nods. "Let's get it over with."

Glory glances over at me before continuing with, "I would just like to remind you of how reasonable I have been, ensuring Connie's wellbeing. Your services will not be required all the time. You will both be free to live your lives. Provisions have also been made for you both, a place to call your home separate from this coven, if you like. I would like to think of this as more of a part-nership."

"Okay," is Peter's curt reply.

Glory nods. "In return, I would advise you not to test me. Any action you take to remove this tether, or act against it, well..." she glances at me again, "... you remember the fail-safe we have in place."

"I agree to your terms, Glory. Or should I call you master?" He sneers.

Glory's eyes hold his, the fire in his seeming to ignite hers as she bites back, saying, "If it makes you feel better." She shifts her gaze to the witch at her side. "Morgan, shall we?"

Morgan prizes Peter's fingers from mine and places his arms in Glory's hands, taking what looks like old lengths of ribbons and lashing their hands together. As she goes along, some of the ties change color to the same goldish hue Peter casts around, and everything shines and absorbs into her skin. Over and over again, Glory absorbs the glow.

Morgan continues for over an hour. After a while, I notice Peter sways, and the more he does, the more Morgan watches him, taking less notice of what she is doing. She becomes more interested in tracing her bony fingers against the skin of his forearms, and every time she does, the golden light rises to the surface and fades under the pressure.

Like he is made of light.

Glory hasn't noticed because her eyes are closed.

I find myself moving toward Morgan as she crouches close to his skin. Even her expression looks like one of wonder. Up close, it looks like his veins are filled with gold.

"What is that?" I whisper to Morgan.

But my words break something, and Glory's eyes snap awake.

"It is done," she declares, pulling her hands out of the remaining ribbons, releasing Peter, and letting him fall into the shallow waters of the swamp.

Chapter Twenty

Lorna

The tan line that runs down Lisette's back mesmerizes me as I run my forefinger along where light meets dark. Ever so softly, she murmurs, the noise stirring an emotion deep in my core. Her wild mop of hair is splayed across her pillow. She is sound asleep, but sleep evades me on this night, as it has done for the last several. The nights have turned sticky hot in New Orleans.

Of course, the heat is only part of the reason. I'm also aware my friends are drifting, although I have no idea what is to be done about it. The weeks have turned into a month since Glory left, taking Morgan with her, and no one has heard a word from them since. Leaving us all without a direction to head, without a mission in mind.

It seems like we have won.

That there is nothing left to do but live our lives.

A languid calm echoes around the corners of the apartment. My feelings for Lisette grow, and she talks about me living in New Orleans with her on a permanent basis. Marie goes back to tending her shop and guiding those in need, her old spirit guide returning with neither hide nor hair of the mysterious Boots. Connie seems a permanent fixture on the roof, sunning herself like a cat for endless hours. Peter lingers around Connie, cooking our food and drinking his way through bottle after bottle of rye whiskey.

They drift, and their conversation seems to be reserved for each other alone.

At first, Marie hated having him around still, but as the days have turned into weeks, she's gotten used to their presence. Kind of like specters. He's lined the windows with boxes of strawberries, tomatoes, rosemary, and lemon plants. The foliage has started to creep up the frames. When he is not with Connie, he sits and tends to his plants, watching as if they are precious jewels when they come to life in his hands.

Maybe a drink is what I need, to help sleep take me. To make me not feel so disturbed by this sense of quiet.

I pull my T-shirt on, slip my feet into my slippers, and make for the kitchen, hoping there is at least some liquor left in the apartment. I open the cupboard doors with as little noise as possible. No joy. *Just my luck.*

A door clicks in the silence behind me, and my heart skips a beat, but as I turn, I see it's Peter in the darkness, his joggers slung low over his hips.

"Looking for this?" He holds up a half-empty bottle of whiskey.

"Actually, yes. I can't sleep." I hold my hand out to take it from him but, at the last second, he holds it up out of reach, leaving me swiping the air, a devious smile on his face. "Don't be a dick," I tell him.

Peter rolls his eyes but hands me the bottle.

I walk across the kitchen to get a glass and some ice. Then, remembering Lisette sometimes keeps cigarettes in the kitchen drawer, I take one out, feeling in the mood for it.

"I thought you quit?" he asks as he positions himself by the window.

"I have," I say and light up. "I don't know, just a weird night."

"Hmm..." He looks back out the window, the night's dim glow casting shadows across his face. "It's the moon, when it's full like this." He closes his eyes. "And the air is still like tonight, it's gravity. It feels good. Like the pull of the ocean. It's steadying."

I give a quiet chuckle. "I can't feel the moon's gravity, Peter."

"Why not?" He comes and sits down opposite me. "Not as much as me, but it's there. You are connected to everything, the same as me."

I look at him for a while, his eyes keen in the darkness. His hair appears white in the moonlight.

"Is everything okay? With you?" I ask.

"Why wouldn't it be?" he questions and takes the liquor back.

I don't know how to answer that. Because it seems too quiet?

His eyes flick down to the cigarette I'm holding and, extracting it from my fingers, he takes a long drag, letting the smoke fill his lungs before breathing it out.

"You usually prefer the hard stuff." I grin.

"That I do." His eyes gleam in the darkness with all the implications behind the words, but he doesn't elaborate. And for the first time, I wonder about the high he is chasing with his constant indulgence. And whether that indulgence is really him holding back.

Peter peers out the window. "It's weird, isn't it?" He pauses for a beat. "It's all over. No battles left to fight. All those wheels which were set in motion when my mother died. It all ends here." He fixes me with a hard stare. "What we've been fighting and running toward since we were seventeen."

196

"Is that what feels wrong?" I half smile. "That somehow we are all okay?"

He laughs, taking another drink. "How fucked up are we?" His fingers trace the back of my hand. "Are you happy, Lorna?"

I feel taken aback by the suddenness of the question. "I think so. Like you said, the quietness is unsettling. I didn't think we would ever have a quiet life. But, yes, I am happy with Lisette. She makes me happy." I beam at him and finally see a smile meet his eyes.

"I am so glad to hear that. You deserve that, Lor. All you've ever done is be a loyal friend to Connie, to me, at times when I certainly did not deserve it. I will never forget that, or you."

I swallow hard. "Peter, why does it sound like you're saying goodbye?"

He laughs again, the walls of humor gone up behind his eyes. "I'm not, I promise. I know, we don't do the mushy stuff, right?"

"Peter, it's okay. It's okay for you to breathe for a minute."

Peter's eyes seem to flicker with something he wants to say but doesn't. "I wouldn't go that far."

I frown at him. "Are you worried about Glory? What she'll have you do?"

"No, I'm not," he says, leaning back in his chair.

Whatever I saw for a brief second is long gone now.

"Whatever it is, it won't affect you or Connie. You two are safe and that is all that matters."

I feel like there is more I need to say, but he is already on his feet and heading back to his room, leaving the bottle of whiskey for me. "Good night, Lorna."

———

Something in Connie's laugh stops me as I'm about to open my bedroom door. I peek around the door to see she is lying face down on the sofa. Peter's hands are on the ceiling, a foot either side of her back.

"Just do it." She laughs.

"I can't." He pads his feet. "It feels weird."

"It needs to crack, Peter. Stop being a baby."

I watch Peter put one foot on her shoulder blade, leaning some weight onto it before quickly taking it off again. "I can't... it's too weird."

"I do it to you all the time."

"It's different. You are like five foot nothing. I'm six foot two of pure muscle."

Connie cackles, and I have to bite my lip to stop myself from joining.

"Please, you are six foot two of pure Jack Daniels."

He laughs with her. "Okay, okay." He places both feet on her back and, with a quick twist, an audible *crack* rings out. Jumping off, he does a little jog on the spot.

"Wow. That feels good." Connie rolls to sit up, and I finally enter the room.

"Hi, you two."

Peter gives me a nod, but Connie moves her hair to cover the right side of her face, an action not lost on him.

"You okay, Connie? Not in your usual suntrap this morning."

"I think my back has seized up from lying on the concrete. I might give it a rest today." She gets up and moves off the sofa and into an armchair away from me.

"Maybe we should get out of the apartment, go to a bar or something?" I suggest. "Or we could go shopping, Connie."

Her eyes drift to Peter, who isn't saying anything, instead

making coffee with his back to us. "I think I would rather just stay here."

Peter brings us both a cup of coffee, handing me mine before giving Connie hers. Hoisting himself up over the arms so he can slide into the chair behind her, she pushes herself up so she is half leaning against him.

"You need to leave at some point," he tells her. "Maybe you should go with Lorna."

She buries her head on his shoulder. "I don't want to leave you."

He soothes his hand down her face. "I can come with you, then."

"I'm not ready. Don't make me."

She wraps her coffee-free arm around his neck, and he gives me an apologetic look, wrapping his arms around her. "I won't do anything. It's okay."

Connie stays there, nuzzled in him.

"Morning, guys." Lisette strides out of the bedroom and helps herself to some of the coffee still in the pot. "Anything for breakfast?"

"There are blueberry pancakes in the oven," Peter tells her.

She makes a small squeal of joy and opens the oven door to take the top pancake before moving to look out of the window at the bright morning. "I wonder when this heatwave will break."

Peter whispers into Connie's ear, "Do you mind if I let it rain?"

Connie shakes her head. "Of course not." She smiles. "I don't mind the rain."

"But you prefer the sun."

"I adore the sun."

"I like giving you what you want. But it's a good day for rain. What else can I give you instead?"

I stop listening, and Lisette plonks herself beside me, hooking her arm over my knee. Switching on the television, she passes me a piece of pancake just as the rain starts beating down on the window.

"Look at that." Lisette smiles at me. "I swear, we have to go out and do a rain dance in that."

Lisette and I make plans for the evening, then get dressed and ready for the day, pottering about the apartment. Connie remains curled up in Peter's arms, barely moving or talking to anyone else for the rest of the morning. In their own bubble, the two of them whisper to each other.

When Lisette and I leave hours later, they haven't moved.

"What do you think will happen to them?" Lisette asks me over dinner.

"What do you mean?"

Lisette shrugs, popping another shrimp into her mouth. "I don't know. It seems like they are finding it hard to move on. Like, what are they going to do, stay in that apartment forever?"

"I think Connie is still recovering. Trying to get used to it."

"How do you get used to something like that?"

"Not much choice," I say, focusing on my food under the scrutiny of Lisette's eyes on me.

"Lorna..." she hedges, "... you have a future here, you know, with me?"

I can't help but smile as I take her hand across the table.

"I think I am falling in love with you."

My heart pounds in my chest. "Really?"

With an enthusiastic nod, she states, "I love you, Lorna."

"I love you, Lisette," I tell her without hesitation.

She stands up, grabs me from across the table, and kisses me hard on the mouth, earning us a few *whoops* from the tables nearby.

"So..." she sits back down and goes back to her food nonchalantly, "... I was thinking... you should come back to Avery Island with me this weekend. Meet my ma and pa."

"Really?" I sound like a broken record.

"Sure. They are dying to meet this new girl their daughter can't stop talking about."

"You talk about me to your parents?"

"Of course. Ma always wants to know what goes on in my love life, *cher*. Not a lot happens on the island, so she relies on the gossip from the big city." She laughs. "Don't your parents do the same?"

I shake my head. "They don't ask. The closest they ever showed interest about my love life was to tell me they didn't approve of Peter."

"You were with Peter?"

"No." I almost choke on my drink. "No, never. They just assumed because we are close."

She gives me a look. "They know, though, right?"

I swallow hard. "I guess it never came up. We live in a small village. I suppose I never really labeled myself that way anyway."

"But... the girl you loved before."

"Anna."

"Anna. She is the only other person you've loved?"

"Yes, she was the first. Lis, you have to understand. I never meant to fall in love with her. It all happened so gradually. She was my best friend first. It was like, there was all this darkness and in it was Anna. It felt like a crazy whirlwind."

She gives a quiet nod.

"But it's so different with you. It feels more normal."

"Wow." Lisette hits me with a dry look.

"Not in a bad way, in a real way. Lis, I don't need that darkness to love you. I want to stay. I want to stay with you and live a life that is real. You know, I want us to argue about washing up and take trips to see your parents. I want to do that as well as dance in the rain and face the dark times. I want it all."

Lisette bites her lip. "Well, why didn't you say that before?" She beams, and she's beautiful. "I feel the same way."

We finish our dinner and drinks before roaming the reawakened streets. The rain has cleared, leaving the air feeling fresh, like New Orleans has taken a deep breath.

As we near Marie's shop, we see her approaching with Frankie, arm in arm with him. It's clear they've had a few drinks too as we chat with each other and enter the apartment.

Connie and Peter are in the same chair we left them in, Connie fast asleep on Peter's chest.

"Sorry," Lisette whispers as his eyes flicker open, seeing us all filtering in.

Marie and Frankie move to the table with their bottle of wine.

Groggy, Peter gets to his feet, sweeping Connie, who does not stir, up in his arms.

"Why don't you join us?" I ask him.

"Not tonight." He smiles back at me, retreating into their room.

The next morning, heavy rain pounds against the apartment windows.

Connie and Peter are gone.

Part Two

Chapter Twenty-One

Connie

The day Peter made it rain is our last in New Orleans.

We have a need to be away. Somewhere on our own. Somewhere neither of us has to hide.

Peter calls Glory.

Some of the ribbon that was used in the tether ritual remains tied around his wrist, a means of being called on but also a way of signaling to the coven. Glory said we would be provided for. It took traveling for three days to the coast of Ireland and then another day across the north of England with Glory and another witch we recognized from the clearing—Gareth—to an uninhabited island off the north coast of Scotland.

A wild, beautiful place with a single house in the middle which somehow looks old and new at the same time.

"This place is yours." Glory and Gareth watch us with guarded expressions. "It is heavily warded, so no one will be able to find you here. Only Gareth and I know this place."

Peter doesn't speak to them, addressing me instead. "Do you like it?"

I gaze at the two-story house. It looks like something out of a fairy tale, pale and bright against the stormy Scottish weather. *I can't believe it's ours.*

"It's somewhere where you don't have to hide. A place where we can be ourselves."

"I love it," I tell him.

Gareth eyes Glory, who glances at Peter as they make their departure. "We will give you some time to settle in. Expect our call in two months."

They leave on the same boat they brought us here on, telling Peter a boat will be sent when he is needed.

The house is supplied with everything we could ever need. Peter follows me from room to room while I look through each cupboard, then turn every tap on and off again. I run my fingers across the luxurious fabrics of the curtains, the porcelain of the roll-top bath, the cherry wood of the four-poster bed.

"Glory is just giving all of this to us?" I ask, feeling incredulous, like I am being bought.

"To you." He watches me from across the bedroom. "I may have said you were finding the eye difficult. That you were unable to leave the apartment, and I wanted somewhere you felt safe to be yourself. So she found this."

"Why? Why would she do this for me?"

"To keep me sweet. Compliant." He crosses the room to look out at the wild storm, closing his eyes as it passes and the sun breaks through the clouds.

"Two months," I murmur.

"I know. Let's not think about it." He pulls away from the window, walking back toward me and stopping at the edge of the bed. "We have two months not to think, to just live and be still. Let's have it. Let's have this moment, Connie, where we don't think about anything else."

"Okay." I edge closer. "Just me and you, on an island. Our island. What do you want to do?" I bite my lip. I know his answer as he reaches his hand out toward me, taking it and pulling me closer.

"Tell me." His eyes burn hot into mine. "Tell me you are mine."

"I am yours," I say, my heart in my throat.

"Forever?"

"I am yours forever," I tell him, and his mouth finds mine, kissing me long and slow.

For the next two months, we barely move out of that room. We don't think about anything else. We don't need much of anything to survive, just each other, and I gorge myself on him, determined not to take much notice of the days. I don't want to live in fear of the one when he has to leave.

We know it's time when the tether ribbon burns hot on his wrist, and the next day Gareth appears at the island dock with a boat to take him. He kisses me like his life depends on it and then he is gone.

I wander.

Rattle around the house like I am haunting it.

The house has a phone and a television. But the television bores me, and I spend hours staring at the phone, wondering if I should call Lorna, my mum, or Jamie. *What would I tell them?*

I spend hours in the bath, marveling how my skin never puckers. I stare at my hands, then at my reflection. I study my green eye for ages. I walk the length of the island and wonder if the water is too cold to swim in.

Mostly, I read and wait for Peter.

He is gone for two weeks.

At first, I think something has crashed on the island or there has been a small earthquake with how the whole island shakes.

When I open the front door, he is already right in front of my face. His eyes are black, his pupils fully dilated and quivering in the whites. He doesn't need to tell me what Glory has had him do.

His breathing is ragged, and he pushes his arms around me, taking me backward until I land hard against the wall, a crack shuddering through the house. His eyes struggle to focus on mine as he licks his lips. I know I should say something, but I haven't spoken in two weeks.

"I-I..." He shakes his head, his words vibrating around the whole house. "I can't come down," he confesses as his eyes contract and dilate again.

His hand slides into mine, pushing it farther above my head as his knees find their way between my legs, his breath hot on my neck. I try to breathe but can only gasp at the sudden onslaught. The power drips off him, making me shake. Making both of us shake.

"I need to share it with you," he whispers into my ear.

My body reacts to his, to feeling him close again, so I don't realize at first quite what he means. "Peter, no—" I start, but it's already too late.

His breaths come heavy as he releases some of the energy into me, some of the souls, my hand in his own starting to glow white hot. My senses become confused, the feeling of the souls so overwhelming I almost don't notice he is removing clothing. I can't tell which feels better. Peter, his body against mine as he takes me where he stands, or the power of the souls he is offloading.

When he finishes, his knees buckle, leaving us both in a breathless heap on the floor. I can't catch my breath, so I lie here and stare at the ceiling, the chandelier glittering above me. It's so pretty, like fairies dancing in the light.

I wonder if there are fairies in this world.

Wouldn't that be wonderful?

Wouldn't it be absolute magic to have a chandelier of fairies dancing in the light?

Peter gets to his feet, although the light from the chandelier is so divine, I almost don't notice. "I'm going for a shower." He marches off, leaving me lying on the floor.

I can't be bothered to get up but notice the front door is still open. My legs are too shaky to stand, and it feels too good for me to care. I don't get up until I feel another shudder ripple through the house.

I wobble to my feet, the insides of my legs feeling a little bruised. As I climb the stairs, I follow the sounds of running water to our en suite bathroom. Peeking my head around the shower, I see fractured tiles and Peter leaning with one hand against the wall, and his head hung under the shower.

"You okay?" I ask, wondering what I've done wrong.

He shakes his head before whirling around to study me. His eyes still look huge, but they aren't contracting as much now. "I'm sorry." He drags his hand over his eyes. "I'm so sorry I pounced on you like that."

"It's okay." I smile, trying to move his hand away from his face.

"You told me to stop, and I didn't." He tries to get away.

"I was talking about the souls, not you." I try to reassure him, but he still tries to escape me. "But it was fine. I am fine."

"It didn't make any difference. I couldn't stop, Connie."

I let him move away to rest his forehead against the tiles under the shower. "Fuck." He slams his fist into the tiles again, sending another crack up the wall.

"Feel better?" I pop my hip at him.

"Not even remotely," he answers, still not looking at me.

I stare at the back of his head for a moment. "How many was it?"

He lets what seems to be his first real breath out, and a long, defeated sigh, hanging his head lower. "Hundreds. Maybe close to three hundred, maybe two-seventy? I'm not sure."

"Do you want to talk about it?"

"No."

"You didn't like it?" I realize I am soaked through, my dress turning transparent.

"Connie..." His words come out strangled as he gives his attention to me once more. "I am mad about what I just did to *you*, not them. Listen, this is not supposed to be your burden. I am—"

"No, you listen. We're partners. We are in this together. If what you need is to share that load, then share it, Peter. You caught me by surprise is all. I mean, geez, I haven't seen you in two weeks." I move closer, taking his chin in my hand so he can't look away. "Do you think I can't take it? That I'm not strong enough?"

"Of course, I know you are strong enough. I just—"

"No," I tell him. "You are what I need. *All* of you. Let me be what you need too. It's the only way this works. We chose each other, remember?"

For a second, I think he is going to tell me no, but his stance shifts, his eyes hold mine, and he nods. His chin still in my palm, and I pull him closer again, kissing him more slowly this time. I want to enjoy every inch of him. He deepens our kiss, snaking his hands around my back, reaching down to lift the hem of my dress over my head, then turning me so I can enjoy the full warmth of the shower. Kissing my neck, down my chest, the fight and the fury are gone.

Now, he only whispers, "I adore you," over and over into my skin.

The following months, while heavenly, pass all too fast. Sometimes I wonder if maybe we died and now, we *are* in heaven, the sun always shining on our island. Then I remember he will be called away soon, and I will be alone once more.

Glory sent him back with seeds for the garden, so we spend most of our time outside, growing all our favorite foods. All Peter needs are the seeds. Everything else is grown in moments. I've adopted Peter's habit of never wearing anything on my feet. My soles becoming hardened to the ground, I feel more rooted to the island.

Time passes and, as expected, Peter is called away again.

I spend most of my time in the garden, eating strawberries off the vines and keeping the weeds at bay. The dirt gets under my fingernails, and I don't seem able to shift it. The sun continues to shine, and I bask in it for hours on end. I study my reflection, noticing the silver strands of my hair have turned white.

I wait for Peter.

By chance, I am looking out of the upstairs window, watching the sea, when I see the boat sailing up to the dock. I watch as Peter puts a foot down onto the wooden slats and the whole island shakes, but something is wrong. He topples backward, sending the little boat swaying violently while Gareth staggers to try and stay standing.

I fly as fast as my feet will carry me down the stairs, opening the door and running toward the beach. Gareth's arm is around Peter as he heaves him out of the boat and flat onto his back on the jetty. Without a glance back, he drives away.

Peter's limbs are like jelly as I try to bring him around when I reach him. The dock creaks under his weight. Close up, I see golden pulses of energy rippling under his skin.

"Peter." I try to shake him awake, startled by how his whole eyes are black with the dilation of his pupils. "How many?"

He blinks back at me, his breathing heavy, something close to hurt and confusion in his eyes. "Over a thousand," he manages to get out.

I squeeze my eyes shut.

Don't cry, Connie. Don't let him see you cry.

I hold on tight to his hands. "You have to give me some."

"No." He pulls his hands away from me, rolling over so he can drag himself off the jetty and through the grass. "No, I can take it. It was too many. Glory won't make that mistake again. I just need to deal with it."

The glowing light pulses along his arms as he drags himself toward the house.

"What is happening?"

"My body is struggling to contain it."

"You look like you are about to explode."

"I feel like it." He half laughs.

"Peter." I stop his crawling and roll him so he is flat on his back, looking up at the blue sky. Straddling his chest to keep him where he is, I kneel and order, "Give me some. Now."

He takes a deep breath before drawing his hands up to either side of my face. The glow burns until it feels so hot I can barely stand it. The only sound is our heavy pants. When he stops and I feel fat with souls too, Peter loses consciousness. All I can do is lie next to him in the grass, almost failing to notice the vines that wrap around me are coming from him.

I don't remember moving back to the house, but Peter sleeps for days. When he wakes, he uses the phone to call Glory to tell her he wants a guitar for me, a hive with bees, and juniper seeds.

Gareth arrives two days later with his order. We build the hive and grow wildflowers. Peter brings the juniper to fruition and shows me how to make home-brewed gin in the bathtub. His hair turns as white as snow, and we notice my roots do the same. Glory tells us it is the trauma of absorbing the souls. Peter's eyes don't return to normal, now remaining black orbs rimmed in a fraction of brown.

He is quiet.

We make love—in our bed, in the garden, the kitchen.
Anywhere, everywhere.
And he is quiet.
Only whispering, *"I adore you,"* over and over into my skin.

Peter is gone again.
  I wait.
  I play my guitar. I tend to the garden.
  I wait.
  I make gin. I spend hours in the bath.
  I wait.
  I wonder if I should jump into the sea. I bask in the garden.
  I wait.
  I am alone.
  Until one day when I notice something shimmering in the wildflowers moving toward me. I watch until the greenish skin glitters in the eternal sunlight, writhing toward me. Without hesitation, the snake wraps around my wrist and palm, nestling there. I bring it to my face, watching as its tongue tickles the fluttering pulse point of my wrist. It remains there until the sun goes down and I retreat inside.

Peter returns, the island shaking with his first step back on it. I'm in the garden when it happens. I run through the house, my heart pounding in my chest at what state I'll find him in this time. He is already in the hall, eyes black and power dripping off every inch of him.
  But he is on his feet.

I don't think.

My body slams into his with such force it almost knocks him over. His mouth finds mine as I wrap my legs around him. I am so glad he is home, that he is okay, because part of me was missing, and now, it has just walked through the front door.

"I love you, Peter. I love you," I tell him. "I love you forever."

His skin shudders, and he doesn't say anything, only stares at me. As if I am the stars and the moon. Silently, he carries me up the stairs.

Something is changing. I feel the rough texture of vines twisting around my feet and arms, binding me to him. It's all coming from him. He looks at me like it all ends with me. I am everything. It is consuming to mean so much. Like I am the center of the universe.

He holds it in until we are in our room, then he kisses me so slowly I think it might kill me. The power echoes all around us, the house creaking under the strain of it. His restraint almost too much, I claw at his skin, demanding more, until finally he lets go. He devours me. The souls' glow reverberates around his skin, transferring to mine.

I can't have him close enough, deep enough. He clings to me like a savage, like I am the only thing left to hold onto.

Consuming.

The years pass.

My time measured by when I am with him and when I am without.

With the passage of time, Peter smiles less and less, and he clings to me with such ferocity that I think it should destroy me.

The hive produces rich honey. When he is home, I watch him

eat honeycombs with his eyes closed in sweet satisfaction, the combs crunching as the sticky, amber-tinted nectar coats his hands and chin. It is mesmerizing, addictive as he is, to watch him eat it.

I make elderflower gin.

Peter makes more demands of Glory, and everything I could ever want arrives at the house. Books and seeds, paintings, and a record player.

My hair turns pure white—there is nothing left of the brunette. My hair is as white as Peter's, and I discover there is something under the paleness of my skin. A sheen, a faint pattern of intricate white lines, like snakeskin, shimmers in patches over my arms and torso. Peter spends hours examining it and telling me it is so beautiful, that I am his, how he adores me, adores me, adores me.

The snakes find me. More and more come to the island. Some brave the treacherous sea, others stow away on the boat that brings Peter back to me. Once, one came wrapped around Gareth's wrist. He said nothing, only studied me with hard fury-filled eyes as it slithered from him over my bare shoulder. I wondered at the time what private battles he is fighting to make his eyes so violent.

Sometimes, my snakes wrap around my wrist and sleep as I make gin in the bathtub, or lie across me when I bask in the sun.

The island becomes more and more Peter. Every time he sets foot back on it, it bends more to his will. So gradual I almost don't notice, the cracks in the house fill with vines and the roots of the trees that now cover the island. When Peter is gone, I roam the rooms, running my hands over the roots, feeling him everywhere. He doesn't need seeds to create anymore—everything comes from him.

Peter affects everything. This isn't just a place for me to hide. It's a place for Peter to breathe, to let everything out. For him to create instead of burn.

The cherry wood of our four-poster peeks through thick vines as moss creeps into the mattress and forms a canopy of wisteria. Our bedroom looks reclaimed by the earth.

I wonder how long it has been.

Then Peter comes home, and I run to him. Heavy with souls, smelling of earth and death, his lips, hands, vines everywhere, finding every inch of my skin as he climbs the stairs with me wrapped around him. I always tell him I love him, forever, forever, forever. His vines wrap deeper, and he fills himself on me. The snakes that live in the canopy wrap around my wrists, around Peter's, attracted to the power.

The house creaks and sways.

And the years pass.

Chapter Twenty Two

Peter

The dull *boom, boom, boom* of Connie's heart sounds in my ear.

I can't remember how long I've been lying here between her legs with my head on her chest, her hands running lazily through my hair as she hums away to herself. The adder that has been wrapped around her wrist wakes up and uncoils to make its way back to the bedpost, then slithers up to the canopy.

I lift my head up, moving my hand from around her back to trace the patch of iridescent snakeskin on her chest and wonder if, one day, she will shed her skin and emerge an even more magnificent creature. Something more god-like than me. A wonder of the fucking universe.

I want to stay here forever, my favorite place on the planet, and not be forced into answering Glory's call. Something is building inside of me. With every execution at Glory's command, I feel the rot eating away at my soul.

"Tell me what you're thinking." Connie runs her delicate fingers against the sharpness of my cheekbones. *Has it been hours or days since we spoke? How tight can I hold onto her before I lose my grip, and everything else in the process?*

"I am thinking..." I start, moving my head back to her chest. "I am thinking that one day I won't be able to stop. I don't think Glory's command will be enough to stop me."

Connie's hands stop fussing me. "Is that possible? With the tether?"

"I'm not sure. I've never wanted to test the boundaries of it. But one day, it won't matter... it won't be enough." I close my eyes, listen to the beat of her heart, pull her closer. "My father was right. I will destroy this world someday. I won't stop until everything is gone."

Connie pushes me up at my shoulders, forcing me to face her, concern written all over her face. "Glory won't let that happen. She—"

"Con, the tether is weak." I rub my eyes, moving away from her, now regretting bringing it up. We could have hundreds of years before I go nuclear. "Somehow, I just know it is. Forget I mentioned it. I'm fidgety because her call will come any day now. You know I don't like leaving you."

"How can I forget that?" She gets up, crossing the room and throwing on a thin dressing gown. "Glory doesn't want this world destroyed. She said so herself."

The laugh I give her is devoid of all traces of humor. "You have no idea what she wants. The stuff she has me do... it's fucking horrific."

Connie stands still for a while, the light of the dawn through the window making her look like some kind of angel. "So why don't you tell me?"

"I can't." I shake my head, sinking back to look at the canopy. Making all the Lily of the Valley bloom, I close my eyes to breathe it in. "I don't want you to see me that way. Can't you be

218

the one person in my life who doesn't look at me like I'm a monster?"

"You are not a monster." She moves back over, lying her head on my chest, also breathing in the sweet scent.

"You don't know what I have done."

"At the coven's bidding."

"At the coven's bidding," I repeat. Hollow words hardly a consolation. Glory may point, but that doesn't mean I don't love every blood-soaked minute of it deep inside.

Connie shifts about, her deep breath reverberating in my ear, an action I've come to recognize as an indicator she is about to say something she thinks I won't like.

"I've been thinking, and this may be the perfect time. Maybe next time you leave, I can come with you."

"What?" I move away from her, her face suggesting she is being nothing but reasonable. "I tell you I am the literal end of days, and your reaction is, what? You want to watch?"

"Of course not, Peter." She rolls her eyes, getting back to her feet. "Maybe it will make a difference with me being there. You always say that I cool you down."

"It is out of the question," I tell her. I don't mean to sound so harsh.

The fire inside me burns as she paces away from me, running her hand across one of the vines at the window frame she looks out of. As she does, the tickle of her touch tremors across my skin.

"I need to get off this island," she says so low I almost don't hear her.

That murderous voice in the back of my head flares, rages as it tells me she is leaving me.

"You want to leave?" I ask, my voice fracturing.

Connie rubs her throat, looking a little confused, as if something should be there. Something we have both forgotten. "I don't even know how long I've been here. I can't remember what it feels like to have rain on my face, or eat a burger, or talk to anyone else. I think I'm ready to go back."

My chest heaves at the thought of Connie out in the world again. "How? You look even more different now than the day we left." I hear the spite in my own words and cringe inside but I don't let her see as she turns to me.

Her brow furrowed, she takes an accusing step toward me and asks, "Am I a prisoner here?"

"I can make it rain for you. I can bring different food. I can—"

"Am I a prisoner, Peter?" she demands.

The heat ravages my body, fueling the fire inside. "*You are mine*," I shout as I loom over her.

Still so tiny and delicate, but so different now, her face is alive with passion, the same fire filling her emerald eyes. Yet she doesn't say anything.

After glowering at each other for a good minute, she walks away. Going to the wardrobe, she pulls out the first real clothes in years and frantically tugs them on.

"What are you doing?"

"I am leaving," she says, yanking a top over her head.

I half smirk. "With a snake wrapped around your ankle?"

She jigs it off in annoyance, not at all seeing the funny side.

"There is no way of getting off this island," I remind her.

"You said it yourself. Glory will call and you have to answer. I am getting on that boat, Peter. I would rather come with you, but I will go somewhere else if I need to."

"You are not going anywhere." I growl at her.

"I am not the one with a master," she seethes through her teeth. "*You* are *not* my master."

Something in me shifts, and the rage starts to subside because she is right. She does not belong to me. I entered the tether, not her. I push my hands through my hair, easing my stance and turning away to go back downstairs. If she wants to leave, I cannot stop her. I don't blame her for wanting to leave me. She knows what I do when I leave her. It was always only a matter of time before she didn't want a murderer in her bed.

On the kitchen table is one of the last bottles of red wine. I grab it and plonk myself on the backsteps to watch the last of the sunrise. I've spent so long hating the thought that I am the creature my father envisioned, I forgot to hate the fact that I am also every inch my mother—psychotic, alcoholic, and taker of prisoners, apparently. Our way of protecting others is to cage them. I am also full of fear, just like my mother. Fear that Connie will one day come to her senses and leave. For good.

Connie pads up next to me, taking a seat on the step, and holding a small tub with a honeycomb in it.

"Eat," she tells me, pushing the tub into my hands and collecting the bottle, taking a long drink herself. "It was a low blow... the thing I said about the master."

"You weren't wrong," I reply without looking at her.

She shifts forward, hugging her knees and looking at her toes. "You did this for me. You saved my life."

"It wouldn't have needed saving in the first place if it weren't for me." I take the wine back from her. "You don't owe me anything," I state and then finish the bottle.

She shoots a glance at me before returning to her toes. "I know how you see yourself, Peter. I know you think that you are the villain."

"I *know* I'm the villain, Connie," I interrupt.

"Right." She nods. "You are the villain. But I need you to understand something, Peter. Even if you are the villain, I don't care."

I meet her green eyes.

"If you are the villain, then I am too."

I open my mouth to talk, but nothing comes out. I don't know how she can say that. She is everything I live for. The only goodness that lingers around me.

She rests her head on my shoulder. "You brought me here so that I didn't have to hide, but I don't want you to always have to hide part of who you are from me."

I give a dry chuckle. "The murderous side?"

"Yes," she murmurs, leaning into me. "I love even the murderous part. Turns out, I am a freak, after all." She pauses for a minute. "Why is she making you do it?"

I rub my eyes, recalling Glory's tirades. "Glory believes the Earth is on track for the next extinction, when mankind will be wiped out for good. She told me magic has slowly been leaving this world, that it has become overpopulated, and the Earth cannot cope. She and Gareth say most covens believe in a natural order, a cycle of life, that this extinction is just a continuation of that natural order."

Connie tilts her head up and frowns. "I think I follow. So, what does this have to do with you?"

"Well, in Glory's words, I can break that cycle. She is trying to tip the balance back in favor of mankind."

"By having you kill people? Pretty weird way of saving the world."

The corners of my lips turn into a grimace. "It's the way I'm doing it. Her idea is that, if we can take out enough of the population, I can throw the extinction off course and give the Earth a chance to heal."

Connie's hand moves to her mouth with her inhale. "That is horrifying. All those people."

"Millions of people."

"Millions?" Her eyes go even wider.

"I'm not there yet. But it's a lot." I look up at the morning sky. "Ironic, really. She thinks she is saving the world, but in reality, she is setting me on a path to destroy it anyway. All that death... it's addictive, and you know how I am. Sometimes the cycle cannot be stopped."

Connie scoots closer, putting her hand on my arm. "I'm so sorry, Peter."

"Why? This is what I was built for, Connie." I look into her eyes. "All those bodies, all that death, and I am always at the center. Except, it never bothers me. I am nothing close to human anymore. All I am is fire and rage. I want to burn and grow. I am not the judge... I am the executioner."

"You are the arrow," she repeats the words I said to her what feels like a lifetime ago.

"I do not want to be the hunter," I admit. "I want to destroy and rebuild. It is all instinct. My instinct. Glory's tether is not enough to hold it."

"We need to talk to Glory."

"And say what? That the tether I've never tested will not hold. She will think it's a ploy for me to stop. To get out of the contract."

"Why don't we test it, then? Show her she needs to stop."

I shake my head. "I cannot risk your safety. She still has a fail-safe. Something that could kill you." I put my hand over her stomach. "I haven't been able to figure out what that is. Besides, Glory thinks she is winning. She won't give up."

Connie looks at me hard, taking my hand. "It is a risk worth taking. We need to start pushing at the tether, just enough to make her stop what she's doing, and then we can tell her what it is doing to you. She won't carry on if she thinks her current path will lead to the same outcome."

"And the extinction?" I ask, keeping my tone light, not giving much thought to the catastrophe pushing the tether could lead to.

Connie gives me a little shove. "One apocalypse at a time, maybe?"

Right on cue, the ribbon at my wrist burns hot.

Gareth is coming.

Connie gages my reaction, and I hold her close. "Connie, please stay here." I see her brow furrow, so I console her. "I agree to your plan, okay? Just give me some time to get my head around it. How to push the tether without getting you killed. Please?"

"Peter..."

I know she is going to argue. "For me, Connie. Stay. Just a while longer."

She doesn't answer.

Her face becomes set, and she walks back inside, leaving me feeling like a wounded animal.

Chapter Twenty-Three

Sorcha

Meath is once again a hive of activity when Lily and I return. Not surprising—the world has changed a lot in the last five years. Maybe not to the common person. Most people would say it has always been this way, or that it is an inevitable part of nature.

Few know what is actually happening.

Thousands are dying. Floods and famine. Earthquakes and long-dormant volcanoes are being forced back into life. The deaths are indiscriminate. Of course, many covens across the globe have fallen into line with Glory. All past indiscretions are forgiven. If you are not with her, you stand aside. Nobody is daring to oppose her vision or stand in the way of the juggernaut at her disposal.

Not even me.

I stay well out of his way.

It appears I was wrong, and he is hers to control after all.

After a year, I began to see the change in them too—Glory and Gareth starting to relax. Despite a rocky start, they were getting comfortable. Satisfied that their beast was muzzled. Glory was true to her word. She never bought him to Ireland, not to her home.

But after a year, I had to escape, sick of my skin prickling every time they said his name. More and more uneasy with the casual way I overheard Glory and Gareth talking through their plans for world domination, how to bring the world back to apparent balance. As far as I know, it was only ever death and destruction. The rebuild would come later, they told me.

I couldn't help but start to doubt Glory. That kind of control can only go to one's head. Glory has always been a fierce warrior and has had so much taken from her, yet I can't help wondering how much blood she can stomach.

The fire seems to fuel Gareth as he becomes even more rage-filled and driven. He has always been attracted to power. Even Lily started to feel uncomfortable in her old home. So we returned to my long-forgotten home of Osogbo, recharging ourselves in the sacred forests of my ancestors and wading in the Osun, the only place I feel detached from him. Surrounded by souls departing from this world. Free souls, journeying beyond. The Osogbo coven, not agreeing with Glory's means but understanding her end, are keeping well out of the way.

Though after four years, Lily has started to miss her home and feels like she needs to reconnect with Glory. Therefore, we're back in Meath. We are surprised to see the ancient underground home the Irish coven has resided in for centuries has changed much in the time we've been gone. A great dome now sits on top of the mound, full glass windows facing Newgrange.

Lily gives a little chuckle at the sight of it. "Do you think she is sending a message?" She raises her eyebrows at me.

"The past is well and truly in the past." I smirk. "She has reclaimed her homeland and will be damned if anyone tries to force her from it again."

Lily smiles at the modern structure. "I can't believe she did it. She never once gave up faith that we would return here one day."

I turn to my face my friend, the setting sun forming around her head. "Do you think she will be pleased to see us?"

"Of course, Cia." Lily beams. "We are her family."

I take her hand as we push forward and make our way through the bustling halls, so many faces I don't recognize. The coven has grown, more than doubled in numbers, in the last four years.

"Sorcha," a familiar voice calls out.

I look across to see Glory standing near the entrance of the main meeting hall, her face full of the warmth of a mother. My heart thumps at the sight, and in two short steps, I am in her arms.

"You look so well." She holds me close.

I pull back to gaze upon her. There are a few more lines in her skin than the last time I saw her, her face is more tanned, and she carries a weariness in her eyes. "It is so good to see you," I tell her.

She gives Lily the same warm smile, pulling her into her arms. "I am afraid you are just missing us. A team of us are on our way out. A mission to Jakarta." She looks between the both of us. "But you are staying? Both of you?"

"Of course," we both say in unison.

"We just got here." I laugh, relieved to see Glory's easiness. "We have so much to catch up on. Like that monstrosity on top of the mound," I tease her.

Glory's easy laugh echoes all around. "I know. I have to say I can't stand the thing myself. It was Gareth's idea. We needed a bigger place for full coven meetings. This place cannot hold us all any longer." She rubs a nostalgic palm across the heavy oak door to the central meeting room, looking lost in thought. "But there is something about seeing the sunrise and sunset on the solstice from those tall windows. It almost makes you feel like you were here all those thousands of years ago, truly connected to the cosmos."

I chance a grin at Lily, who smirks back at me.

She puts a gentle hand on Glory. "We can't wait to see it."

Glory takes her hand, giving it a squeeze. "Not tonight. The sun is almost set. You two go down to the dining hall. The others will be so pleased to see you. Eat, drink, sleep. Rest well." She places her rough hand on my cheek. "It is so good to see you. We will not be gone long. I think Gareth is back. I need to find him and then we will depart. Two weeks, tops," she tells us before making her way toward the entrance.

"She seems well." Lily eyes me, her words loaded, and leads me toward the kitchen.

"That she does." I plod along behind her. "I'll catch you up, Lil. I'm just going to drop our things." I hold up our luggage, and Lily gives a nod and carries on as I take a nearby passage to our room before circling back to the main meeting room, brushing against unfamiliar faces. None seem bothered to see me.

Right before I reach the corridor, I spot a new door, one I've never seen before. It must be the entrance to the glass dome. I can't resist. Maybe I'll catch the last of the sunset. I open the door and creep up the dark stairs, and am soon met with windows that must be fifteen feet high. Seven panels across, from up high seeing the beautiful vista of Meath, the last of the sun's rays hitting the grassy tops of Brú na Bóinne, making them look almost white. My breath catches in my throat. Glory is right. It's so moving—the feeling washes over me. Primal and primitive, the home of the first witches.

I cross the darkening room, placing my hands on the glass as if I could reach out and touch them. They feel so close. The last of the sun's light disappears, plunging me into darkness. It feels good to take a moment by myself.

It's strange to hear the flush of a toilet, a juxtaposition to the calm of the view, and the light switch flipping on from someone entering the room. My eyes squint at the sudden brightness as I spin to find the source.

He stops dead in his tracks when he sees me by the window. My body goes into revolt, not sure if I should run or stand my ground. He looks so different. His hair is a shock of white, his eyes are black orbs standing out against the tan of his skin, and his face is no longer soft and boyish but sharp and deadly.

"H-how?" I stutter. "How are you here?"

His eyes narrow. "How are *you* here?"

"I..." I need to pull it together. "I can't feel you."

His stance relaxes as he smirks a bit. Peter throws the towel he is holding back into the bathroom. "You are not the only one protected by a witch's cloaking spell." He crosses to a far corner, turning his back on me to examine some bottles there. "Do you think she wants them to know when I am coming?" He half turns back with a sly smile. "Kind of ruins the element of surprise." He pours himself a drink. "Although, I have to admit, I prefer it when they beg for their lives." He pours another drink. "There is something quite intoxicating about the screams of those who have lost all hope."

I keep my back to the window, trying to keep from shaking as he saunters over, holding out one of the glasses to me, which I don't take. His eyes rake up my body, and I have to tell myself not to tremble.

He cocks his head from a few feet away. "What? No witty retort, Sorcha? After all these years." He inches closer to me. "This is all you have? Silence. How disappointing."

I stare defiantly into his black eyes. "Your father would be so proud..." I get out through clenched teeth, "... to see the animal you have become."

"There she is," he whispers, dropping one of the glasses and slamming his hand to the window by my head.

My senses warp by the vibrating of the glass window and his breath hot in my ear.

"I killed my father and fed him to pigs. He has nothing to do with what I am." He pulls away to look at me, yet he's still so close I can smell the whiskey on his breath. "You are the one who should be proud... you're the one who did this to me."

I let out a shaky breath, looking over his shoulder.

Keep your feelings inside, Sorcha. Don't let him see that inside, you are screaming.

"Peter, I—"

"If you say sorry, I will rip you apart."

"Why don't you?" I meet those cold eyes burning with ice once more. "Just rip me apart, Peter. Kill me if it will make you happy."

His eyes glance down to my lips, then the scorch marks that still decorate my neck. "Why would I do that, Sorcha?" He ghosts his nose along the burns. "Why kill you when torturing you is so sweet?"

With that, his rough tongue licks my neck, from its base right up to my ear, as his chest rises and falls with my own. Against my own will, a moan escapes my lips at the touch.

Peter stops, giving a humorless laugh, and raises his head to look at me again. "After all this time?" He smirks.

"I hate you." I seethe.

The sentiment seems to amuse him as he ogles me up and down like he's appraising my outfit. Running his finger along the V-neck of my top, the touch of his skin on mine feels like fire. "Take it off," he commands.

And although I try to fight it, fight it with every inch of my being, I do as he says. Unwrapping my top and dropping it to the floor, the shaking is no longer in control. I'm caught between fury, so desperately wanting him to touch me, and the anticipation of what will happen next.

He regards me for a moment, licking his lips. Lips I so badly want to taste. Moving so close that they are almost on mine, I refuse to give in first. His body feels so hot, still so familiar.

"I want you to remember this moment, Sorcha."

His voice sounds like velvet, and I can almost taste the whiskey.

"I want you to remember how much you want this, and how much I don't want you."

My eyes snap back up in recoil as his mouth twists into a cruel smile, taking half an inch backward. "Connie was right. This is alpha bullshit, isn't it?" His eyes glitter at the thought. "You just can't say no to me, can you?"

"You son of a bitch." I try to push him away, almost hissing at her name.

But Peter is on me again, pushing me against the glass, the hard planes of his body putting pressure on my soft curves. "No, no, no." He searches my face. "This is just too sweet to miss. You have to go on in this world knowing I do *not* want you. My father did *not* want you. Even this coven. Do you think they would choose you over me?"

"Stop." I bite down the lump in my throat.

He lets me go, moving away to hold up his arms, throwing his head back and cackling at the ceiling. "Shit. I haven't felt this good in weeks."

"Peter, please. I can explain... what happened with Anna."

"Don't." He moves so fast, slamming me so hard into the glass that it cracks. "You never get to say her name."

I feel the first tear slide down my face. "How can you say these things? You are my—"

"Don't!" He growls, drawing me closer again. "Don't even think about saying that word."

I squeeze my eyes shut. "I know you feel it too. No matter how hard you try, Peter, I know you do. She is not enough."

His grip squeezes. "You have no idea what she is." He pulls me tighter to him so I have nowhere else to look. "She is the only light in all my darkness... she is all the goodness I have. She is what I live for. But you, Sorcha... you have an eternity of my wrath. It will never be satisfied. You are right. We are connected in some way, and I will use it to make sure your suffering never ends. I will personally take everything from you, this coven, everything you care about. I will take it all from you."

His breaths come hard against my chest, leaving me trembling in his hands. I try to find my ability to fight back. I need to fight back, but in this moment, I have nothing. All I can do is stare into the black depths of his eyes. The violence in them is terrifying and addictive at the same time.

Just breathe.

I hear the footsteps at the same time as Peter, his eyes now traveling to the door. As soon as he sees Lily's slender frame, he takes a good step away from me, all the threat melting out of him.

Lily eyes me with curiosity as I scramble to get my top back on, then to Peter. "Am I interrupting something?" she muses.

"Not at all." He pushes his hair out of his eyes, turning to Lily with ease. "Just getting reacquainted with Sorcha after she so rudely came into my room unannounced."

My stomach ices over. "Your room? They built this for you?"

"Where else do you keep your pet god?" he says with nonchalance, shrugging and looking at Lily again. "I don't do well underground."

"So, you are Peter?" She crosses her arms at him.

"You've heard about me?" His eyes sparkle at her.

"All bad." She smirks.

"Oh, I hope so. And you are?"

"Lily." She holds out her hand for him to shake, which he takes, letting him pull her forward.

"Such a pleasure to meet a friend of Sorcha's," he tells her.

I can't seem to look away from what's happening in front of me, or Lily's easy smile for him.

Glory appears in the doorway behind her, her eyes widening at the sight of Peter, Lily's hands in his as he sends Lily of the Valley winding around her arms, much to her delight.

"What is happening here?" Her booming voice echoes around the room as she takes in the cracked window. Her eyes land hard on Peter, who takes his hands off Lily and holds them up as he walks toward her.

"They found me. I think the trip should be postponed. You know where I will be." He stops by Glory in the doorway, dipping his head to her ear. "Word to the wise. When I am here, she shouldn't be."

He walks off without another word.

Chapter Twenty Four

Connie

As I stand at the cliff edge and watch the waves crash against the island, I wonder if I could survive the fall. The Scottish sea must feel like ice. Or maybe the unnatural warm climate Peter has created here has heated it up.

I've thought about jumping before. I wonder if, somehow, he would feel it across the hundreds of miles between us.

I question where he is.

What he is doing.

I close my eyes and try to picture it.

Sometimes, I imagine him as some kind of Aztec god, standing at an altar with lines upon lines of willing sacrifices giving themselves to him. Other times, it's much more like the clearing, bloody and dirty, as he slices his way through hordes of people while they try to flee.

The truth is probably somewhere in between.

Still, I can't help being shocked how it is hundreds at a time. Or why the thought doesn't bother me that much.

I head back to the house, running my fingers over the tops of the wildflowers, petulantly knocking some of their heads off, and spotting some of my snakes basking between the poppies. I think I might join them, curl up and go to sleep in the high sun, but I hear a faint call and think I must be imagining things.

"Connie?"

I hear it again. The voice sounds familiar, something from another life.

My heart jumps into overdrive as I crouch down in the long flowers. I hear it yet again, now closer. I don't know what to do. It can't be Peter. The earth shudders every time he steps foot on this island, and besides, he only left not much more than a day ago.

Try not to panic, Connie.

I pick up the adder closest to me, and it coils around my wrist. I pray it will strike if I need it to.

"Connie?" the voice calls again.

I take a deep breath, trying to ready myself to pounce as the source of the voice rounds the corner of the house, shielding their eyes from the sun.

My heart beats double time as my brain catches up. I can't believe who is standing there, on my island. I release the snake back into the grass, and little by little, I rise from my hiding place. I don't know why, but my chest heaves and an involuntary sob leaves my lips as I run as fast as my feet will take me.

Jamie barely has chance to register it's me before the force of my body hits him. Jumping into his arms, he almost misses catching me as I wrap my arms and legs around him.

"H-how?" I stammer through my tears. "You're here? Are you really here?" I hold on so tight to him.

Jamie laughs. I feel his hands move to my ribs, trying to pry me off him. I let my feet touch the ground and take a step away, moving my hair over my eye, and look up into his familiar blue eyes. Jamie has lost the roundness in his face, and stubble adorns his chin. He looks like a man.

His eyes search my left one, not giving much away, taking in the white hair and alabaster skin. After studying me for a few moments, he reaches up and nudges my hair away from my face to see my right eye.

"Connie," he says my name again with such tenderness.

I take another step away, pushing my hair over my face again.

"Peter tried to prepare me. He said you would look different." His eyes are filled with sympathy.

I look down, noticing my earth-worn feet, the hem of my long, cream-colored dress covered in dirt, and my white hair so long it reaches my elbows and is probably full of leaves. I smooth it down—no signs of any leaves. *That's something, I guess.*

"Peter?" I say after a moment.

"Yeah. I have to admit I was surprised when he called. He said you would like to see me. I assumed you knew I was coming," he says, looking a little nonplussed at my shaky reaction.

I shake my head a little, looking at my toes. Peter didn't mention he was doing this for me. But then, I hadn't spoken to him much before he left, still in a mood about not being able to go with him.

"Connie?" Jamie brings me out of my thoughts.

"Do you want to come inside?" I ask, motioning to the house.

Not waiting for him to answer, I walk toward the back porch. I can't help but feel a tad guilty that Peter was trying to do something nice and I was ignoring him when he left. Then I catch myself and feel a little peeved at how he fills my every thought. Jamie is here. On the island. It has been so long since I've seen a friend.

Jamie is here.

It has been Peter and me for so long that I can't remember how to talk to anyone else.

Jamie follows me into the kitchen.

"Do you want something to drink? I have elderflower gin." I open the refrigerator. "Or cordial, or water. Or do you want something to eat? We have honey, from our own bees." I glance up at him to see he is hanging back in the doorway, his eyes scanning the kitchen. I do the same, active in my surveyance for the first time, noticing the large tree root emerging through the floor and the ivy growing upside down on the ceiling.

Other than that, I keep the kitchen spotless. When you have as much time on your hands as I do, cleaning becomes a hobby.

"You look so different," I tell him.

His eyes snap back to me, and the corner of his lip turn up. *I suppose I surpass him in that aspect.*

"How long has it been?"

Jamie runs a finger over a small crack in the nearby wall, his eyes curious. "Over five years." He looks back at me with something bordering reproach.

I tip my head, not wanting to acknowledge the lump in my throat. *Has it really been five years?* "Did you see Peter?"

"No, just spoke to him on the phone." He gives me a half smile. "I was so surprised when he called. I almost thought it was a trick. And then some angry Irish dude showed up at my door. After five years, I almost didn't come."

I give him a long look, making elderflower cordial and handing him a glass before retreating to the other side of the kitchen. "I'm glad you did."

He takes a long sip, not taking his eyes off me.

"You know, Peter looks different too. Weird, right? We are the immortal ones, and yet, we are the ones who look super different. You look good... the same, just a little older. The beard suits you." I haven't had a ramble in a long time. "How is everyone? Are you still in touch with Lauren?"

"Yeah." He huffs a breath out. "Actually, I married her."

That information knocks the wind out of me. "You're married?"

He nods, holding up his left hand to reveal a wedding ring on his finger. "And..." He pulls out his phone, his face beaming as he crosses the kitchen to stand next to me and show me a photo of a chubby-faced baby, who shares his same blue eyes. "Max is eighteen months now." He is brimming with pride. "And baby number two is on its way. It's early days. You are the first person I've told outside of my mum and Lauren's parents."

I look from him to the picture again, and for some reason, I want to cry. In an instant, something that feels like regret pools in my stomach. *This could have been the life I had with him. Simple. Temporary. Happy.* I gulp as I peer down at the smiling baby.

"I'm so happy for you, Jay."

"I always wanted to be a dad." His voice is full of pride. "You know... do a better job than mine did."

I nod, blinking away my tears and sitting down at the table, pulling my knees up to my chest. He sits opposite me, his eyes still wide at the sight of me. *It feels like he is drinking me in.*

"When did you get married?" I ask, needing to fill the silence.

"Almost three years ago. It was small, obviously. I would have invited you, but, you know... I had no idea how to reach you. Even Lorna had no clue."

I feel hot again. "Lorna came to your wedding?"

"Of course." He smiles. "She brought Lis too."

"You've met Lisette?"

"A few times. She was the talk of the reception. They were wild. Everyone loved Lisette, and Lorna is so happy. They're married too, you know."

I can't say anything. My breath rushes out of me. I get up out of my chair and pace the kitchen, then look in a few cupboards but find no wine. Peter always brings it home with him. I could call the mainland, but it will take hours to get here. *Screw it.* I throw open the refrigerator door and down one of the small vials of elderflower gin, which makes my eyes water all over again and has me spluttering.

"Are you okay?" Jamie asks, looking a little alarmed.

No. I am definitely not okay.

What did I expect? That the world would stand still like I did? Five whole years I haven't left my island. I've been alone with my snakes. Making gin and contemplating jumping in the sea.

For five years, I have thought about jumping into the sea.

Five years!

"Connie," Jamie says when I don't answer. "Where have you been all of this time?"

Here.

I can't say it out loud. I have been here for five years, waiting for Peter.

The earth shakes, and the foundation of the house moves. Jamie is on his feet, coming toward me, yelling, "Earthquake!" He tries to move me to safety, but I dodge his grasp and am out of the kitchen.

Peter is almost at the door when I collide into him, jumping into his arms. The vines bind around my legs and wrists as I do. Relief floods my body. It feels good to have him back, even though he shouldn't be here yet. It's only been days, and I feel that he is not laden with souls. From the open door, I see a boat—still empty —waits at the jetty behind him.

"You're back? Already?"

He nods, snaking his hands around my waist and carrying me

back to the house. "We should test the tether, right? I left Ireland, told Glory we had to postpone the mission."

"Why?" I ask as he steps over the threshold.

"Sorcha. I saw Sorcha."

I freeze, trying to wiggle out of the vines.

"Nothing happened. I just wanted to tell you." He takes my chin, stopping at the bottom of the stairs, his eyes resting on my lips. "It's just... it bought up a lot of forgotten feelings and I had to see you. I don't know what I would have done if you hadn't taken me back..." His voice trails off and when I look into his black eyes, they look so desperate, I kiss him. His hands move down my legs to push up my dress, moving dangerously close to my center as he climbs the stairs. My breath becomes hard to catch.

Until the sound of someone clearing their throat makes me stop and look down the hall.

"Jamie." This time, when I try to wiggle free, Peter lets me.

"Er... don't mind me." He gives an award chuckle as I race back downstairs to him.

"I am so sorry. I completely forgot you were here. Peter—"

His footsteps make me turn around to see him sullenly marching down the stairs. "What are you doing here?"

"Uh... you invited me." Jamie takes a step back from him.

"Well, I thought I would be gone longer. I'm back now. Can you go?"

"Are you serious?" Jamie looks from Peter to me.

"No," I tell him. "You have to stay... you just got here. How long are you staying?"

Jamie still looks uncertain, his gaze fixed on Peter. "I was planning to stay the weekend. That's what I said on the phone."

Before I have chance to reply, Peter huffs off. "Well, that is just fantastic." He marches into the kitchen, slamming the French door so hard the glass shatters all over the floor.

I glower behind him and remember I was mad at him before he left. I'm furious now. *How can he be mad? I'm the one who has missed five years being stuck here. I haven't lived in half a decade. And now he is mad my friend is here at his own request.*

"Shall I go?" Jamie peers down at me, searching my face.

"No, you should not," I say and stalk into the kitchen, making sure to march my feet all over the broken glass while trying not to wince at the pain.

Jamie follows me with cautious footsteps as we walk in to find Peter standing in front of the refrigerator, downing at least three vials of gin.

I don't say a word. Instead, I saunter past, leaving a trail of bloody footprints behind me and start slamming the empty vials around. I practically feel him rolling his eyes, until he looks down at the floor.

"Connie." He turns around swiftly and, lifting me at my waist, places me on the table, then kneels at my feet to look at all the glass shards. It's like watching an ice cube melt—all his frustration fades away as he picks the glass out of my feet. "You have to be careful, or your skin will heal over the glass." He glances up at me. "Can you please look after yourself?"

"Why?" I shrug. "You do everything for me."

He shakes his head. "We both know that's not true."

Peter takes his time picking the glass out while I watch. The concentration on his face is adorable as he pours water to clean my wounds. He notices me staring, and his eyes turn a fraction darker, and, rather than use his hands, he runs his tongue along the sole of my foot, the same healing glow there.

I bite my lip. "You're bad," I whisper.

"I know," he tells me, rising again and pushing his hips between my legs, towering over me. I thread my fingers into his hair.

Again, I am distracted by a movement near the door—Jamie trying to make his escape.

Shit. Jamie.

I keep forgetting he is here, and I feel a tad ashamed that this is literally all I have been doing for five years.

Peter lets out an audible groan, also remembering Jamie again, and moves away from me and goes to the refrigerator to retrieve more vials, drinking at least two more before returning his gaze to me. The darkness in his eyes glitters.

"I am going up, Connie. You are welcome to join me." He prowls around the table and pauses in front of Jamie, moving so close his chest is almost touching Jamie's. "You should stay. You never know... you might even enjoy yourself."

He looks back to me, giving a little eyebrow raise, and takes off upstairs, leaving Jamie in a state of shock, who has nowhere else to look except at me, then at the table.

I can't help but bite my thumb and grin. I don't think I've ever seen Jamie lost for words. I shuffle off the table and make my way over, and he shakes his head a few times, searching for the words to say. I take his hand, peering up at him through my lashes.

"You should stay. I want you to." My heart hammers in my chest as I wind my fingers into his. "For old times' sake."

I lead him out to the hall and toward the stairs, gentle and slow enough so if he wants to stop, he can. But he doesn't. He looks mildly scared, but not enough to stop.

"You okay?" I ask as we get to the top of the stairs, his eyes wandering across the vines and moss that cover the steps and walls. I can't remember when it got this much.

He doesn't say anything, only nods.

I inch open the door to our bedroom to see Peter standing by the dresser. When he sees me come in with Jamie, he gives me the most wicked grin. I try to give him a warning look. Jamie lets go of my hand, marveling at the epicenter that is our room, not much of the walls visible through the vines, hanging wisteria, and Lily of the Valley. Our room smells so sweet it is enough to make one's mouth water.

"Here..." Peter says to him, "... you might want this." He throws him a vial of gin, which Jamie catches with ease.

Looking down at it, I see the question of why forming on his lips. When Peter pulls his black T-shirt off and looks at us, exposing his tanned skin and lean frame, Jamie wastes no time in undoing the vial and downing its contents then spluttering a little.

Nerves tingle over my skin, along with the slight sensation of being a touch vexed by how Peter looks like he has achieved some great victory. Jamie stares at me as Peter moves to sit on the edge of the bed in front of us, my nerves reflected in his expression.

I eye Peter.

"Play nice," I tell him.

"I intend to," is all he says, giving me an ushering dip of the head as if to say, *"Continue."*

Although I'm not quite sure how to.

I pivot toward Jamie, whose nerves have evolved into appearing somewhat scared. I know Peter can hear my heartbeat, and I remember our hearts beat in rhythm now, so when my heart pounds, Peter's does too. That knowledge gives me confidence as I put a hand on either side of Jamie's face, making him look only at me. He is so different, but so familiar at the same time.

"Connie..." he says my name, nothing else.

The anticipation fills me, fills Peter. We take a collective breath.

"It's okay," I say, making my voice as soothing as possible. "We are going to make you feel so good." I almost can't believe the words have left my mouth, so I kiss him before I get the chance to think better of it.

It only takes him a second to relax into it, for his hands to find my waist. Despite the years, it feels the same—comforting, nostalgic. I rise onto my toes to wrap my arms around his neck and press my body to his. Pulling back, he takes a deep breath and smiles. But it falters when he realizes Peter is watching. His confidence wanes a little as Peter gets to his feet, slow, almost feline-like, and advances on us.

His black eyes are serious and fixed on Jamie.

I find myself taking my own deep breath watching as his eyes flick down to Jamie's lips before he grabs the back of his neck and crushes his lips to Jamie's.

Jamie's body tenses for a moment before relenting, his breath deepening to kiss Peter back.

I've never seen Peter kiss anyone else. A jolt passes through me as I comprehend this is what he looks like kissing me, gorgeous and deadly. Watching them is intoxicating. So sexy.

Jamie's hand slides up Peter's bare chest, and Peter stops for a moment to take my hand and pull me toward them. Turning Jamie with a touch before kissing him again, I join, placing kisses along Jamie's neck, making him gasp as the back of his legs hit the bed. We pull the T-shirt up over his head as he falls back, his eyes wide with desire and a sprinkling of fear.

Before we join him, I stop to look at Peter, who grabs my face and kisses me too. The kiss is deep and reverberating, and the Lily of the Valley comes alive and blooms within the canopy.

Giving me another devilish smile, we return our attentions to Jamie.

When I wake up, it's dark.

My head is on Peter's chest with another arm wrapped around

my waist. Jamie's arm. I glance at Peter, who is fast asleep and looking his usual gorgeous self, before wiggling around to regard Jamie, who appears so peaceful.

It feels selfish—*but oh so good*—to have Jamie with us. I trace my fingers along his features, so familiar, the home I have long left. In a way, I wish I could keep him too.

Jamie's eyes flicker open to look at me, and instinctively, I move my hand over my eye.

"You don't have to do that." He nudges my hand away.

"You were amazing," I tell him, not able to keep the grin from playing across my lips.

He regards me for a minute before looking down to realize the other hand under my neck is Peter's.

Jamie's whole face changes as he exclaims, "Shit. I did that. I can't believe I did that."

He is out of bed in a flash, frantic in his search for his clothes and causing such a commotion Peter wakes up.

"Jamie, calm down." I try to soothe him.

"What's going on?" Peter sleepily props himself up on his elbow, his hair falling into his eyes to watch Jamie flapping about the room.

Jamie stops and looks at him, the color flooding his face while he decides what to say. "I have never done this before," he says directly to Peter.

Peter gives him a smirk, fishing a rogue vial of gin off the floor. "Neither have I," he tells Jamie with a shrug.

Jamie rubs the back of his head, and it's obvious this doesn't make him feel an inch better. "I... I'm not gay," he mumbles.

Peter gives him a strange look. "Why would I care?"

Jamie rubs his eyes. "This can't be happening." He looks between us both. "I'm married."

That gets more of a reaction out of Peter. "You're married? When did that happen?" he asks, sitting up for the first time.

But Jamie has had enough of us and stalks downstairs.

Peter looks at me, raising his eyebrows as he asks, "Do I need to sort this out?"

"No." I breathe in. "Let's just give him a minute." I eye Peter as he lies back down, running his hands through his hair.

"You know, Glory will probably be here in the next few days. I might have to leave soon." He plays with the edges of my fingertips. "He can stay if you want. You know... something to keep you amused."

I can't help but be taken aback. "You heard him, he's married." Peter gives a shrug, so I add, "And he has kids."

Peter shoots up. "I didn't know that."

"Yeah, well, he does. So he can't stay. Besides, that's not what I want. I want you, Peter, to be with you."

"You know I want that too." He rolls over on his side, pushing my hair from my face. "But I also know it's possible to have feelings for two people, and I want you to be happy here."

I take his hand that is resting on my face. "I want to come with you. I want the world, Peter."

His eyes go soft. "You want the world?"

It feels like an impossible ask. "To live in it again. To be part of it. What is the point of living forever if I'm not really living?"

Peter stares at me hard for a moment, taking a deep breath. "Okay. You can leave, but you can't come with me on missions. You may be okay with it, but I don't want you to see what she has me do. That's the deal, all right?"

"Okay." I grin.

He huffs out a deep breath, letting his head fall back onto the pillow as if I will be the actual death of him. I should go check that

Jamie hasn't gorged himself on our gin store, but I pause when a thought occurs to me.

"You said you know what it feels like to have feelings for two people. You were talking about Sorcha?"

He nods, sitting up to face me. "You have to understand, it never meant I wanted you any less. I always wanted you... *will* always want *you*. Forever."

"You entered servitude for me." I smile.

"And I would again," he admits, running a hand through his hair. "I don't know. I was young and stupid, and I went about everything wrong. If I'd handled it better..." He trails off, looking down at my hand.

"You wanted us both. That's what you desired."

"Connie, it never meant I loved you less. You will always be enough."

"I know," I say gently, letting out a big breath of my own. I can't really be mad at his admission. He just slept with my ex-boyfriend and me, for heaven's sake. "With Sorcha, I'm sorry. Maybe we can—"

"No." He looks up straight away. "That is not what I am saying at all. It's different now. I can never forgive her for what she did. That is not what I am asking." He looks toward the door where Jamie left, his expression changing. "I didn't plan this. I really forgot he was here." He looks hurt. "I'm not trying to trick you into anything, Connie. We had fun, right?"

"Of course we did," I admit. "Unexpected, but fun." Peter gives me a half smile. "So, this is what you want? More of this? Not with Jamie, obviously, but you know. You don't mind if it's men?"

Peter eyes me, giving a slow shake of his head. "No, I don't mind."

I give him a little grin. I suppose we have always been so

wrapped up in each other that we've never had this conversation. "Has it always been that way for you? Women? Men?"

"Other?" Peter chuckles, sitting up a little and rubbing his head like he's never thought about it, which is typical. "Well, you and Sorcha are the only two people I've been with, and Jamie now, I suppose. My focus is pretty much one track when I want something. But I guess I don't discriminate. No."

I don't know why the thought excites me, and it seems to catch in my throat. A feeling he senses as he gathers himself up to loom over me, his knuckles pressing into the moss-filled mattress. I inch away from him a little, despite my knees making way for him, my calves sliding down his legs. "You are wild," I tell him, letting my fingers fall down his chest. "To love and to kill indiscriminately."

His darkness sparkles at the thought, and he rubs his nose along mine before kissing me. "Very poetic."

His kisses become more urgent along my neck, his hands running along my body, pulling me to him. "But you are still mine. If we do this, we only do it together," he says in my ear.

He kisses a trail down my chest, lower and lower.

"Yes," I agree.

Chapter Twenty-Five

Connie

When I wake up again, the sun is cascading through the window, catching the lilac shades of the wisteria, and Peter is in his usual sleeping position with his head on my chest.

Jamie must have slept on the sofa.

I've lost five years like this.

I run my hands through Peter's snow-white hair, over his now angular features, the ripples in his lean back. I guess five years isn't enough to have my fill of him. However, I know I am ready for a change, and it seems like a compromise has been made.

I manage to get myself out from under him without waking him up, and I throw on a long-sleeved dress and head downstairs to find Jamie. While not in the living room, it does look like he slept here. Instead, I find him sitting in the kitchen with his head in his hands.

I lean my hip against the door frame, not wanting to sneak up on him. "Are you okay? Sorry I didn't come find you last night. I must've gotten distracted."

Jamie lets out a weary breath. "Yeah, I heard."

"Sorry about that." I'm not sure if my skin is capable of blushing anymore. I enter and plonk myself in the chair opposite him, noticing he looks tired. "This is literally what I have been doing for five years. I've been here. With him."

"Huh." Jamie half smiles. "One hell of a honeymoon period."

I chuckle. "Yeah, well, he is insatiable."

The color rises in Jamie's cheeks, as he knows this fact all too well now.

I cock my head at him. "Do you want some tea?"

He nods, and as I get back up and potter around the kitchen, I feel his eyes on my back.

"You shouldn't feel guilty, Jay. It was just one time, one night of hedonism. We had fun and let's just leave it at that. You'll probably never see us again, so please don't let what happened here ruin what you have at home."

I've not faced him, but I hear his chair scrape back over the wood. "I won't see you again?"

I turn in surprise as he comes over next to me. "Jamie, I will just complicate things for you..." I start.

"You always have." He gives me a grin.

I laugh despite myself and place a hand on his chest. *How can it feel so normal to be around him after all this time?*

"I've missed you like crazy," he says. "Things are uber weird here, and you and Peter are dangerously codependent, but despite all of that, it's so good to see you."

I tilt my head and smile. "You too."

My heart does a little skip at how he is looking at me. I rise onto my toes and lean into my hand on his chest as his hands rest as light as air on my hips. My eyes flutter closed as my lips find his, light and tentative. As if fragile, like our kiss could shatter at any moment. All this time, and all these feelings, I love him. Not as much as Peter—it can never be that much. But enough for it to feel so good to have him again.

He pulls away and rests his forehead on mine with his eyes closed. I watch him, not knowing what to expect, and think about how this strange situation is affecting him. As he licks his lips, I almost feel the tumultuous emotions mixing around his head and in his heart. When I notice some of the vines shudder, I move myself away from him.

"Peter is up," I tell him and continue making the tea, leaving Jamie leaning against the counter, trying to compose himself, as Peter walks in disheveled but wearing clothes, for which I am thankful.

He crosses the kitchen and pulls me in for a quick kiss, ignoring Jamie, who doesn't know where to put himself. Peter lets me go to acknowledge Jamie, who is fidgeting all over the place. Giving him a frown, he asks, "Everything okay?"

"Yep." Jamie nods.

Peter gives me a glance as if we might need to start worrying for Jamie's sanity, but instead leaves the kitchen and goes into the garden.

I eye him as he lets out a huge breath. "Can you relax?" I chuckle.

"Is he going to kill me?" Jamie asks, his voice hushed and serious.

This makes me burst out laughing. "Of course not. That's just how he looks now. He is always serious, and he makes the earth shake, and he... I don't know. I know he is a lot to be around." I bite my lip. "You looked pretty comfortable with him yesterday."

"Connie..." he starts.

"What? It was hot," I tease, handing him his tea and earning myself an eye roll.

"You two are weird."

I playfully nudge my hip against him in response.

The backdoor swings open as Peter comes in carrying a large slab of honeycomb and sliding it onto the table, a few stray bees following him. He snaps off a piece, holding it to me as I pass him his own tea.

"Smell this." He holds the small comb under my nose, the honey already running down to his wrist. "Smells like the lavender you planted."

I breathe it in. It does. His eyes stay fixed on me as I bite the honeycomb out of his hand.

Wow. It tastes like it too.

"That's gorgeous," I tell him.

"I know." He licks the honey off his thumb while sitting down at the table, then breaks off more of the honeycomb and eats it. The combs crunch in his teeth as the golden honey coats his hands and slides down his chin.

I have a sense of jealousy of the honeycombs being devoured by him, how he greedily licks his fingers as he eats. *How ridiculous, to feel jealous of honey.* After a moment, he looks up, glancing from me to Jamie. Jamie is also intently watching him eat. Maybe not so ridiculous because Jamie also looks like he wants to be honeycomb.

Peter shoots a questioning look from Jamie back to me. I give him a little shrug. Some things never change. It amazes me that Peter still does not realize the effect he has on those around him. How mesmerizing it is to watch him eat the sweet treat. Peter gets to his feet, slow and cautious, snapping off some more comb and approaching Jamie, who appears to be frozen again.

"You want to try some?" Peter asks, his voice low and smooth.

I know, in a way, he is attempting to make himself not threatening. The result is somewhat seductive.

Jamie doesn't say anything. He swallows hard.

Peter glances at me, but I am as intrigued as Jamie to see what

Peter will do. He looks down, drawing his first two fingers along the inside of the comb, coating them, before pushing them into Jamie's mouth.

Jamie's hands grip the counter until his knuckles are white, and I know that feeling. *Boy do I know that feeling.* He makes a small noise of satisfaction at the delicious treat. Peter's dark eyes on him, my own mouth watering, I take his other hand, still coated, and bring his fingers to my lips too to suck all the honey from them. Peter's chest rises as he leans his head back in pleasure. He closes his eyes for a moment before his fingers grip my face, bringing me closer. I think he is about to kiss me when the kitchen door flies open with a loud crack.

Glory and Gareth are standing in the doorway, their eyes taking in the presumably strange sight of Peter's hands covered in honey, his fingers in mine and Jamie's mouths.

It is only a second before he takes them away.

"Erm... can you give me a minute?" he asks Glory.

It's the first time in the five years I have known Gareth to look even a tad amused.

Glory, not so much.

"You left. And you stole a boat." She enters the kitchen, walking around our table as Peter positions himself in front of Jamie and me. "I did not say you could do that."

I hear the smirk in Peter's voice when he replies, "But you didn't say I couldn't do it either."

Glory stares at him for a long time, her eyes hard and unforgiving. I don't think she has ever set foot in this house. "I agree to your terms," she says after a moment's pause. "When you are in Meath, Sorcha will not be."

Peter eases his stance.

"But no more stealing. Not here. The locals will notice."

"That's fair," he agrees.

She glances at Gareth, who doesn't seem too bothered by Peter's absconding but *is* looking at Jamie and me rather curiously. "Time to go, Peter," he says, nodding his head toward the door.

"I need five minutes," Peter tells him.

Gareth raises his eyebrows before shifting them back in my direction. "Is that all?"

"Oh, you're a comedian now?" Peter spits back at him.

Gareth laughs, looking between all three of us and leaving the house, followed by Glory.

Peter takes a deep breath, turning back to Jamie and me. But Jamie speaks first, "I know that guy."

"Yeah, he's a dick," Peter tells him before focusing on me. "I have to go. I said you can come, but next time. I need to speak to Glory about what she can do to keep you safe when I am not around."

I open my mouth to argue, cut off when he turns to Jamie next. "Jamie, you are welcome to stay. Longer, I mean, if you want."

Jamie looks between us. "I-I can't," he stutters, turning to me. "Connie, I can't leave Lauren and Max. I'm sorry."

"You have nothing to be sorry about. You should go." I rub his arm.

It doesn't take them long to collect their things. Before they board Glory's boat, Peter kisses me goodbye and Jamie pulls me in for a long hug.

Peter never looks back when he leaves, but Jamie does. Standing at the back of the boat, his lifts his arm to wave at me.

I don't think I will ever see him again.

———

Alone again.

The brightness of the sun seems fake.

The house feels even more empty.

I make more gin. I eat strawberries. I lie in the bath watching the strands of my white hair floating around my shoulders. I time how long I can hold my breath.

Then a thought occurs to me, and I push myself upward, out of the bath, and run through the house and out into the garden, all the way to the end of the island.

I don't stop and think.

I simply throw myself as far as I can.

Off the cliff edge and straight into the icy Scottish waters.

It's so cold it takes my breath away.

I splutter to the surface while the waves crash around me and notice that the cliff face from this angle looks so much higher. I struggle to bring my breathing under control.

Oh shit, Connie, what have you done?

I force my limbs into action, swimming back toward the rock to find a place to climb up, but I slip on the jagged rocks and fall into the water again.

My teeth chatter together so hard I think they might break when my body hits the freezing water.

For a second, I think I see a flash of white hair on the top of the cliff but decide I must be seeing things. I swim as hard as I can along the coastline of the island until I find a gap low enough for me to climb up, the sharp rocks cutting into my hands and feet. At last, I heave myself over the cliff, naked, crying and covered in blood.

Lying in the sun-soaked grass, I bawl. *I am so unbelievably stupid.*

When I can cry no more, I roll up onto my knees and limp back to the house. Bloody, dirty footprints follow me as I whimper through the kitchen, taking a cardigan off the chair and wrapping it around my bruised, cut-up body. I start to cry again. I only hope these are all healed by the time Peter is home so I don't have to tell him about how stupid I've been.

A flash of movement catches my eye and, before I know it, I am being thrown into the wall of the hallway. I don't even have time to cry out as my bare feet stumble over all the shattered glass I haven't cleaned up yet.

Two vice-like hands grip my arms and slam me over and over into the wall, and the house shakes and creaks. I can't see through my tears, the pain in my arms and back as I hit the wall is excruciating. Everything has happened so fast. Blood fills my mouth, and I realize I must have bitten my tongue.

"Why you? Why *you?*" a voice hisses at me. Their vice-like grip moves from my arms to around my throat, cutting off my air supply.

I struggle to breathe. Using my now free arm to try and grab them, I manage to connect, my nails landing in flesh. When I shake my hair back, I see the rage-filled silver eyes of Sorcha staring into me. Choking me.

I'm not strong enough. I claw at her hands. I can't even make any words to tell her to stop, or that Peter will kill her. Out of the corner of my eye, I see one of my adders writhing along the floor and reach my toes out toward it, praying it will come to my aid. Closing my eyes under the pressure, I feel its smooth skin wrap up my leg, traveling under my cardigan and out of my sleeve, clamping its fangs hard into Sorcha's arm. She yelps, taking a step back and throwing my snake across the room. I almost cry out to it, but all I can do is land in a heap on the floor and gasp for breath.

I am on my own.

Sorcha straightens up to look down at me. She looks exactly the same as the last time I saw her, beautiful and powerful, and like she hates every inch of me.

"Look at what he has done to you." She heaves me up by the

front of my cardigan, this time resting me against the wall. Her hand pushes my wet hair back to examine my snake eye. Shaking her head in contempt, she asks, "Why are you so special? You are not built to be loved this way, with so much violence."

I pant.

Why today? Why when I am all cut up from the rocks?

"He's not like that. Not with me," I say, breathless, through gritted teeth.

Sorcha laughs, a real laugh, like I am being funny. "Just look at yourself, Connie." She shoves a handful of my white hair in my face. "Look at what you are. Are you really so stupid?" She presses hard on me, and I turn my face, trying to escape her, wishing I wasn't wearing only my cardigan and that my feet were not cut so bad I can hardly stand. "He should be mine," she seethes into my ear. "He is *my mate*. He was *made for me*. You know that, right? If you would just die, he would see that."

I force myself to look at her, the fury in her eyes, and I don't know how to stop it. For the first time, I notice the burn marks on her neck.

I will not go down cowering against a wall.

I grab the scar tissue, causing her to wince. "It is you who is burned, Sorcha," I get out through my teeth. "Do you think he will ever forgive you?"

"He will understand. Eventually." She presses, biting the air by my face. "When you are gone, he will understand. It is better to be whole."

But I see a fraction of doubt in her eyes. I try to give a sure smile, as much as I can through the pain, claiming, "I am the *only one*." I grimace at her. "I am the *only one* who loves him without any fear. I see you, and you are so fucking scared of him. You are pathetic."

Sorcha growls at me, forcing her forearm against my neck and her knee into my abdomen. All I can do is claw at her face like a wild animal. *Please, help,* I think. Some of the snakes climb down and wrap around me, hissing at her. She looks savage, grabbing some of them off and throwing them to the floor, but there is not enough, and the pressure on my neck is too much.

My head is getting light.

My vision blurs.

She shrieks at another bite.

But it is not enough.

The earth shakes.

The house creaks, and the vines around me come alive.

I drop to the floor. Coughing, clutching my throat, stars in my eyes, I push my back to the wall, looking around for her, expecting her to be on me again any second.

I push my hair away in time to see Peter's fist collide with her chest, sending her flying to the wall. The house vibrates, some of the concrete dusting the floor of the hall as they pummel each other. The vines back in their place, another punch cracks across her face like thunder, and Sorcha is losing. A kick to her abdomen sends her hurtling toward me, stopping just short. Then Peter is standing above her. Hit after hit, the flat packing sound of knuckles on skin, until the blood from his knuckles splatters my face.

He draws his fist back again.

"Peter, stop," I shout, his fist freezing an inch from her face.

His chest heaving, he notices me for the first time. The cold look in his eyes softens as he takes me in—completely sodden, crumpled against the wall with only my thin cardigan wrapped around me, cut up, and covered in blood. The snakes, which are hovering close by, hiss as he moves toward me. His eyes are all over my body, his hands running over my skin, feeling all the wounds there, the cuts from the rocks, the bruising around my neck and abdomen from Sorcha. His expression becomes feral and furious.

He scoops me up in his arms as Glory and Gareth appear in the doorway, surveying the bloody scene. Glory's eyes widen when she sees Sorcha's bloody form clutching at consciousness.

I stay in Peter's arms. I know now that he will never leave me here again as he addresses Glory.

"She has no idea what she has just done," he tells her, stepping over Sorcha and taking me upstairs. "I want you *all* out of my fucking house."

Chapter Twenty-Six

Peter

Under the flashing lights of the darkened nightclub, Connie dances like her life depends on it. From my place at the bar, she looks like an angel, a beacon of light in the sea of darkness. The pure white of her skin and hair shines under the artificial light, her glittering white dress blending with her skin. The only things standing out are the solid gold cuff in the shape of a snake around her wrist and the ruby-encrusted patch over her right eye.

The bodies around her stay close, and so many gazes travel toward her, some with desire, some with confusion when they catch the shimmer of her snakeskin markings when the light hits just right.

I stay hidden in the shadows, for now.

The changes in the world have not been lost on her or the effect I have on it. How the crowds of the busy Florence streets part as I walk through, a human instinct to avoid me. The weight of my gravity so heavy now, I naturally push out an orbit everywhere I go. People try to maintain their distance until they are forced to cross the event horizon, then there is no turning back.

Of course, Connie now carries no trace of the attack. The same night she received them, I healed all her cuts and bruises, held her under the soothing water of the shower, washed the blood away, and cradled her until she didn't shake anymore.

I stayed by her side until she fell asleep.

Only when the snakes make their way out of the canopy and set up their beds for the night in the crook of her arm or wrapped around an ankle do I leave and make my way back down to Glory's boat. At some point, Glory or Gareth had cleaned up the blood and glass from the floor. I suspect Gareth.

As I round on the boat, I see him standing outside, his back to the island, looking out to the mist-filled sea. It's a starless night. He turns around to face me at the creaking of the jetty, no longer looking so spiteful, but calm and careful.

"She must have followed us when we left to come and get you. I am sorry, Peter. It was not something we anticipated. Sorcha has not been with the coven for four years. I did not think she would come back. Classic bad timing. I would never have brought you back to Meath if I knew she was there. Glory has a soft spot for her, but I was glad to be rid of her."

I give a simple nod, not expecting Gareth to be so reasonable. In fact, I'd been surprised when he turned around to follow me when I knew something was wrong back here on the island.

Talk about testing the tether.

Glory was furious when I turned around, although I can't remember her giving me a direct command to stop. Strange that it

261

was Gareth who understood when I said something was wrong with Connie, and I had to go. I could have sworn a look of concern for Connie's safety had flashed across his face. He followed and, when he did, Glory did too. Maybe he always suspected Sorcha would try something like this.

"What will you do with her?" I ask him.

"She is bound now." He smirks. "She's not like you. She won't escape the bindings. Unless, that is, you want to kill her? I am sure I can distract Glory, if that is what you want."

The hatred sparkles in his dark eyes, the heat there catching, and I step into the boat so I draw level with him. Gareth, sharing my height, meets my gaze exactly, almost willing me to accept the challenge so he can watch Sorcha's demise. The sheer fantasy of what I might do to her spirals through me.

"You are a hateful creature, aren't you, Gareth?" I advance on him.

He barks out a laugh, his mouth twisting into a lopsided grin, and I don't recall ever seeing him smile before. "You know what she thinks you are to her, right? Your father was one twisted son of a bitch."

Anger flares in my chest as he matches my movement, his rage-filled eyes meeting mine.

He doesn't flinch. "Don't you ever wonder, Peter? Why you are what you are, while Sorcha is so weak? He made you to be a pair, to be the strength in each other. He was hoping to topple governments with you both, but I have watched you blow volcanoes and move the surface of the earth like it is nothing. Your destruction knows no limits. You are so much more than what even he meant for you to be."

I cock my head at him. "Gareth, if I didn't know better, I would think you are starting to like me."

"I can't lie... I am intrigued by you."

I glower at him for a moment, and he returns my stare. It's difficult to tell the color of his eyes for the fire in them. However, his body betrays him the slightest as he moistens his lips.

I twist my face into a sneer as I draw a fraction closer. "Have you thought about it, Gareth? Have you found yourself wondering about all the ways I could make you scream into a pillow?"

He says nothing. Only his rage ripples against my skin and, in this moment, I so want to howl with laughter. Because I am not sure if he wants to kiss me or stab me, and I kind of like it. Whether he likes it or not, I get under his skin.

I can only imagine how much it would test the tether if Connie and I took him to bed. I wonder if Glory would think of it as a betrayal. I wonder what I could do with all his rage.

The cabin doors open, and Glory joins us on the deck.

"I thought I heard you two talking." Glory rubs her head with a weary hand. "Peter, let's take a break. Gareth and I will take Sorcha back to Meath, and we will hold her there until we decide what do to next."

Gareth continues to smolder at me, but I give Glory a nod and climb out of their boat.

"We'll be leaving this house," I tell her. "I won't leave Connie here again. Glory, we need a plan for her protection while I am on missions. That's the one thing she can't see. I won't have her see that."

. . .

Glory gave me a funny look but agreed to my request. Two days later, Gareth was back to collect us and was decidedly quiet, not looking at me. I felt his fury simmering under the surface as he drove us to the mainland and then to the airport. I'd watched him in his rearview mirror, staring at the road ahead without a backward glance, as Connie chatted away, full of excitement while looking out of the windows at the passing countryside.

Only when we arrived at the airport did he acknowledge us, throwing Connie a small black velvet box.

"It's from Glory." He grunted out the words as she opened it to discover a ruby-encrusted eye patch. "We'll be in touch," was all he said to me.

Florence is where we ended up, and Connie seems happy.

A shopping trip and a meal later, I found myself in a night club. A band Connie liked happened to be playing, so I talked us in, and now I'm watching Connie in a sea of people once more.

I can't help but think of Gareth's words. *Why* am *I so much more?* Then I think of Connie's words, how she wants the world. I close my eyes for a moment against the thump of the music, thinking of Gareth's eyes smoldering into mine, the sight of Jamie's hands on Connie's body.

A rotting feeling slides under my skin.

Time to move.

I get to my feet, taking my time in my approach, the crowd parting as I make my way to her, my posture stiff through the movement of bodies. Many eyes follow me, probably noting how I look the opposite of her, dancing on her toes in a glittering white dress while I am tall and heavy in my uniform of black.

Noticing me, she reaches up to wrap her arms around my

neck. Moving against me, she is oblivious to the eyes on us. But I can't relax—that rotting feeling flares and sinks into my stomach.

Something is very, very wrong with me.

"Tell me what you want," I purr into her ear.

She beams up at me, turning her back to my chest to dance against me, my hands running greedily over her hips.

"Do you mean *who* I want?" She smiles.

I chuckle into her ear. "Okay, who do you want?"

She looks around as she sways her hips against mine and reaches up to run her hands through my hair. "Who do you want?" she asks after a moment.

Connie wants the world, and I don't know how to give it to her. I spin her so she is facing me again. "Let me give something to you. You just have to tell me what."

"Peter." She puts her hand on my chest, slowing her dancing. "You can stop feeling guilty about what happened with Sorcha. It's not your fault."

"That's not what this is about."

Except, *is* that what this is about?

Having her back in the world feels confusing. Living in this world feels alien even to me. The last five years have been missions and the island. Death and love. The rot of Glory's tether eating away at me. I am not human. I don't know how to be.

Something in my face must give it away because Connie reaches up and strokes my cheek. "Let's get out of here."

She leads me out of the club and into the warm, crowded street, watching me with a guarded expression. "Are you okay?" she asks after a while. "Have I done something wrong? You seem on edge."

I hold on tight to her hand. "I guess I need to adapt again too. I don't know how to do this anymore."

Connie clicks her tongue. "I'm glad I'm not the only one. It's a bit overwhelming to be around so many people again. It feels like I might understand a little of what you felt when you and Anna first came to Wixford. You know, very little."

"You're right. It was like this but times by a thousand. I'll get used to it again."

"Right." She seems to float next to me, and I think she might drift away if I am not careful. "But, maybe we should call it a night?"

I agree, and we make our way back to our hotel. Our room is luxurious but almost clinical-feeling. I now associate Connie with snakes and hanging vines, not high thread counts and king-sized beds. I try to work out what she's thinking as she runs her fingers across the sheets, moving to the window to look out at the well-lit street below. I stand with my back to the door and watch as she regards herself in the mirror in front of the bed, so polished it casts a glow in the moonlight.

I can't place my finger on what is wrong. A quietness between us seems to be stretching out, like an ocean, over the last couple of days.

After a few minutes of staring at her reflection, Connie pulls off the eye patch and turns back to me. "Do we need to talk? You have been so quiet of late, and so much seems to have happened... with Jamie and Sorcha. Even Gareth seemed off. Are we okay?"

"Of course," I tell her, the feeling of poison rising in my blood. I don't know how to articulate the words.

"You haven't really touched me since you healed me. Is it something to do with Sorcha?"

"No." I stay at my place by the door. "I don't know."

Connie dips her head, looking at her feet and wiggling her sandals off. We fall into silence again. *Maybe I feel edgy because of the postponement of the mission.* They have been regular—every four months—for years. *Perhaps I need to snatch one soul to take the edge off. Maybe that will curb the rot.* Glory won't know if I take one soul, not at her command—*the tether is weak.*

One sweet soul.

The tether is weak.

I should test the tether.

My head feels like it's swimming.

Will one soul be enough? Maybe I should claim a few. It couldn't hurt.

"Peter. Are you feeling okay?" Connie is right in front of me, her green eyes searching.

The heat flares under my skin. "I don't know," I answer. "I think something is wrong with me. Being here, I feel out of sync. I don't know... maybe it's been too long since I have been on mission. Or maybe it's being away from the island. I'm not sure." My breathing quickens, and I close my eyes to lean my forehead to hers. It feels so cool. "Connie, I don't know what to do."

She looks at me hard, sliding her hands onto my chest. "You could make this place look more like home," she suggests.

I place my hand on the wall, not moving away from her, letting the vines climb there. It's small, but it makes a difference as I begin to relax, letting them cover some of the room like extensions of myself. Using my other hand to pull her closer, I push my palm up her back to find her skin, winding Lily of the Valley into her hair. Moving my head to breathe it in.

So sweet, like home.

She's like home.

"I'm so sorry, Connie," I tell her and try to breathe.

"Stop. You don't need to be sorry." She holds me close, and her skin feels so good on mine, so cool, quenching me.

The vines extend, covering the wall and up onto the ceiling. I roll my head down onto her shoulder. *I could hold onto her forever.* "Tell me what to do, Connie," I whisper.

Her skin ripples underneath me as she pushes me back to hold me at arm's length. "Just kiss me. Kiss me until you feel better."

I stop the tide of vines and flowers and move my hands to her face. Grasping on as hard as I can without hurting her, I work my mouth against hers, the tension finally ebbing away.

Thinking only of her, of her lips on mine.

That she is mine.

Even out in this world, she is still mine.

I need to cling to that.

I kiss her, my tongue exploring her mouth. I can't stop. Everything else is melting away.

"Peter..." She gasps while pulling away from me. "I need you to touch me now."

Feeling more in control at last, I move my hands, picking her up to wrap her legs around me. My kisses travel down her neck as she throws her head back, and we both fall onto the bed.

"Tell me again." I moan into her ear. "Tell me it's only me."

"It's only you, Peter." She gasps.

"I adore you," I tell her over and over again. Into her skin. Into her mouth. Everywhere. I want to be everywhere.

Through the night, the room transforms while the vines coil around us. Flowers bloom all over the room, from the Lily of the Valley in Connie's hair that grows into the mattress, while Jasmine works into the window frames, and the floorboards creak with orange lily. When the sun comes up, and I take the first deep breath since the attack, our room looks more like an Italian woodland than a hotel suite.

While following Connie through Florence, we consume everything in sight. Rather than death and destruction, it is sex and abundance, saturating ourselves with prosecco and amaretto, and meeting strangers in bars we like the look of.

We drink and make them fall in love with us. Never with influence—simply with what we are. Different and consumed by each other, we saturate into their pores until they are drunk on us.

At first only men, and then women too, or anyone who catches our fancy or who are intrigued enough by us to come close.

The time ticks slowly by.

In the day, Connie sits by the Fountain of Neptune in the Piazza della Signoria while I watch her. I can't take my eyes off her —she fills my vison. Is she okay? Is she happy? What does she need? Sometimes she tries to remind me to look up and around, to appreciate the beautiful sights Florence has to offer, ancient and glorious. But nothing compares to her. I feel myself doing it, moving possessively around her, watching every moment, every glint of the sun off her skin, the way the corners of her mouth pull up when she catches me.

To consume and be consumed.

Sometimes she notices what is on the television—a nation devastated by a long-dormant volcano now alive once more. The lingering effects of a power plant meltdown caused by an earthquake. Nations recovering from tsunamis, wildfires, tornadoes, and rising sea levels. Her eyes widen at me. *"Yes,"* I confirm. *"It is me, all me."* My numbers are not in the hundreds or even thousands. More like hundreds of thousands.

The hotel creaks under the orange lily that now cascades everywhere, through the floors and reception, the Jasmine taking over the windows. The people outside wonder at it as they pass, my influence making them forget as soon as they are out of sight.

Connie's fingers trace the edges of the lily's petals, and I feel the reverberations around my skin. One of the Italian men we have slept with comes back to the hotel for us. She watches my hands on him, touching her own lips as I kiss him before she joins us. He becomes a nightly fixture. I think his name is Marco.

The hotel creaks and sways, the flowers climbing right up to the roof, weighing heavy on the structure.

The time passes.

Quietly, I watch Connie as she sightsees during the days. Then, the night is alive as we make love to Marco. The scent of so much Jasmine fills the city.

Until the time comes and the ribbon on my wrist burns hot.

The next morning, Glory is in the foyer of the hotel.

Chapter Twenty Seven

Peter

"**T**ime to go," Glory tells me, the corner of her mouth twitching slightly.

I eye her with suspicion. "Where is Gareth?"

She cocks an eyebrow. "I thought I would come instead. I didn't think you would be disappointed not to see him."

I shrug.

"He'll meet us at the airport. Besides..." she looks around at the flora-filled lobby, "... I had to come and see what is happening. The witches we stationed here for Connie's protection are fascinated by what you are doing." She traces a finger over a nearby orange lily. "What is it that you are doing here?"

I glance around at the hotel. It now looks like it's been reclaimed by a forest. Putting my hands into the pockets of my jeans, I'm not sure what to tell her. Because creating life feels good, not the terrible adrenaline of killing, but sensual and calming. The deaths make me high, to take so much, but when I give, there's a different type of ecstasy to enjoy.

I shrug, tapping my finger on the lily she touched and turning

271

it to ash. "You would have me destroy it all. Death is not my only gift, Glory."

Glory's eyes turn a shade darker. "You think me a monster?"

"It takes one to know one," I tell her, not meeting her gaze.

"Jakarta, for two weeks. I'll wait outside while you say goodbye to her and, um... whomever else you have up there," she adds with a smirk.

I roll my eyes. Obviously, the witches stationed in Florence have been reporting back everything they see. Including Connie's and my nocturnal habits.

My goodbye with Connie is short and sweet. She is too sleepy to say a proper goodbye. I hesitate but do leave Marco in bed with her. At least she will have someone to occupy her while I am gone.

The travel to Jakarta is uncomfortable. My skin feels tight. This is the first time I've left Connie since the attack, and my mind constantly wanders back to her.

What is she doing? Is she doing Marco? What if she's still roaming the streets at night—no, she wouldn't do that. We only do that together.

The thoughts make my head fuzzy. I feel agitated that Gareth is not talking to me.

Hateful prick.

I don't know why I care, but it annoys the hell out of me. It doesn't take long for me to start fantasizing about the different ways I could kill him.

The witches seem nervous. When I am not close, Glory whispers into Gareth's ear, and I'm curious about what she is saying.

Has Gareth aged a bit since he has been my handler?

I wonder how many unnatural years his witch life has granted him. How, in five years of knowing him, I have asked him so little about himself.

Five years.

Why did Glory come for me on her own this time? Gareth always comes for me.

The rot sets in like poison. I feel it twisting around my organs. Pulling at me.

The witches watch me.

The murderous voice in my head tells me I could test the tether by slaughtering them all.

Test the tether.

Test the tether.

We should test the tether.

Connie's words rattle around my brain.

I want the world.

Her lips on Jamie, Marco. Me.

Connie's green snake eye.

Dipping her pale fingers into the cool waters of the Fountain of Neptune. So fragile.

My Connie.

My Connie.

"Peter." Gareth's hand shoves my shoulder from behind, and I hear him hiss into my ear, "Get your shit together, you fucking psychopath."

I peer around and realize I am on a beach, looking out toward an enchanting island. Glory stands on the shoreline about ten feet in front of me, the waves breaking over her boots.

I adjust my head back a fraction. "I don't remember getting here," I whisper to him.

"I don't know what is wrong with you, but you need to get it together. Focus on the mission," he whispers back, glancing at Glory and moving away.

Instinct now tells me he is not supposed to be talking to me.

I glimpse back to the island Glory is staring at, then catch on that she is talking as she turns to look at me. "Maybe a tidal wave? It only needs a few hundred."

I flex my neck. The moon is in a good place for one. I close my eyes and welcome the feeling of the moon's gravity against me. It's better by the water. As I pull my hands back, the tide Glory is standing in moves with me like a symphony. *I could play these waters like Mozart.*

"How about a tsunami?" I offer, the tremors of excitement passing through me while I churn the water around her.

"A tidal wave is enough. The population is only about ten thousand or so."

I heave a long, slow breath out. The tether is *so* weak, and my power is *so* strong. I shake my head, then find myself rounding on Gareth and giving him my biggest grin, which must be bordering on maniacal. His answering expression is part warning, part annoyance, and he shakes his head a fraction.

"I am going to take that island," I tell him, the certainty of my actions becoming more clear and the waves of excitement coursing up my legs like electricity.

In a heartbeat, I wade past Glory, who commands, "Peter, no. The wave is enough. A few hundred is all you will take."

It is a direct command—I can hear it in her voice—but I definitely do not care. The tether is too weak to stop me. I raise my fist, gathering my strength up through my legs and into my arm. All this power. I push against the rot. I want this island, and I won't stop until it is gone and everyone is dead, dead, dead.

"Peter, stop," she yells, and I'm kind of aware of Gareth pulling her back as I release, slamming my fist into the ground.

The ground shakes and cracks. The waters swell, pulling back the beginnings of my tsunami. Terrible and beautiful, my breath leaves me, and I know I am going to throw myself into it.

Her face is furious when I look back. "I guess I will see you back in Ireland," I say with a smirk.

It's the last thing I say to her before I launch myself into the water and set off in the island's direction.

Now, there are no more thoughts, only the consuming need to claim every last one of the ten thousand souls who reside here and then send the whole island to the depths of the ocean.

I ride the swell of the sea and get dragged ashore. Getting to my feet, people are already fleeing inland, their cries loud over the chaos of the wave taking out their boats and cars. The wave is like an extension of me. In a quick jerk of my shoulders, I call the souls already claimed, and they fly through the air, hitting my body as I walk. I dig my nails into my forearm, wincing at the temporary pain of tearing my own flesh off. Those who notice the unnatural sight of the white glow of souls hitting my skin won't have long. As the souls hit, I feel my pupils shiver and contract.

Ten thousand souls.

I have never taken so many at one time.

It's like an overdose, coming on so strong my knees almost buckle.

My small blade now in my hand, I'm feeling righteous. Slashing at random passers-by trying to flee. To love and to kill indiscriminately, just as Connie said, a symphony of blood and water. I throw my hands toward the island, bringing forward another terrible wave, sending more people into my path to slice my way through.

The blood splatters.

The souls hit me.

Over and over.

I am death.

I am the dark and terrible night.

A black hole, hungry and insatiable, ready to eat everything in sight.

So many claimed by the water and my knife, but neither can go quick enough. I know what to do. I bite down hard on my lip and taste the blood. Stopping my slashing to stand still for a moment, I raise my hands to the skies. Feeling the gentle pull of the moon, I slam both fists into the ground, breaking a few of my fingers, which will heal all too soon. The wet asphalt cracks, and people around me fall through, deep into the earth, their screams like a symphony of music vibrating through my muscles.

Keeping my stance, I pull the waters to me, crashing them over the island, roaring inland, taking sacrifice after sacrifice as the island starts sinking. The water covers everything until, eventually, the wall of ocean hits me too. Pushing me, crushing, farther, deeper and deeper as the whole island sinks, along with every single person on it.

The noise of the sinking earth is unlike anything I have ever heard. Colossal. What I would imagine it sounds like when a meteor hits the Earth. The weight of the souls continues to hit, pulling me farther and farther, my skin illuminating under strain, contrasting with the crushing pressure of the water.

Until I am glowing.

To die. *Oh, to die.* Instead, I will sit bloated at the bottom of the ocean for a millennia until, maybe, I am discovered like a long-forgotten artifact. My muscles atrophied with the loss of oxygen, yet preserved like the bodies in Pompeii.

I sink farther and deeper while the souls continue to hit.

It's so dark now, and I'm not sure if my eyes are closed or not.

I am glad for the crushing feeling.

To lose myself to the darkness.

Chapter Twenty-Eight

Sorcha

It's been weeks, maybe months, when the door of my cell creaks open, revealing a sliver of Glory in the doorway. She looks tired, more so than I have ever seen her. Her hair is as flat as her countenance, her eyes dull from sleepless nights.

I've been left here to rot. Glory never thought to give me a direct order as I've never been much of a threat. She certainly made her choice when she locked me here in the coven's cells. She'd told me she would decide what to do with me when she got back. I'd heard Gareth saying I should be left to rot for a hundred years. His hatred for me has grown over time—the bile festered after Rue's death. Maybe she was more to him at one point. He always looked up to her power. Maybe he grew on her too—maybe they were something to each other when Glory sent her to destroy Peter.

Maybe that is why he hates me so much.

Although part of me suspects that, witch or no, there is only a certain amount of time you can be around Peter before you start to love him. The power drips out of him and infects everything. It

277

only took me one meeting, one lick, one hand on my throat to be driven mad by him again.

And now, I have been locked up.

For the good of everyone.

Glory appears exhausted, but there is still a fraction of defiance flaring in her eyes as she looks at me in the dim light of the cell.

"There is something you should see," she says simply, nodding her head for me to follow her.

So, I obey and she leads me down winding corridor after winding, deserted corridor.

Where is everyone?

The halls feel hollow, and Glory's silence is haunting.

We draw near the corridor where my room is situated, and a dread feeling creeps into my stomach, making its home there, when I see Gareth standing by my closed door.

His eyes are so hateful like he would burn me alive if he could. When he opens his mouth, his words are venom.

"Every action has a reaction, Sorcha." He shakes his head a fraction. "Why is it always others who pay the price?"

Glory shoots him a stern look but doesn't offer any words of reproach. My mouth is like sand. I can't talk, and I desperately don't want to know what is behind that door.

"He is under control again, for now," Glory tells me, her voice also laced with simmering anger. "But your little stunt has put everything at risk. Years of work, of fine balance, now all on a knife's edge."

However, her words seem a distant echo as I reach for the door ever so slowly. A terrible, awful feeling claws at me. I know I don't want to see. But I *have* to see.

Gareth steps back so I can have full view of my room. It is no longer earthy and comforting but painted crimson, smelling like tainted copper. I can't see at first, can't quite make out what I am looking at.

There's just red.

So much red.

Then, I spot a clump of stringy blonde hair, stuck like glue to the dresser. As I move into my room, my feet slip on something. Slimy. Gooey. When I slide, I realize it's skin. The hammer comes crashing down with the understanding of not *what* this is, but *who* it is, and they are everywhere.

The noise doesn't come from my mouth but my chest. Feral. It's more than a scream, more than terror. My feet take me backward, and I slip in the pooling of Lily's blood. There is so much blood. And flesh. So much so there isn't even a body to clutch onto.

I careen back into Gareth and Glory.

I cannot breathe.

I've never seen such horror.

Only Glory clutches onto me, sliding down the wall to cradle me in her arms. I have no words. I am only grief.

And acceptance.

This is what he threatened—that he would take everything from me. It's his only promise to me, to make me suffer. I should have known this was coming, but I never expected it to be so cruel.

So savage.

I cry in Glory's arms. Defeated. Done. I should have left his pet alone.

Lily is dead because of *me*.

She suffered unspeakable torture because of *me*.

"Were there others?" I get out between gasps.

"Yes." Gareth's voice is ice. "But Lily was the only one mutilated. Lily was personal." His tone carries blame, which I deserve with all that I am.

I sob, clutching onto Glory's arm. She strokes my hair like I'm a child once more. "How?" I make out, my voice on the verge of shattering. "How did this happen?"

Glory doesn't answer straight away, but I feel her turn her face to Gareth. Something is wrong. I look up into Gareth's furious face once more, his visage now set.

"How could he do this to the coven? I thought the tether protected them," I press, regaining some composure.

Gareth stalks away from me, dragging his hand down his face.

"Sorcha, the tether." Glory's voice shakes and cracks. When I look at her, her face is white, a sheen of sweat glistening there. "We did what we had to, but the tether..."

Oh my God.

Glory continues, "The tether was not possible. He was already too strong to be held. It was a trick. It's all been a trick."

"No." The word gargles in my mouth. "No!" I bury my face in my hands. "No. He has been doing your bidding for five years."

"He believes what he wants to believe. So he can blame me for the bloodshed. He needs to be controlled. He acts on my commands to protect the girl."

Rage bubbles out of my lips and I scream. So loud the ground shakes, the earthen walls crumbling dust at our feet. I cry out until I am spent, bringing my forehead to rest on my knees.

"You fools," I whisper. "We are all such fools. And Morgan?"

"There was a spell," Glory tells me. "A tracer spell so I will always know where he is. Morgan made it look like something more than it was. She put the fail-safe in place so he would never test the tether." Glory glances toward Gareth. "He is becoming unstable, though. There won't be any more missions. We need to regroup. He will not break away with the fail-safe in place."

I blink at Glory. "What is the fail-safe?"

"We cannot use it. If we lose the girl, then we are all lost."

I've never seen Glory look so desperate before. It's all slipping through her fingers. The empire she has built is constructed on quicksand. And it's sinking. *We will all go down with her.*

I can't help feeling my bitter resentment toward Connie. "How can one insignificant person cause so much trouble? He was made for *me*," I mutter to myself.

"He has that connection to you, as was his father's initial intention." Glory's wild eyes hone in on mine. "He cares enough about you to do this." She gestures to Lily's remains. "We might have been wrong. Maybe *you* are the key."

"It will never work," Gareth says between his gritted teeth.

Glory's desperation seeps out of her eyes and into mine.

"We need to show him we are in control. You need to be there when we activate the fail-safe. We will remove Connie, and you will be there when we do. You bring that monster to heel, Sorcha. And bring him back to Meath."

"Glory..." Gareth's voice is tight.

"Do I need to tell you again?" Glory's eyes turn on Gareth in fury as he sets his jaw and, with a simple nod, leaves us. Glory looks back at me, her eyes burning bright with the first flickers of madness. Burning into me. The stench of Lily's blood, so close.

"He is your birthright, Sorcha."

I feel the command well up inside Glory, something I have always suspected but never confirmed. Until now.

"You will go to New Orleans, and you will claim our god."

Chapter Twenty Nine

Connie

My fingers ride the wave of the hot New Orleans' air while I watch the airport fade into the distance until it's nothing but rolling highway and the smell of hot asphalt.

I am beside myself that I am going to see Lorna again. The snakeskin pattern on my white skin glistens in the sun as I hold my hand out of the window, catching the breeze. It's funny, how used to it I have gotten. The patches have grown over the years, and the faint pattern now covers more of me than my plain ivory skin.

Peter is silent beside me. Not looking out the window, rather at the back of the driver's seat headrest. He is still as a statue, his hands clasped in front of him and his knuckles white. I think they might snap under the pressure if he isn't careful. I wonder if his body could hold the marks of scars what one might see, lightning trees would adorn his arms, grizzly stab wounds in his chest, entry and exit wounds of arrows in his legs. I ponder what other injuries he has sustained on his travels that I will never know about. Instead, he looks immaculate, beautiful, and deadly.

I rake my eyes over him. He is not looking at me.

He's been like this since he got back. Quiet, way quieter than usual. He's only put his hands on me a few times since we left Italy, quick and furious. Not like himself.

I open my mouth to tell him to speak, but my attention is caught by something on the radio and Peter's sharp inhale of breath.

"Can you turn that up?" I ask the driver, who obliges.

For the first time, Peter moves, turning his head to look out the window, his knee starting to shake.

"A nation in mourning and panic. As Indonesia continues to count their losses, which are now guessed to be somewhere near ten thousand, the bodies continue to wash up on the mainland. A midnight vigil will be held tonight in Jakarta to mourn the loss. Geologists continue to be baffled by the events of three weeks ago, where one of the small islands off the coast was swallowed up by a crack in the ocean floor..."

My heart is in my mouth as I look at Peter, who will still not meet my gaze.

"Awful, isn't it?" the taxi driver says, but I don't register his words. "Looks like it really is the end of the world. A lot of strange stuff has been happening. God help us all."

"*Ten thousand,* Peter?" I breathe out, ignoring the driver.

Peter closes his eyes, his knee all but rocking the car now. "Test the tether, right?" He brings up the base of his palms to rest his forehead on. "I screwed up."

"Ten thousand?" I parrot. "How are you standing? You didn't give me any. What?" I struggle to find the words, to comprehend the magnitude. "How did you come down?"

He pinches the bridge of his nose, exhaling a long breath. "I don't even remember getting out of the water. The next thing I knew, I was back in Ireland."

"Ireland?" My heart takes a swan dive.

Ireland leads back to one wretched person.

He brings his eyes to mine for the first time and admits, "I went for Sorcha."

Rage flares up in my lungs, and I am about ready to slap the hell out of him because he thinks her body is stronger than mine, more capable.

"To kill her," he clarifies after a moment of reading my face. "I wanted to kill her, not sleep with her, Connie. All I could think about was her attacking you and how you were all cut up. I failed you. I told you I would be there to protect you and I wasn't." He sighs, looking out of the window again. "But I couldn't find her."

My rage subsides. "So, what did you do?"

"Something bad," he says to the window. Closing his eyes, he knows I'll ask. And he will tell me.

"What did you do?" I coax, taking his hand. "Look at me, Peter."

He faces me, his black eyes so desperate not to share this side of himself with me, but it's the last piece, and I find I need it so desperately. I might lose him without it. Lose him to the darkness, to a place I cannot follow.

He swallows.

"Sorcha has a friend there... or lover, I'm not sure which, but someone who means something to her. I couldn't find Sorcha, but I found her. She was called Lily. They were screaming through the halls. I was still so high from all the souls. Ten thousand souls. I-I found Lily."

"You killed her?"

Peter gulps. "I skinned her."

My own skin shudders while the prickles of his darkness ride me like a wave.

I nod.

"With my bare hands."

His eyes look so desperate, like saucers that could slip off the edge of the universe.

"And..." he pauses, looking down at my hand and tracing the snakeskin pattern there, "... I ate her heart."

All the blood rushes out of my head, and I can't think. I chance a look at the driver, who is staring, horrified, in the rearview mirror.

Noticing, Peter leans forward and whispers into his ear, "Do yourself a favor and forget this conversation."

He turns back to the window.

For some reason, the only thing I can think to say is, "But you are a vegetarian."

Despite himself, he laughs and looks at me for a few seconds before rubbing his eyes, sinking his elbows to his knees.

I make a snap decision and give my attention to the driver. "This is an important conversation, so take the long route, will you? Drive around the block if you have to. I will let you know when we are done."

The cab driver's gaze flicks to Peter in the rearview, who inclines his head an inch, consenting in confirmation. That is all he needs to exert his influence over anyone these days. It wraps and curls around everything, like its own entity desiring to be used. My head has been in the sand for long enough.

"The tether?" I ask, returning my focus to Peter.

"The tether is bullshit," he says into his hands. "It's either too weak or broken." He chances a look at my stomach. "I can't risk falling out of line. Glory is pissed but, for now, she thinks it's all Sorcha's fault for attacking you. You are safe. Glory needs me on her side."

A grade-A mess.

I gaze out the window for a while. The hot sunlight of a beautiful day shines down. This world is so full of wonder, and I want it all. To see it, to feel it. I need the dark and the light.

I turn back to him, and he still has his face buried.

"So..." I stretch the word. *How do I show him that I am his, that I want him, all of him?* "What did it taste like?"

He shifts his face from his hands to gawp at me. His eyes are black, so black. "The heart?" His voice is strained. "I don't know. I can't remember. It's all a blur. I just remember the blood." He takes a hard swallow. "Everywhere."

I lick my lips, then move with caution. Seduction and danger is oozing off me like one of my snakes—like him—crawling and slithering until I am sitting on top of him, so he can only look at me, leaning so close our lips are almost touching. If I smell like honey, then he smells like the countryside dew on a summer morning with the faint scent of death tingeing his edges.

"Then tell me what it felt like," I say and flick my tongue against his lips.

His breath hitches and he glances down at my lips. "You really want to know?"

I nod, realizing I truly do. "What I want is for you to describe it to me."

He swallows, and the air thickens around us as his chest inhales against my own. "It felt powerful... like I'd lost myself. To pull someone apart... it is a primitive, primal thing." He sets his eyes on my lips again. His words a velvet whisper when he adds, "Intimate... and horrifying."

In that moment, as I stare into his eyes with my breaths constricting, the only thing I feel is jealousy. Pure jealousy. Lily got to know how it feels. How wonderful it must be to be ripped apart by Peter.

It must be glorious to be truly devoured.

My head swims as his power saturates the air around us,

turning it heavy until there is nothing else I can do but kiss him. He kisses me in return, urgently, with everything. His whole body. I find my fingers on the buttons of his jeans, pushing them down as his hands slide over my legs, then up inside my dress.

"I envy her," I murmur. "If only I could know that sensation, how it feels to be torn apart by you."

The next breath out of him is ragged. I move into position, our bodies sliding together, and his face twists with pleasure. His dark eyes watching me, always.

"Stop hiding yourself from me. Let me be terrible with you." I breathe into his ear, causing his body to jerk against mine, a primal sound leaving my lips at the movement and the noise of strangled pleasure from him as he slides his hand up to my throat, pulling me harder to him.

Letting go at last.

"I want it all, Peter. Next time, I *will* be with you. I want *all* of you," I say between pants.

His breaths shallow now, he claims my lips again, nodding, *yes, yes, I can have it all*. His lips find the skin of my neck as I claim control of momentum. His eyes darken even as his jaw slackens. All I have is need, a need for him as his fingers dig into my thighs. My hands clasping the back of his neck, and he leans his head back to watch the way I move on top of him.

When I moan, he is almost undone.

Peter closes his eyes as I bite down hard on his lip.

I realize a thousand lifetimes will never be enough. I will never burn, never tire. The world could burn, and I would remain. Me and him.

Eternal as the stars. Burning hot.

Because I adore him, adore him, adore him. Every bloody, murderous, terrible inch.

I writhe and deepen my kiss, clasping hard onto his neck.

Claiming...

He is mine.

He is mine.

HE. IS. MINE.

I can't let go.

We can't let go.

His breaths are so shallow now. Pulling my hair back, pushing my eye patch away so he can look at me. Really look at me. Truly see me. Like I see him.

His eyes close as he falls over the edge, and I fall with him.

Chapter Thirty

Lorna

A pair of slim arms the color of ivory wrap tight around my neck and threaten to choke me. Connie rushes from the taxi so fast I barely get a chance to recognize it's her. I return her embrace and notice her frame is still as slight as I remember. A slice of home I have missed.

She buries her face in my neck, and I look over her shoulder into eyes long changed by the last five years.

Black orbs with no hint of their old softness stare back at me.

Tears fill my eyes. "Peter." I hadn't meant to say his name. Or breathe it, rather.

"Hello, Lorna." The hint of a smile tugs at the corner of his mouth. "It's been a while."

I almost choke. *Yes, it has been a while.* Five years ago, they vanished into the night, and no one heard from them again. Until a week ago when Peter called out of the blue, saying they needed to see a friendly face. I'd been so shocked all I could say was, "Yes, they could come. Of course it would be amazing to see them." But

289

I hadn't counted on how much it would break my heart to have them here in front of me.

My breath gets knocked out of me all over again when Connie releases me from her embrace and pulls away a little to look at me, and I can see her. White hair, white skin, the white gleam of a snakeskin pattern in certain patches of skin, pink lips, a green eye, and the glint of a ruby eye patch. She looks like she has walked out of a fairy tale.

"Connie." I grip her arms tight while my eyes rake over her body, her tiny white dress. "You look—"

"I know, I know," she says with a shrug, waving a hand. "I look different. You look amazing, just the same. The nose piercing suits you." She beams. "We have so much to catch up on. Jamie said you are married now."

"You spoke to Jamie?"

"He didn't say?" Connie starts but doesn't have chance to finish as Peter wraps an arm around her waist.

"Maybe you can hold all of your questions until we are inside?" he purrs into her ear.

She gives me an apologetic look as I lead her into Lisette and my apartment. Connie wastes no time and wanders around, her fingers tracing over the beading covering the window and the leaves of the spider plants, perusing our wall hangings. Peter stands aside, holding their bag, and watches her investigations.

He is still and serious as she picks up my book from the kitchen counter and flips through a few pages. *How can they be so different?* Peter seems to weigh a ton while Connie is made of air.

"Where did you go?" I ask after a few minutes of Connie inspecting the apartment.

She glances at Peter.

"Scotland. For the most part," he says.

290

"You couldn't have called? Or at least said goodbye?" I'm impressed I am able to keep my voice even.

Something in Peter's eyes flickers. "It was easier that way. I knew you would be okay with Lisette. Not just okay, but better off with her. Whatever Glory had planned, I didn't want you near it."

"And?" I ask, looking at my nails. "What did she have planned?"

He takes a breath, stepping farther into the apartment. "You watch the news?"

I tip my head. I've always had my suspicions. He doesn't need to say it for me to know. Peter is ravaged by his actions. His face is more drawn and serious, his hair so white it looks like ice but still curling into his eyes, the only softness in his appearance.

We fall into an uncomfortable silence.

"Is Marie still in New Orleans?" Peter asks after a while.

"Yes," I answer cautiously. "Why do you ask?"

"I am in need of her advice."

I feel the blood pool in my cheeks a little. "So this isn't a social visit?"

"Of course it is," Connie says, coming back to me. "I have missed you so much. Time has flown by... in the blink of an eye. I'm sorry we have left it for so long."

"I've missed you too, Con." My voice hovers above a whisper as I pull her to me again. This time, it's me who holds her close enough to almost crush her bones. "Come on, let's go and see Marie," I say when I release her.

The walk to Marie's shop is strange. In a way, it feels like no time has passed. Connie chats with the speed of someone who has not spoken to anyone in years, like she has a need to use all the words she possesses. She wants to know everything about my life —*and now*. What my wedding was like, what my life with Lisette is like, what we have been up to, how often I speak to Jamie, how often I go home. She is careful to avoid the subject of her mum. Often, I haven't answered one question in full before she is on to the next.

I can't take my eyes off her, and neither can everyone else who walks past. Her hair is as white as Peter's now, and her skin almost matches. The fact that she wears all-white clothes only makes her stand out even more. Along with the green of her normal eye, the sparkling red rubies of the eye patch she wears, and a gold bangle in the shape of a snake, there's no hint of the self-consciousness she harbored five years ago.

Peter walks a few paces behind us, the busy street parting so no one brushes us. The few times I chance a glance back at him, his face is serious. He's a little thinner now, and his icy hair contrasts with his tanned skin and his uniform of black. They make quite the pair. I wonder if people can tell they are not of this world. It seems so obvious. I didn't realize how much five years could change them into beings who do not look human anymore.

They're too beautiful, too different.

As we round into Marie's shop, I see Marie in the doorway, placing the closed sign and beckoning us inside. She must be expecting us.

I ask Peter, "Does Marie know you are coming?"

"No," he says without further explanation, moving ahead of us to go in. "What have you heard?" he asks Marie as we file in behind him.

She doesn't answer right away, instead locking the door behind us and moving toward the front.

"Not much," she replies, her shoulders hunching while leaning her back to the counter to look at him, old caution reigniting in her eyes. "Not everything coming across the veil is about you." She rubs her head, leaving the impressions of her fingers in her dark skin. "You are here about the pomegranate seed?"

Peter nods.

"Pomegranate seed?" Connie asks.

"It was the fail-safe," Peter tells her. "I have never been able to figure it out." He holds out his hand to Connie, beckoning her to him and placing his hand over her stomach.

Marie follows suit and does the same, tracing delicate finger-tips over Connie's belly.

"Pomegranate seeds are deeply rooted in mythology and have strong connections to the underworld." She peers at Connie. "This is old magic."

Peter chews his lip. "I need to know how to get rid of it."

Marie's eyes widen as she takes a step away. "Why do you think I will help you? It was part of the bargain."

"Marie, I cannot keep following Glory's command." He lowers his tone a notch. "Something dreadful will happen if I do. It's already starting."

I see the confusion flare in Marie's face as she searches his.

He approaches her with caution, as if Marie is a skittish animal before he takes her hand and places it over his heart. "I am not here to threaten you. I know I have done nothing to win your loyalty. Please, just think about it."

I cast a nervous glance at Connie, who is watching him, unwavering.

Marie looks at me for a second and then nods. "I will make inquiries."

He breathes out a sigh of relief. "Thank you." He turns to Connie, putting an arm around her, and says, "Let's go and get a drink."

"They look like something out of the *Addams Family*," Lisette says into my ear at the bar later as we watch Peter and Connie dance together. The noise is so loud there is no chance they will overhear us. Under the flashing lights, the low beat, they are entwined with each other.

I giggle.

"Any ideas why they are here after so long?"

"They need Marie's help," I say into her ear over the music.

Lisette rolls her eyes. "Figures." She doesn't ask me to elaborate.

"They are my best friends, Lis. I love them."

She gives me a warm look, rubbing my arms. "I know you do. But they take advantage of that, honey. They take advantage of everything." Lisette shakes her head, looking away. "They haven't paid for one drink since they got here, and they're ordering the good stuff. All they do is take," she adds.

"That's not fair. Neither of them asked for this."

"I know." She holds her hands up. "But what's that saying about *with great power* and all of that? He could be healing the world, not getting hammered."

"It's not his choice."

Lisette chews on her lip as we look at them again. They seem to have found a couple to dance with. "They make each other worse, not better." She looks at her hands. "*Cher*, I don't want you to get hurt again."

"I know," I say quietly, then notice Connie break away and head to the bar again. "Hold that thought, Lis."

I make my way over to the bar, to Connie, who is ordering top-shelf tequila.

"Hey."

"Hey," she greets me with drunken enthusiasm. "Do you want one?"

"Sure."

I watch the bartender pour another silver tequila next to the three already poured.

"Put it on the tab," she tells him before raising a glass to clink my own. Peter must have told the bar staff to give her anything she wants. We both drink our shots before Connie continues to sink the other two.

I raise my eyebrows at her.

"Man. I have missed tequila." She laughs.

I glance at the dance floor to see the couple they were dancing with are now pretty much draped around Peter. I look from them back to Connie. "He's not okay, is he?"

Connie muses on my words for a while until I think she won't answer me.

We simply watch Peter.

"No," she says after a minute of our observations, turning back to the bartender and motioning for more drinks. "So much destruction," she says without meeting my gaze. "And I am powerless. Three more, please," she says when he comes over. Looking at the grain of the bar, she all but whispers, "Lorna, all I can do is hold on. Try to hold him together while what she is doing tears him apart." She sinks another tequila. "There is no balance here."

I tear my eyes away from him and look at Connie who, at last, meets my eye. Her normal eye glistens, it's black rim still marked.

"I don't know what else to do, Lor. I think I am close to losing him." She swallows hard before downing another.

"Connie..." I start as she drinks the last tequila, swaying so much she has to steady herself on the bar, "... is this helping?"

I look back at Peter, who is now watching her from across the room.

"Lor, it is the only thing that helps."

The girl Peter has been dancing with runs a long nail along his cheek, but his eyes remain firm on Connie.

She drags her eye from him to peer up at me. "Do you want to know what will happen tonight? We will leave this bar and take them both back to our hotel room." Connie allows her lids to close, swaying her head to the music. "And he will keep us awake for hours. Every plant and flower in the building will bloom because of us." She looks at me again, her expression distant. "You want to know why? Because this can't be all he is. He is not just death. He is beautiful." A stray tear runs down Connie's face, glinting against the pale of her skin before she swipes it away. "God, I am so sorry, Lorna. I am really drunk. Pay no attention to me."

Without another word, she moves back into the crowd. Peter prizes himself away from the couple and pushes his hands into Connie's hair, moving her close, bringing her head to his chest, and holding it close to him.

My breath catches in my throat. A sick feeling grows in my stomach that has nothing to do with the tequila. I push my way back to Lisette, who is nodding along to the beat.

"Lis, we have to go."

"What's happened? What did she say?"

I push my hands through my hair, trying to collect my thoughts. "I don't know. I need to see Marie. See what she has found."

Lisette puts a steadying palm on my shaking hands that I hadn't even noticed were tremoring. "Lorna, slow down."

We glance back to Connie and Peter, who are still in the middle of the dance floor in the throes of the music.

"I have an awful feeling that something terrible is about to happen."

Lisette doesn't say anything else, only follows me out of the bar, and we make our way down the bustling street toward

Marie's. My skin prickles and I bring my denim jacket close around my chest, wishing my feet could move faster.

Marie's shop is dark, of course, but this doesn't stop me from pounding on the door.

Lisette does the more practical thing and calls Marie a few times.

"*Cher*, she must be out. Or in bed. Are you sure this can't wait until the morning?"

I push my hands through my hair, feeling sick and sweaty. "I've known them long enough to know when something is *really* wrong. He's too quiet, and I have *never* seen Connie like that. She is so close to snapping, Lis. I feel it somewhere deep inside of me. She isn't going to make it. She can't. I can't. Remember, before, when she almost..." But I can't finish, nor can I breathe as I clutch my chest. "They only came here because they're out of options. But they don't even know it yet."

"Lorna," Lisette tries to comfort me. "They are just really drunk. You've all had far too much to drink tonight." She can't hide the alarm on her face.

I sink my back to the window of the shop, trying to steady myself. "You don't understand, Lis. He is part of me. I can feel it."

"What—"

The light in the shop comes on, Marie swings the door open, and I almost fall in after it.

"Heavens." Marie pulls me into her arms. "What is happening?"

I push away and stride into the shop, rounding on her. "Please tell me there is a way, Marie. To remove the seed. A way for it to disappear and them along with it?"

Marie looks from Lisette to me, with caution the only expression she wears. "I wish there was a way to help your friends. I really do, Lorna."

I try to take deep breaths.

Marie continues, "They should leave New Orleans. It is not safe here for them. They should keep moving."

"Who are you?" Lisette asks, and I glance up to the open window to see Sorcha standing there, her silver eyes glinting in the moonlight.

Her eyes bore into mine. "Where are they?" she demands.

A feral noise erupts from me as I throw myself at her. While my fist collides with her face, it makes not a hint of impact, and she easily swirls me around, catching my throat and turning me to Lisette and Marie, holding me fast.

"Where. Are. They?" she demands once more, exposing more of my neck to my wife.

"They are staying at the Monteleone," Lisette says, her hands up, fear across her face.

Sorcha gives a half laugh. "See you around, Lorna," she whispers into my ear, then pushes me toward Lisette, who catches me in her arms as Sorcha disappears into the night.

"Who was that?" Lisette asks.

I don't answer. Instead, I throw my bag onto the counter and frantically look for my phone. I dial Peter, but no luck. My fingers feel too big and clumsy to do anything productive as I dial Connie's number and hope to God it's the same one. *Out of service.*

Shit.

I try Peter again. He'd called me to let me know that they were coming.

Pick up. Pick up.

I dial again.

On my third try, a breathless Connie answers the phone, "We are kind of in the middle of something here." She giggles.

Relief floods my body. "Connie, Sorcha is coming."

"What?" Her breathy, playful voice is gone in an instant.

I hear Peter say something in the background, along with other voices I don't recognize. I assume the couple from the bar.

"Connie. Sorcha is here in New Orleans, and she is coming to your hotel," I reiterate.

"Sorcha is here," she tells Peter.

"Why would they send her?" he asks in the background.

"You two should go," I say loud enough to bring her back to me.

Silence.

"Connie?"

"L-Lorna." Connie's voice breaks. "I am sorry we left before. We will come back for you, I promise."

"It's okay," I utter. "Don't make promises you can't keep. Just go. As long as you are both okay, I will be fine."

"I love you, Lor," she tells me.

"I love you too."

She clicks off the line, and I fall into Lisette's arms once again.

Chapter Thirty-One

Peter

The clammy air of the New Orleans' night clings to my skin as Connie and I spill out onto the streets, wondering if I should make it rain, or perhaps blow a gale.

I glance up and down the street, taking in the people bustling past with little regard for either of us and instead, going back to giving me a wide berth as they pass. I take Connie's hand and walk to the waterfront.

"Why would the coven send Sorcha?" I ask again when we've put some distance between our hotel and ourselves. "It makes no sense. They hate her as much as I do. Gareth does, at least."

"Gareth is not the one calling the shots," Connie says, stumbling into my side.

I steady her. "I can take Sorcha."

"You sure about that?" a venomous voice sounds behind me, giving me only a fraction of a second to register her before I feel a thundering hit in my kidney that sends me five feet forward and onto the grass of Woldenberg Park.

Connie rushes to my side as my brain catches up.

I look up to see Sorcha showing a band around her wrist that looks like mine. "The tracer spell can only get me so close. I couldn't believe my luck when I saw your friend rushing into that magic shop." She shakes her head, almost tutting. "You went too far this time. No more playing nice." The band on her wrist glows. "You shouldn't have done that to Lily."

The park isn't busy at this time of night, but those who are crossing pay us no mind. Sorcha must be cloaking us from them. She might be able to shield them from seeing us, but she won't be able to hide my thunderstorms. I rise, allowing the clouds to roll in, the rumble sounding in the distance.

"Think of it as long due retribution for my sister. Why would *you* come here? Do you really think you stand a chance against me?"

"No," Sorcha admits. "But that is not what I am here for." Her eyes flick to Connie.

I attempt to put my body into a protective stance in front of her, but the second I do, Connie doubles over, clutching her stomach and tears springing in her eyes.

"Connie." I grasp her arms to steady her as she winces and falls to her knees. Her body convulses, and the faint signature scent of the pomegranate becomes stronger.

"What are you doing?" I spin back to Sorcha but don't dare to move away from Connie, who is struggling for breath.

"I'm not doing anything. I am only the messenger. Did you really think she'd let you take out an island? Kill her coven. And there would be no consequences?"

"No," I whisper, clutching onto Connie, moving my hands to her panic-stricken face. "They can't do this. She can't do this." I grit my teeth, placing my hands on Connie's belly.

Her eyes shut tight in agony.

There is nothing I can do.

Nothing for me to heal.

The fail-safe.

Underneath it all, I'd assumed it must be as useless as the tether. "Connie, talk to me. What should I do?"

"Peter." Sorcha maintains her distance. "It is Connie who is holding you back. The coven is yours. I am yours. We are your people. You will see. It is the way it always has been... the way it should be. We serve the coven, not ourselves."

I hear her but don't.

Connie straightens up a little, her terrified eyes fixed onto mine while clawing at her throat, her blood oozing and becoming thick.

Then I see it. At first, I think it is mud seeping from the corners of her mouth, but then I make out the winding branches protruding. All I can do is stand by, horror-stricken as the bark chokes her. Green leaves sprout and wind around her face, traveling around her neck and weaving down her body, consuming her whole.

I attempt to break the branches away, but it's all moving too fast. Connie's breaths begin to fail. Trying to take her hand, I reach out to reassure her it will be okay, that I will fix this, but she is out of reach, and the tree is unstoppable, covering every inch of her snow-white skin until there is more tree than Connie.

"No. No. No." It's all I've been able to say, although I haven't noticed myself saying it. I can't believe what I have witnessed.

She's disappeared right in front of my eyes, and her branches now hang over me, huge pomegranates blooming before me.

"No," I whisper again, my fingers running over the bark, trying to find a trace of her. Perhaps a knot in the wood that resembles a snake eye. "No."

"Her soul belongs to the underworld now," Sorcha tells me. "She was never supposed to be yours."

I shake my head, stalking around the Connie tree. "This isn't supposed to happen." My knees buckle and I slide down the trunk to the ground. "This can't be real."

Sorcha crouches in front of me, pushing the hair from my eyes, her silver ones full of warmth and sympathy. "It's time for you to come home, Peter."

My breaths come shallow now, my head spins, and I know my body is going into shock. I cup my head with my shaking hands. "No. No. No."

"You will be okay. I promise. I promise it will be okay. I have fallen in love with a mortal before. I know how you feel. I will help you get through this."

The tequila rolls in my stomach, and I am sick, coating the ground between my knees. "No." I loll my head back onto the Connie tree to look at Sorcha, and her hand slides into mine, warm and familiar. *I don't know what is happening.* "No. I will wait." The tears drip from my face. "All souls are recycled, right? I will wait. I can wait for her to come back." I recoil my fingers from her grasp.

"Peter—"

"No. I will wait. She will come back to me. She will. I am hers."

"The coven needs you."

"I am hers," I hear myself say, but it already sounds so far away.

I don't want to look at Sorcha anymore, so I close my eyes.

Everything is becoming distant as I trace the rough edges of the bark with my trembling fingers, the grass around coming alive at my touch. *So many souls. I have taken so many. Given Connie so many. She will come back to me soon. I will wait by the Connie tree until she comes back. I am hers. I feel certain she will know where to find me.*

I feel myself start to fade.

I sense Sorcha moving away and hear her talking to someone. This was not what she expected. She expected a fight. Telling whoever is on the other end that I'm going into shock- and asking what she should do.

Something moves in the branches of the tree, and I peer up to see a huge snake wrapping around the trunk, coiling toward me. Huge green, slitted eyes. My vision blurs.

Someone is calling my name. I think it's Sorcha, but I can't tell.

For a second, I think the snake is going to bite, although it looks big enough to swallow me whole. I have a fleeting thought where I hope it will. It reminds me of Morgan's snakes sliding over Connie's body, mixing with the souls. My souls. I press my hand to the bark of the tree. My Connie tree.

Only when I breathe, it breathes too. I feel the bark move against my back as the entire pomegranate tree takes a breath.

Sorcha's hands are on me, grabbing the front of my shirt and pulling me to my feet and away. I watch, horrified, as the fruits behind me fall, smash to the ground, and send seeds everywhere. Like bloody orbs, they coat the grass. The tree starts falling in on itself. The bark crumbling in, oozes red. Pomegranate seeds spill everywhere, and the snake slithers to the ground, circling the base of the tree while we observe in growing horror.

Sorcha and I jump back when a hand punches through the bark. A slim, pale hand breaking through, covered in seeds. Sorcha is too stunned to move, but I step over the circling snake—it lets me cross—and push into the tree so I can better reach the hand. Ripping the bark with my bare hands, more seeds slosh to the floor as I pull the hand and the body it is attached to forward, back into this world.

Connie. Slender and naked, looking the way she always looked, her long dark hair shining under the sticky residue of the fruit, both eyes emerald and bright—and human. Yet she is different. Glowing. Smiling. A creature never before seen in this world.

"How?" I breathe out, touching her bare skin, no longer patterned with snakeskin.

Connie reaches her hands up to touch my face as if *I* am something to be wondered at. "Before, I was a chrysalis." She leans into my touch. "Watch." She runs her hand across her skin, revealing the snakeskin once more.

"You are a god." I gaze back into her eyes, but she is so much more. She is *everything*.

"I don't think so. I think I am something in between. I heard you call. I couldn't leave you. You are mine, and I am yours."

"Connie..." I can't believe it. There are a million things I want to say.

"No." Sorcha finally finds her voice, although I'd forgotten she was here.

The miracle of Connie reborn is too much.

"This is not possible," she seethes, shaking with rage. "You are supposed to die. Why? What makes you so special?"

Sorcha advances on us, grabbing Connie by the throat and pushing her into the remains of the pomegranate tree.

"It's time for you to let go, Sorcha," Connie says, her tone gentle, though her voice is commanding.

Sorcha tightens her grip.

"Peter." Connie gasps, bringing me to myself because I am too busy marveling at how magnificent she is. I open the skies and hit Sorcha with a strike of lightning, sending her away from Connie and leaving her heaving on the floor.

In a way, in this moment, I feel sorry for her.

I turn to advance, but Connie holds me back. "Let me." She prowls toward Sorcha, reminding me of her weaving snake with her movements.

"You couldn't have just walked away." Connie's skin ripples, changing from her own back to the pale skin of a snake. "You will never leave us alone, will you?" Her brown hair changes, dripping like white paint down the length as she molts.

The snake follows her advance, hissing at Sorcha as Connie stands in front of her.

Her voice is measured and so assertive it fires goose bumps over my skin. "He will never be yours. Because he belongs to no one." She crouches down close to Sorcha, and both of her eyes transform to the green of the snake. "He is mine because that is what he chooses. And you will never understand that." She tilts her head.

I have lost the ability to breathe.

"It is better for you this way."

The behemoth snake rears, but Connie strikes first, plunging her hand hard into Sorcha's chest. Sorcha gasps, her chest rising with Connie's hand, and she takes her last breath as Connie rips her heart from her body.

Bringing it up, she marvels at it for a few seconds, bloody in her hand, before tossing it away to her snake with only a shrug. The snake devours it whole.

Connie stalks toward me, changing back before my eyes, until she is standing in front of me, covered in pomegranate and blood, yes, but looking like Connie again.

Her emerald eyes stare up into mine. Unmarked. Strangely, I don't think I have felt better in my life. The sludge of the rot from doing Glory's work shifts.

I swallow hard as I look at her.

"So, what do we do now?" she asks.

A wicked smile stretches across my lips. It has been so long since I felt the true urge to smile. "Now. We go to Ireland."

Chapter Thirty-Two

Connie

The sun rises across the wild vista of what Peter tells me is called Newgrange. The early morning rays hitting the ancient burial site just right stirs something deep down in my soul, matched in beauty only by the absolute certainty I feel in my bones. The same certainty I have felt before, in the bayou of New Orleans.

This time, it is not fear I feel. Only certainty that I am in the right place.

The wind catches my hair, and it changes from brown to purest white from the corner of my eye. I know Peter is not watching the beauty of the sunrise, only me. Waiting.

"Do you think they know we are coming?" I ask him, my words quiet against the breeze.

"Absolutely."

I look up into his deep brown eyes, noticing they already shiver and bloom under the anticipation. My heart picks up.

"Are you sure about this? I can go in alone," he offers.

"I want to come," I tell him.

He doesn't answer straight away, and the weight of his stare is crushing. "Okay," he says after what feels like forever.

"Give me the knife," I tell him, surprising myself with how strong my voice sounds.

He doesn't move at first, again his eyes boring into mine. Only his breathing becomes heavier, the anticipation building as he shrugs off his jacket and digs his fingers into his forearm, ripping at his flesh.

"Doesn't it hurt? Having it in your body?" I ask, unable to look away.

"You get used to it," he says in a low voice, examining my movements when I shift to take his wrist, pulling his arm toward me, and see the glint of metal. I chew on my lip as I reach into the bloody cavern in his arm, delicate and soft, blood already coating my fingertips as I pull out the blade and hold it up to take a look. This is the first time I have felt its cool metal against my skin.

He watches me, breathing in deep, and a thrill passes through me. Like the electricity I haven't felt from him in years. It rises.

He closes his eyes, motioning his head with the rising wind. "I can smell them." He licks his lips.

I grip the blade tight as his hunger catches. "You should take the souls as you go. If they try to fight, kill them. Kill anyone who is left. I will find Glory."

He doesn't say anything else. With a deep dip of his head, he turns and stalks away from me. I follow a few paces behind, marveling at my palms as they turn the palest of white snakeskin. I know I am stronger in this form.

As Peter walks, his stance changes, and he transforms too. The vines that sometimes hold me to him come free, moving forward to clear the path before him and around the large round wooden door of the main tunnel. The ground at his feet cracks, and he forces his way into the home of the coven. A low rumble echoes and I'm not sure if it comes from the ground or from him.

He vanishes into the darkness of the winding hallways. As I enter, I already hear the screams of those inside. It doesn't sound like I would have thought as I pause to tilt my head and appreciate it. *Almost musical.* I push on through the clear path he is creating.

The coven is like a maze, running deep underground. I follow the sound of the screams, only the noise of my own breathing keeping me company. The fingers of my free hand run against the textured curved walls.

When someone eventually crosses my path, the sight of me pale and covered in scales is enough to cause them a moment of hesitation. A second is all I need. I plunge the small knife deep into their chest. It slices so easily. The shock on their face as I pull it out to strike again—intoxicating.

Three sharp strikes.

My snake eyes keen on them as I let them fall.

Only noticing when I continue on that my cream-colored coat is now covered in their blood, I shrug it to the floor, leaving it behind. The screams become more distant. Their attack—whatever it may have been—does not seem to have been thought out. Not the well-oiled machine I have known before. *They were losing before we even stepped in.*

As I advance, I notice a bloody handprint on a doorframe as a shaft of light reveals the way to the glass dome on top. I make my way up, easing on each step and ensuring no one is lying in wait. This way seems too quiet, but the view from the top of the mound calls to me.

I inch the door open to reveal a huge room. It looks empty. Abandoned. Only a glorious view, as I imagined. The large windows make the view even more breathtaking. *There is something about this place. And it means something. When I came back from the other side, I didn't come back the same.* I push the door a little farther to take a better look and get distracted by movement. Someone is crouched by a table, throwing some things into a bag.

I step fully into the room. "You're not even trying to help them?"

Glory freezes, straightening up to look at me as I edge closer to her, her initial shock fading as she stands back. *She doesn't see me as a threat. Not yet.*

"You ungrateful creatures." She snarls. "After everything I have done for you."

I giggle, incredulous at her claim. "You tried to kill me."

"It looks like it worked." She motions to me. "You should have stayed dead, Connie. Look at that monster you are with. What he is doing to my people down those stairs."

I am beyond repulsed by her. By the notion, she truly believes he is anything other than what she has created. An old ugly belief of an "eye for an eye," Glory does not deserve anything else. Her cruel means of obtaining what she wants makes her the true savage.

"It is everything you deserve. You are true evil for what you have done, to so many, in your ridiculous crusade. For everything you have done to him, for what you have made him do."

She scoffs.

"He is here killing your coven because I told him to, but I wanted you for myself. I killed Sorcha for Anna. But you..." I hold my knife up to her, "... I am going to kill you for him."

Glory's eyes flicker. "You?" The briefest doubt flickers before something of a smirk passes over her face. "You are brave, but stupid. What do you think is going to happen? To him? To the balance?"

The anger rises in my veins as I bare my teeth and let out a cruel laugh. "You think what you are doing is balance. You think that *you* are balance? You are the one who is stupid, Glory." I point his knife at my chest. "*We* are the balance."

Confusion crosses Glory's face for a fraction of a second, but I don't want to hear anything else from her. I lunge forward, swiping the air with the blade, narrowly missing her as she moves away.

Her hand, wrapped in what looks like a binding rope, collides with my face at full force. Lucky for me, it's not enough to slow me down. I swipe again, this time nicking her shoulder. I hear the clear intake of breath.

She is too fast when I move again, ensnaring my arm with the rope and throwing me at the huge window and causing me to drop the knife. She moves to hit me again but, this time, I am too quick for her, and I duck to bring my fist into her stomach, sending her into the shuddering glass.

I stumble to retrieve the knife—it's just out of reach—as Glory lashes the binding rope around my neck, tightening her grip, and the air leaves me. Glory is tall enough to bring me almost off my feet. The tips of my toes teeter on the stone floor until I manage to bring my elbow into her solar plexus. Her breath whooshes out as I lunge forward onto my knees, coughing hard.

I'm crawling toward the knife when I hear the boom of footsteps heavy on the stairs and see boots move into the doorway.

"Glory?"

I look up in time to see Gareth staring down at me.

Shit.

The knife is closer to him than it is to me. He looks from me to the knife and then back at Glory, but he doesn't move. For the second time today, I am saved by someone hesitating. I don't have time to consider it. I've always known Gareth to be a vicious, unhesitating kind of person.

Vines appear and wrap around Gareth, holding him in place, not that he makes any move to fight. Peter comes into view behind him, his hand gliding around Gareth's neck, pushing his head slightly up to look at Glory, who is getting to her feet.

"Watch this," I hear Peter whisper into his ear as he sees me scuttle forward.

Taking up the knife, I throw it back at an advancing Glory with all the force I have, finding its mark in her chest. I follow it as she hits the glass, the squelch sounding against the window. I draw the knife out and drive it home, again and again.

I stop only to watch the fight leave Glory, the light of her long life coming to an end. Her coven—it is over.

She has lost, and we are finally free.

I draw the knife out, letting her sink to the floor.

It is done.

As I stare at her body, I think about her being the third life I have taken. *I hope my last.* I haven't noticed Peter release Gareth until he is standing next to me, his arm grazing mine while he looks down at Glory. The vines, no longer in sight, are back to being part of him.

"It's over." He lets out a long breath.

When I glance up at him, the sun is catching the angles of his face, the white of his hair looking more like an angel in battle than anything else.

He drops his gaze to me. "Are you okay?" he asks.

I nod, turning back to Glory. "Can I have it? It seems fitting." I motion toward Glory's body.

When I peer back up, he's having a hard time hiding his surprise. He doesn't question it, though, and simply goes to Glory, puts a hand against the wound in her chest, and beckons her soul, which the knife has trapped there. Carefully walking back over with his eyes on mine, he pushes it into my chest.

He watches as my breathing shallows.

"What are you?"

I hear a voice behind me and realize I have forgotten all about Gareth. We turn in unison to see him standing by the door. Still fierce and fearless.

"Both of you? What are you?"

Peter gives a smirk, stalking over. Gareth, tall enough to meet his eye, still backs into the wall, taking a hard swallow as Peter leans his hand on the wall by his head.

"How about it?" Peter grins at him, wolf-like. "You can go down with your coven. I will be glad to tear you apart. Slowly, intimately. Or... you are with us. You could join us. I know you are a warrior. That death does not faze you. I have to admit, I am intrigued, too, by you, your fire. It is your choice."

Gareth stares at him with a fiery fervor, vowing, "I am with you."

"That's a good choice." Peter stands back, giving him some breathing room. "Welcome to the new world."

Chapter Thirty-Three

Peter

The world above is a different place to the one when we entered the underground tunnels of the coven.

The air feels fresher, the sun hanging bright and brilliant over Newgrange. As I look into the distance, I spot the outline of a figure standing on top of the monument, their cloak billowing in the breeze.

Gareth shields his face from the brilliant sun. "Is that Morgan?"

I take a few steps forward. She looks majestic from a distance, not grotesque. "How did you find her?" I ask him.

"Signs," he says with a hitch of his shoulders like I should know what that means.

I look back at him, his fierce eyes, and know he is a warrior of a man.

"I am good at reading them, tracking. It is my talent, you could say."

I glance at Connie, who is standing a little behind him.

315

"What are you thinking?" she asks, now looking more like her old self again—dark hair and brilliant emerald eyes—only, now, her skin glows under the weight of her immortality.

"I think we should go to her." I look back to the horizon she is standing on.

Connie comes forward, pushes her fingers through mine, and takes a few steps in the direction of the tombs before looking back to Gareth, who isn't following.

"You two go," he says. "Whatever she has to say, it will not be for me. You can tell me after, if it's something you want to share."

So Connie and I make our way across the hill to the sacred grounds, where Morgan hobbles out to meet us. She doesn't seem at all surprised to see us here.

I stand face to face with her for a minute, not quite knowing what to expect, but she does not feel like a threat. Connie and I stand firm, and I hold resolutely onto her hand.

Morgan's amber eyes gleam in the light, looking more triumphant as she reaches out and takes my arm—now fully healed—and runs her rough fingertips over my skin, which holds no hint of a scar. My blade is safely in Connie's pocket.

"So much for your tether," I say to her for lack of anything useful to say, given the coven she'd allied herself with are all dead, barring Gareth. "It was weak."

Morgan offers me a yellow smile, pulling my arm toward her again. She traces runes into my arm that make sense in my head.

On the contrary, the tether is strong.

I chuckle. "In case you haven't noticed, Glory and her coven are dead. Gareth has switched allegiances. Unless I answer to Gareth now?"

Your tether was never bound to the Irish line.

Her amber eyes flick to Connie, her triumph heightening. My heart drops. "You are kidding?"

Morgan shakes her head.

"How?" I ask.

"What is she saying?" Connie looks up at me, trying to read the shock on my face.

"The tether was weak, Con, because it didn't exist."

Connie's eyes go wide, and she looks from me to Morgan. "Morgan couldn't tether me to Glory because I am tethered to you."

"Me?" Connie breathes out.

Morgan pulls my arm again, tracing frantic patterns.

"She is saying you were not ready before. You needed to transform, to be strong enough to endure it." I almost roll my eyes. "She is saying I will need strong commands."

"How can that be possible? How can you be tethered to me?"

I look back to Morgan but almost don't need the answers. It feels like it is all flooding back to me. Stealing in through her window, I was addicted to her. I *am* addicted to her. When she left, how I wanted to destroy myself. Sharing my dreams. A thousand little things that make sense now, and bit by bit, I am more and more hers.

"Peter." Connie slaps my arm. "What is she saying?"

"She is saying... that I chose you. And you chose me in return." A smile tugs my lips, and I turn more toward Connie. "I think this has been happening gradually. Right from the start. It always felt different around you... calmer."

Morgan clicks her tongue as she turns to Connie herself, tracing more patterns.

"She is saying that she is betting I have never disobeyed a strong command from you. And paid for ones I have."

Connie moves her hand to her chest, looking from Morgan back to me. It is clear she isn't overjoyed by this news.

"Peter, I don't want this kind of power over you. We are supposed to be equal. I..."

My eyes turn back to Morgan as she continues to draw her runes onto me.

"She wants you to know..." I hesitate, trying to keep up with what she is writing, "... that many of the old gods, the tether didn't just bind them to their people... they were devoted. The witches tethered them because they could become out of control, but the gods were devoted to those who held their tethers. They were not slaves, not the old ones."

"You are mine," she says. Her words are gentle, but I recognize the undercurrent of power she holds there now. The tether stronger for her transformation.

"Always have been."

"I..." She struggles to find the right words. "How can I do this?"

"Connie. You are everything that is good about me. This is what you were meant to do."

Morgan frowns a little, and Connie closes her eyes before speaking, "I believe in the good in you. I have seen it so many times."

Morgan is writing on my arm again, nodding at me to translate to Connie.

"She is telling me to listen to you. She said, 'You cannot blame the hurricane for being a hurricane.' We are what we are."

Connie now offers a brilliant smile. "You are the arrow."

"Heavy is the head who wears the crown of the huntress." I smirk.

Connie shakes her head, her eyes widening again, still finding it difficult to take it all in. But everything Morgan is telling us makes so much sense now. The rot in my soul from taking orders from Glory always felt so wrong. I'd bound myself so deeply to Connie, little by little, it feels *right*.

I look back to Morgan. "Everything you have done... it's all been leading up to this. From the fake tether to the pomegranate seed. Why did you help us?"

Morgan's keen eyes gleam.

Because I am glad for a world full of wonder once more.

"What do you mean by that?"

When I woke, the world was a changed place. Magic has long been leaving this plane, creatures with the energy of the First having long left. The world had become dull. The gods left, magic waned, and creatures went extinct. Man's connection to the universe was lost. But this is changing. You woke it up.

"How?"

By being born.

It's like being with Kali again. I am beyond confused as Morgan lowers her gaze to my arm again. Only, this time, she doesn't draw any runes but, instead, sweeps her hand across my forearm and, as she does, a bright gold hue rises in my veins. A sight that has Morgan's nose almost touching my skin.

Connie moves closer, tracing her fingers over the glow. "I've seen this before. In the clearing, when she did whatever it was instead of tether you, and after one of the first missions."

Morgan nods before frantically drawing onto my arm.

It is the blood of the First, she clarifies. *This has not been seen in millennia. Too diluted to be detected in anyone.* She pulls up her sleeve to show the yellowing skin of her arm, running a hand over it to disclose the faintest of glows before returning to the runes. *Even my blood, over two thousand years old, diluted a hundred times more than yours.*

I feel the lump knot in my throat. "My mother?"

She nods.

She was part First. And with her, they made a new god. A new creator.

I don't even know how I feel and don't notice I am shaking so hard until Connie smooths her hands down both of my arms as if to warm me. Morgan drops my arm, calling her falcon to her. She has imparted her side of the story. That is all she has. It is more than I can comprehend right now, yet I cannot help but feel a strange sense of symmetry.

"What did she say?" Connie asks gently when Morgan turns from us.

"My mother... she was part First. It's why I am the way that I am. Why I was always so much stronger, why I am connected to everything." I look down at Connie's hands. "It has to be Boots, right?"

Connie looks from me to Morgan, but she doesn't have the answers. In my heart, I know it is. That feeling of familiarity—he was family. *Why would he take a vested interest in keeping me alive otherwise?*

Morgan strokes her falcon before returning her attention to us, although she is turned to Connie now as she writes, only giving me a nod to relay the message.

"She said that this world is ours now. And that you should take good care of it."

Morgan lets my arm fall, giving me a small nod and a slight bow to Connie before turning and walking away.

We watch until she is well into the distance, then Connie threads her arm through mine, and we start our trek back to Gareth.

"Do you think Boots will come back for you?"

I stop and look down at her, running my thumb along her cheek. "I don't know. But for the first time in a long time, I feel good."

She grins. "What do we do now?"

I laugh, putting my arm around her and pulling her close. Gareth stands up as we approach, walking away from the entrance of the coven and toward us.

"Now, Constance, we do whatever we want."

The End.

.

About the Author

Kerry Williams is an emerging UK author and writer of magical romance, Other Nature being her debut paranormal romance novel. Told from multiple points of view, it will keep you hooked with its twisty plot and boy obsessed.

Copywriter by day, she gets lost in a world of magic at night, either in her writing or in what she reads. Her creative roots cultivated by the writing of the unforgettable Anne Rice, she also adores the work of Erin Morgenstern, Holly Black and J. K. Rowling.

She is an avid cat lady, die hard tea drinker and eternal star gazer. Always known to her family as a daydreamer, her and her young daughter, Ivy, can often be found looking at the moon.

Printed in Great Britain
by Amazon

23041440R00183